SHATTERED WORLD II
RUSSIA

SHATTERED WORLD II
RUSSIA

Scott M. Baker

Also by Scott M. Baker

Novels
Shattered World I: Paris
The Vampire Hunters
Vampyrnomicon
Dominion
Rotter World
Rotter Nation
Rotter Apocalypse
Yeitso

Novellas
Dead Water
Nazi Ghouls From Space
Twilight of the Living Dead
This Is Why We Can't have Nice Things During the Zombie Apocalypse

Anthologies
Cruise of the Living Dead and other Stories
Incident on Ironstone Lane and Other Horror Stories

A Schattenseite Book

Shattered World II: Russia
by Scott M. Baker.
Copyright © 2020. All Rights Reserved.
Print Edition

ISBN-13: 978-0-9963121-7-2

This is a work of fiction. Any resemblance to any actual person, living or dead, events or locales is entirely coincidental.

Cover Art © by Joolz & Jarling – Uwe Jarling & Julie Nicholls 2020
Editing © Michele Thompson 2016
Map © Petar Dekic 2020

To Mitch
My friend, my blood brother, and my mentor.
Thanks for being there for me.

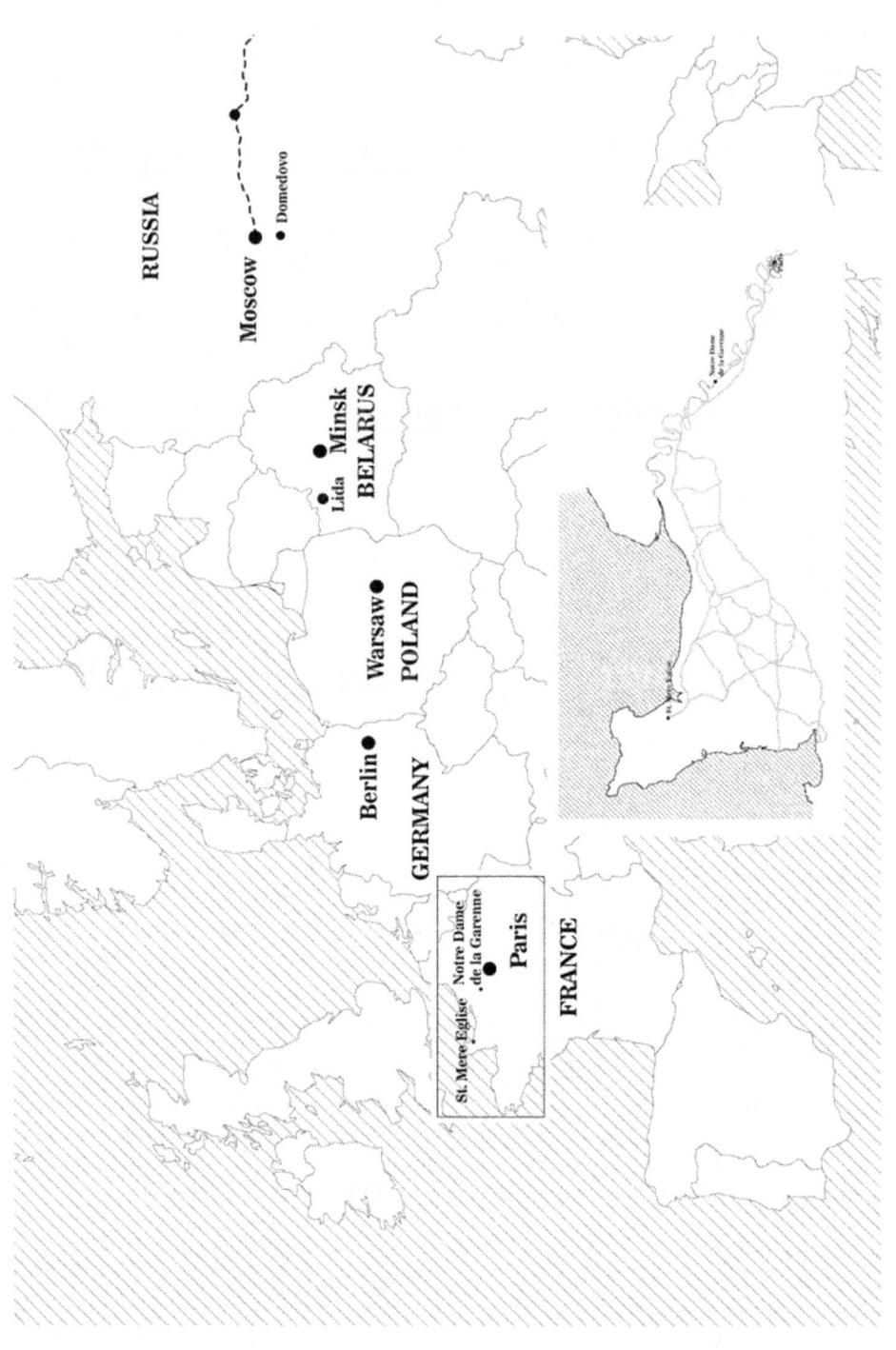

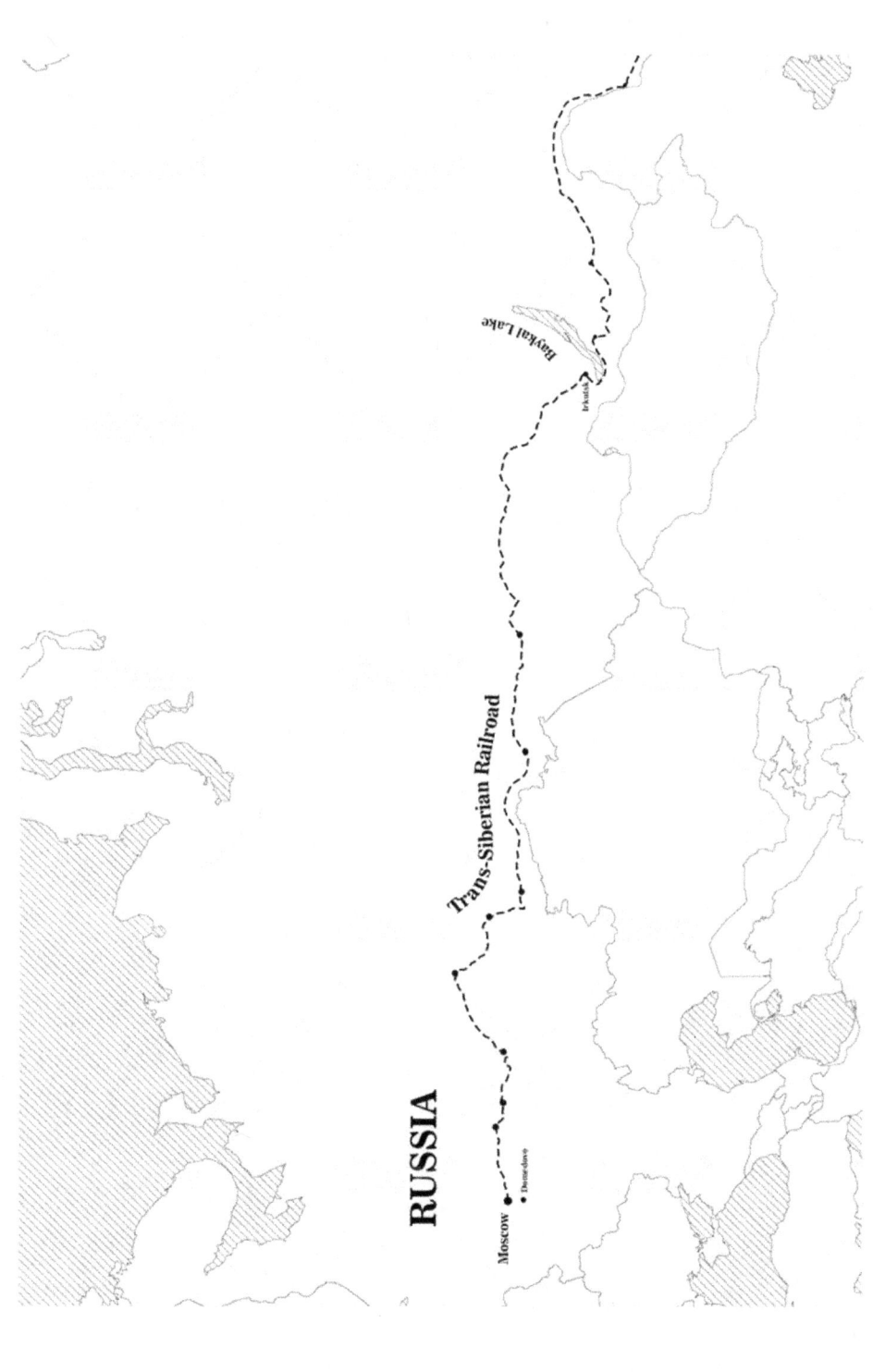

BOOK ONE

CHAPTER ONE

Red Square, Moscow, nine days after the opening of the Russian portal

TEN FLESH EATERS broke through the line and swarmed General Budenny. They were even more frightening up close, like the zombies from American horror films, emaciated corpses with gray leathery skin and dull, milky white eyes. They also had a taste for human flesh. These were the tortured souls condemned to eternal damnation that now walked the Earth because of the portal, the gate to another dimension. Unlike their movie counterparts, a bite from one of these demons would not turn the victim into a flesh eater, although that didn't mean enough of these creatures couldn't strip a man down to his bones if given a chance.

Budenny raised his 9mm Makarov pistol at the flesh eater rushing toward him and fired three rounds into its face. A blue eddy of light, the creature's lifeforce, separated from its body and drifted skyward. The carcass went limp, forward momentum carrying it a few feet until it collapsed and tumbled onto the pavement. The other flesh eaters maneuvered around the body and swarmed the general. He shifted his aim to the next closest and fired three more rounds. The bullets punched into its chest and head, freeing its lifeforce and dropping the corporeal shell. Budenny continued his attack, taking down two more flesh eaters before the breach of his Makarov locked in the open position.

Major Rozhenko stepped in front of Budenny, his AK-47 automatic rifle raised. The major fired into the heads of the last six onrushing flesh eaters, bringing each down. The last fell in front of the major and rolled. Rozhenko stepped back so the carcass wouldn't knock him over, ejected the weapon's empty magazine, and loaded a fresh one.

Rozhenko's eyes pleaded with his commanding officer to end this carnage. "You have to order a retreat."

"No," barked the general.

"But...."

"We can do this." Budenny added under his breath, "We must."

"We" referred to the five thousand soldiers of the Russian Ground Forces surging across Red Square to close the portal that had opened in front of the State Historical Museum in the wake of the scientific accident at the Institute for High Energy Physics in Protvino, seventy miles south of Moscow. The portal measured seventy feet in diameter. The bottom five feet lay buried beneath ground level, melting the surrounding stones and forming a trough. Its circumference shimmered, creating a distorted boundary between the two realms. An endless column of flesh eaters stumbled through, their numbers stretching back into the other dimension as far as the eye could see. They had been pouring into Red Square and spreading out across Moscow since the portal first opened.

The electromagnetic pulse generated during its formation had burnt out all electronic circuitry for thousands of miles, rendering most of the military equipment useless. Not that it mattered. Budenny had scoured armories throughout the Urals to find "old school" weapons to arm his troops—AK-47 Kalashnikov automatic rifles, Makarov semi-automatic pistols, and a dozen TPO-70 heavy infantry flamethrowers left over from the Cold War. He also possessed four ten-man squads, each armed with a Special Atomic Demolition Munition, more commonly known as a "suitcase bomb," a portable low-yield nuclear weapon they would use to blast shut the portal. The general had thought his command would be able to deal with this threat.

To paraphrase von Moltke, no battle plan ever survived first contact with the enemy.

The flesh eaters threatened Budenny's force by their sheer numbers. As his troops advanced up Red Square, they ran into a seemingly impenetrable wall of the demons that slowed their pace. For every flesh eater brought down, twice as many took its place. It had taken nearly an hour to move only a few hundred feet. Their left flank was anchored by Lenin's Mausoleum in front of the Kremlin, with the line of advance stretching across Red Square before swerving north in front of Gum Department Store where the right flank pushed three hundred feet ahead. Two of the nuclear squads had fallen in behind this surge to get closer to the portal. Budenny had used his left flank to distract the bulk of the flesh eaters and give his right flank a chance. As a hedge, he had ordered the remaining two nuclear squads to maneuver toward the mausoleum to make an end run if the opportunity arose. Budenny hoped this would work because his men had already expended more than half their ammunition. Once they were out, the flesh eaters would overwhelm them.

A commotion came from the troops off to his left. Budenny focused his attention beyond the portal toward the northeast corner of the Kremlin, expecting to see more flesh eaters bearing down on them. Rozhenko expressed the disbelief both men felt when he muttered, "You've got to be kidding."

A dragon had emerged from behind the Kremlin wall and centered itself between the citadel and the State Historical Museum. It did not resemble the mythical creatures from the childhood fairy tales his grandmother had told him about dragons protecting the Motherland from foreign invaders. This monster had the shape of a lizard, albeit one that stretched two hundred feet from nose to tail and did not have wings. Its colorization was a deep red streaked with tints of orange. The scales were as thick as armored plates, especially around the head where the chin, nose, and brows extended outward in bony structures, and along the chest and spine where the skin peeked into thick ridges that glowed crimson. The beast crouched as if to lunge yet remained still and observed the battle through a pair of glossy, pitch black eyes.

Rozhenko moved beside Budenny. "General, we have to fall back now while we still have a chance."

Before Budenny could respond, two soldiers, each carrying a flamethrower, raced up on the dragon's flanks and doused it in flames, the one on the right aiming for its head, the other focusing on its massive chest. The behemoth reared up on its hind legs and screeched in agony. When the attack ceased, the dragon had not even been singed. It dropped onto all four legs, lowered the front part of its torso, and leaned its head forward. The glowing ridges along its chest and spine shone in intensity. Budenny sensed the panic that raced through his men.

Rather than fire, the dragon exhaled a cloud of lime green smoke tinted with thousands of crystals. The behemoth swung its head from side to side, producing a cloud that stretched for five hundred feet and expanded above Red Square, forming above the heads of flesh eaters and humans. It floated for several seconds before settling onto the troops. When the first crystal touched a hard surface, it ignited a flame no larger than the head of a lit match, which then kindled the lime green gas around it. The cloud became a raging inferno that burned itself out within seconds, incinerating flesh eaters and Budenny's men, leaving thousands of charred corpses sprawled across the square. A few remaining green crystals smoldered on the blackened skeletons and scorched pavement.

The left flank of Budenny's front panicked and broke into a horde of terrified men, including one of the nuclear squads, all of whom dropped their weapons and ran for the Moskva River. Colonel Yurchenko, who led the other nuclear squad, headed for shelter behind Lenin's Mausoleum. Budenny, Rozhenko, and a dozen soldiers followed, stopping only when they reached the relative safety of the tomb's southern wall.

Several of his men stood their ground inside the square, many aiming for the ridges along the dragon's chest and spine. The behemoth glared at them. A guttural growl emanated from deep within its throat. One of the flamethrowers circled to its right and released a stream of fire that engulfed its head. The growl became an agonized screech. Budenny braced himself for another gas attack. Instead, the dragon lifted its left leg and smashed its foot on top of the flamethrower. The fuel tank exploded, splashing liquid fire on the nearby troops. Those not burnt alive were crushed as the behemoth lowered its head to the pavement and swung it sideways, flinging a score of Budenny's men into the air to be smashed against the Kremlin walls. One brave comrade rushed forward and emptied his AK-47 into the dragon's face, only to be scooped up in its mouth. As the man screamed in pain and terror, the dragon lifted its head and swallowed. The final shreds of discipline among Budenny's left flank collapsed and a panicked escape ensued. Surging ahead, the dragon rampaged through the fleeing men, crushing them under its weight or hurling them aside.

The right flank remained intact and took advantage of the confusion. Moving toward the center of Red Square where the dragon's fire cloud had cleared away the flesh eaters, the other two nuclear squads, protected by one hundred troops, raced for the portal. A handful of new flesh eaters had passed through it to replace those wiped out, more than enough for the Russians to handle. They had closed to within fifty feet when a roar came from Nikolskaya Street, which ran alongside Gum Department Store and entered Red Square near Kazan Cathedral. A second dragon thundered into the plaza. The ridges along its chest and spine glowed crimson. Upon seeing the humans, it exhaled a lime green cloud over the advancing soldiers. The two nuclear squads rushed ahead, trying to plant their devices in the few remaining moments left to them. The crystals struck a hard surface and ignited. In seconds, the cloud became an inferno that incinerated another hundred troops and a score of flesh eaters. An explosion erupted from the fire cloud as one of the nuclear devices misfired, detonating with the equivalent of between ten and fifteen tons of high explosives.

Budenny and the others ducked behind the wall moments before the shock wave slammed into the mausoleum. The entire structure shook. Chunks of red marble broke loose and fell on them. Budenny felt his internal organs compress, fearing for a moment that they might rupture. The mausoleum took the brunt of the force, and the general suffered nothing more severe than a ringing in his ears. Leaning with his back against the wall, he shouted, "Is everyone okay?"

"Yes," Rozhenko responded. Budenny didn't hear the words but instead read his aide's lips.

"Wait here." The general made his way to the corner of the mausoleum and checked on the situation in Red Square. The blast had devastated everything within a two-hundred-foot radius. Those soldiers on the right flank not killed outright had been crushed or maimed from the concussion. Every flesh eaters in the square had been ripped apart, the blue light of their life forces mixing with black smoke as both drifted skyward. Even the dragon had not come through unscathed. The blast had thrown it against the front façade of Gum where it lay amongst a pile of debris. A gaping wound in its abdomen oozed blood and the torn remnants of internal organs. It tried to raise its legs and swing its tail, an effort that ended in a pathetic mewl before the behemoth went limp. For all the destruction it caused, the blast had one positive effect. It had cleared away all obstacles between them and the portal.

"Yurchenko," Budenny ordered. "Move while you have the chance."

The colonel did not waste time responding. He circled Budenny and rushed into Red Square, knowing the others would follow. The general watched as the squad raced toward the portal, confident they would make it.

AS YURCHENKO'S SQUAD approached the portal, half a dozen flesh eaters wandered through onto their side, only to be taken down by a barrage of automatic weapons fire. The squad stopped twenty feet from the opening, most providing suppressing fire against the demons that came through. Yurchenko slid off his backpack, lowered it onto the pavement, and unzipped it to reveal a cylindrical-shaped device eighteen inches in length by four inches in diameter. An LED display and keypad were built into one side. He would set the timer for two minutes, place it against the portal, and then get as far away as possible before the one kiloton explosion detonated and, in theory, blasted shut the portal. Yurchenko unlocked the keypad. The six spaces on the LED device lit up in a series of 0s. Once he typed in 120, he would—

A distorted roar shot across Red Square. The way his squad backed away from the portal told Yurchenko in which direction the sound came. A third dragon raced toward them from the other dimension. It rushed the opening, though still a thousand feet distant, crushing or pushing aside the flesh eaters heading in the same direction. Another roar came from behind him near St. Basil's. The first dragon had reversed direction, abandoning its pursuit of the fleeing humans to defend the portal. It had already approached to within one hundred feet, the ridges along its chest and spine a radiant crimson. The behemoth stopped, crouched low to the ground, and exhaled a cloud of lime green gas.

Yurchenko had a few seconds at most. He set the timer on the LED display to 1. Picking up the device, Yurchenko stepped up to the portal and initiated the countdown.

The first crystal touched one of Yurchenko's men, erupting into a spark that ignited the expanding cloud.

The LED counter switched to 0.

BUDENNY SHUT HIS eyes and ducked behind Lenin's Mausoleum as blinding light flashed across Red Square. Rozhenko scrambled over and threw himself on top of his commanding officer.

The dragon reared back, screeching as wisps of smoke formed on the skin and scales exposed to the fireball. A moment later, the shock wave slammed into the behemoth, tearing it apart and flinging the shattered carcass across the square to land in a bloody heap in front of St. Basil's.

The same shock wave slammed into the mausoleum, shearing off the top layers of marble and the reviewing stand, and dropping the fragments onto those hidden along the southern facade. Rozhenko groaned when a chunk fell on him. Budenny did not hear the major, being only vaguely cognizant of his surroundings for the next minute, sliding in and out of consciousness. When he regained his senses, he heard a low rumbling, and immediately knew what caused the sound.

"Rozhenko, get up. It's over."

The major did not respond. Budenny reached up to shake his shoulder. A warm liquid covered his palm. Rozhenko's body slid down the general's back and onto the marble debris surrounding them. Blood flowed from the torn skin around his crushed skull. His blank eyes stared up. Budenny placed two fingers over the major's lids and closed them. When the general stood, he could not see out of his right eye and the skin on that side of his face felt warm and numb. He would worry about his wounds later. Right now, he needed to confirm that Yurchenko had closed the portal. Placing his left hand against the mausoleum's wall, Budenny stumbled through the debris until he reached the corner of structure.

Smoke and dust shrouded most of Red Square. The rumbling came from a cloud that billowed skyward, the top forming into its familiar mushroom shape. Budenny could not see the section of Red Square where the portal once stood. He leaned against the wall and waited as the dust settled. His heart sank when he saw something shimmer on the other side of the smoke. The blast had not affected the portal. The explosion had penetrated the opening because the dragon and the closest flesh eaters on the other side had been cut down. The portal, however, remained intact. He had lost almost five thousand men to seal off this portal and had been unsuccessful.

Budenny slid down the wall and sat on the rubble from the mausoleum. He laid his head back and closed his eyes, wishing he had died along with the rest of his men. His failure meant that nothing would stop the demons from flooding into Moscow.

CHAPTER TWO

Mont St. Michel, three weeks after the closure of the portal in Paris

J ASON MCCREARY STOOD on the terrace outside of the main doors of the Abbey. He leaned forward with his arms resting on the wall, staring out over the bay. Lucifer, one of his two werehounds, lay curled up at his feet, snoring peacefully. The werehound still had scabs across his back from where a soul vampire had vomited acid on him during the battle inside Notre Dame Cathedral. Although the wounds had hurt for several days, with Lucifer whimpering for much of the journey home, they eventually healed. Lilith stood to Jason's right, her front paws perched on the wall and her tail wagging. She blinked from the wind gusting in from the bay, the same wind that ruffled her shiny black fur. Jason reached out and scratched Lilith behind the ears. She responded by twisting her head to the side and licking his wrist.

The view from the terrace was spectacular. From here, Jason could see most of the surrounding mainland. Off in the distance, across the other side of the bay and past the sandbars and the island outcrop of Tombelaine, sat the coastline of the Cherbourg Peninsula. In the old days, Jason used to stand here for hours watching for any Demon Spawn that approached Mont St. Michel, knowing their arrival would mean the end of the remnants of the civilization they had created. The closure of the interdimensional portal in Paris had destroyed all the demons that had emerged from it, ending the threat to the island city. It had been months since Jason could appreciate the beauty of the view rather than merely its strategic significance.

Jason was learning to embrace the good things in his life. Since returning to Mont St. Michel two weeks ago with the surviving Demon Hunters—the honorific the locals had given them for closing the portal—he had graciously endured the accolades heaped on him and his team by the island residents and the refugees camped along the coast. Everywhere in town the Demon Hunters went they were greeted with handshakes and back slaps. Jacques, the leader of the community, had declared his team heroes and the saviors of mankind. In a celebratory mass a few days ago, Bishop Fiorello referred to them as "God's warriors in the battle against Satan." Jason could not agree more. His team deserved the praise they received. They had faced and overcome insurmountable odds to complete what everyone, including himself, had considered a suicide mission. For his part, though, Jason found it hard to accept the tribute. While everyone now treated him as a retuning hero, they all seemed to forget that when he left for Paris he had been viewed as the city pariah.

In the months following the opening of the portals, everyone at Mont St. Michel had held Jason responsible for the apocalypse. To be fair, no one had blamed him for the incident at the European Organization for Nuclear Research, or CERN, in Geneva. They realized Jason's mother, Dr. Lisa McCreary, had pushed the scientific community to engage in a risky experiment to use five supercolliders around the world to simultaneously generate separate caches of anti-matter and that the consequences of this experiment had created five interdimensional portals. However, the locals ensured that Jason wore the stigma of his mother's infamy. He had endured the staring eyes, the pointed fingers, and the whispers behind his back that he was Dr. Lisa McCreary's son. At the time too immature to know better, Jason had accepted the full burden of responsibility for his mother's failure even though it ate away at him. He joined the search and destroy team that roamed the countryside seeking out approaching Demon Spawn hoping, as Doc had once phrased it, for "suicide by demons." That was until the mission to Paris when Jason had learned that his mother had been warned about the dangers of her plan and had proceeded anyway. The portals were not an accident of scientific curiosity. His mother's intellectual arrogance and refusal to heed warnings were the reason the world now lived in a new Dark Age. That cross he refused to bear. Separating himself from his mother's guilt was the most liberating thing he had done.

Jason still found it difficult to comprehend how events had played themselves out. He had been allowed to accompany the group, despite almost every member of the search and destroy team making it clear they did not want him along, because Andre, the group leader, had insisted. He saw past Jason's weaknesses and relied on his sixth sense to perceive the Demon Spawn's aura to provide the group with an early warning of approaching danger. At first, their confidence in him had seemed misguided. A few days into the trip, Jason's arrogance had led the group into a field of pus zombies where Christophe was infected by spores that turned him into a flesh eater. The entire dynamic had changed when Demon Spawn killed Andre the next day, and the rest of the group turned to Jason for leadership. He still could not ascertain why. Maybe it had been his sixth sense, which gave the group a slight advantage over the demons. Or maybe it was his determination to complete what the team had started that inspired them. It may have been as simple as no one else wanting the burden of command. In any case, Jason took the remainder of the team to Paris and closed the portal. He may have left Mont St. Michel a pariah but he had returned a hero.

None of this changed the fact that their mission, while successful, had been achieved at a terrible cost. When the Demon Hunters had left Mont St. Michel, they had numbered twenty. Only seven of the original group survived. Two deaths bothered him because they were the only people with whom Jason had been close. Eric Fisher, whom he called Doc, had been his mother's colleague. Doc had been at CERN the day the gate opened, had witnessed Jason's mother being sucked into the other dimension, and had gotten Jason to safety. Doc had devised the anti-matter device, so he had accompanied the group to Paris to deploy it, only to be crushed by a Golem moments before seeing his concept put into reality.

Jason had also lost Sasha, who had commanded one of the minigun teams. Her death had hit him harder than the others. Even though she was several years his senior, he had a huge crush on her. Sasha had kept him at arm's length and had treated him more like a little brother than a boyfriend. Jason had not known how much she truly cared until she admitted her affections for him moments before they engaged the Demon Spawn inside Notre Dame Cathedral. Sasha died a few minutes later while distracting a horde of flesh eaters long enough for Jason to use the device. He had been denied the opportunity to say goodbye and, after the battle, could not summon the courage to find Sasha's body and pay last respects, wanting to remember her the way she had been in life. Even worse, he had never gotten the chance to tell Sasha how he really felt about her. By then, Jason had fallen in love with Jeanette. He still possessed strong emotions for Sasha, although he found it difficult to define them. She had filled a space in his life much greater than that of a friend, yet without the shared emotional intimacy of lovers. Sasha had understood him more deeply than anyone else. She had known when to offer him encouragement and when to put him in his place. A bond had existed between the two he could not describe. Jason had once heard Doc use the term soulmate to describe a woman he had been close to in college. Jason had never asked Doc to explain what he meant by soulmate but, from the sound of it, the term accurately described the relationship he had with Sasha.

Lilith barked once, her tail wagging. Jeanette sidled up

beside Lilith and petted her. The werehound shook in excitement, especially when Jeanette placed her hand behind Lilith's ears and scratched.

"Who's a good girl?" Jeanette asked.

She received three licks on the face as her answer.

Jason had never met anyone like Jeanette. They were both sixteen, although she retained the soft, gentle facial features of a teenager despite having the poise and bearing of a warrior. Usually she wore her long brunette hair in a ponytail. Today, it hung down her back and draped over her shoulders, the strands blowing in the wind. Jeanette was as beautiful now as when he had first met her in the town of Notre Dame de la Garenne when the Enclavers had rescued his group from a magma monster. Claude Reno, the head of the Enclavers who had converted an underground World War II bunker into a survivalist camp, had provided Jason's group a safe place to rest for a few days. Jeanette, Reno's niece, led them into Paris and guided them to the portal. Afterwards, she left the Enclave and followed Jason back to Mont St. Michel. Jeanette was the only person who cared for him because of who he was and never judged him for what his mother had done.

When she smiled at him, his heart soared. For a moment, he forgot about everything except her.

"Why didn't you knock on my door this morning so we could have breakfast together?" she asked.

"I skipped breakfast. I came up here to go over what I plan to say to the town council this morning."

"Do you think they'll agree with your suggestion?"

"They'd be foolish not to."

That didn't mean they would go along with his recommendation. Ever since the closing of the portal, Jason had noticed that Jacques and the others were more concerned with maintaining power than rebuilding society and ensuring their future safety. It left him in awe how those who ordered troops into battle without ever having led from the front possessed such a distorted view of the reality of war.

"What if they say no?"

"I'll convince them."

"I know you will." Jeanette hesitated. "Is there any other way to do this?"

Jason leaned against the wall and faced her. "Are you having doubts?"

"No. It has to be done. But is what you're about to propose the best way to carry it out?"

"There is no *good* way. I thought about this for a long time. Every scenario has more cons than pros. This is the one I think we can pull off and, hopefully, the one the council will buy into."

Jeanette maneuvered around Lilith. Stepping up to Jason, she straightened the collar of his jacket and used her right hand to flatten down his shirt. "If I was on the council, I'd vote for you."

Jason chuckled. "You're biased."

"You're right. I am." Jeanette leaned in and kissed him. "Good luck. I'll be waiting for you back at the hotel."

Jason crossed the terrace, leaving Lilith and Lucifer with Jeanette. As he approached the double doors leading into the Abbey he paused, took a deep breath to steady his nerves, and exhaled. Pushing the door aside, Jason entered.

CHAPTER THREE

J ACQUES' OFFICE WAS in the abbot's lodging atop the southern
Romanesque wall surrounding the Abbey, giving it a
commanding view of the island city below. A walkway spanned
the stone stairs that wound up the southeastern façade between
the exterior fortress wall and the Abbey, providing the only
access to his quarters. Jacques kept Jason waiting in the outer
foyer for ten minutes, which irritated him. Not because of the
delay. The inconvenience didn't bother him. Despite all the
accolades heaped upon him, Jason refused to view himself as
privileged or more deserving than anyone else at Mont St.
Michel. While Jason and the others appreciated the gratitude
they received from the local citizens, they did not feel that their
service should place them in an exalted position. Jacques did
this to everyone to remind people that he was in charge. Such
arrogance might have been acceptable if Jacques had led the
mission to Paris or commanded even one of the search and
destroy missions that used to patrol the area keeping the city
safe.

After another five minutes, the door to Jacques' office
opened and a young woman emerged. Jason estimated her to
be his own age, maybe a year older. She stood a few inches
short of six feet. She had a firm body and was exceptionally
pretty, with brunette hair cut into a bob and brown eyes that
were dark and beautiful, yet sad. The woman benefitted from
better grooming and cleaner clothes than the others in town
had access to. Her privileged position must have embarrassed
her because she averted her gaze.

"Jacques will see you now," she whispered.

"Thanks." Jason approached the door. He slowed as he entered the room, pausing long enough to place a hand on the woman's wrist. "Is everything okay?"

The woman's demeanor brightened. "Thank you for asking."

"But you didn't answer me."

"Everything's fine." Her pleasantness faded and she glanced over at Jacques. "Considering."

Jason squeezed her wrist reassuringly and entered. A small fireplace opposite the door provided heat. To the left, three windows with wooden frames overlooked the city, and to the right hung a painting of the Crucifixion taking place in Hell. The furnishings were antique yet basic. A large wooden dining table now used as a map display dominated the center of the office, with the eight chairs that belonged to it placed in empty spaces against the walls. Jacques and Bishop Fiorello stood on one side of the table with their backs to the window and the leaders of the protective force across from them. Jason recognized the symbolism even if no one else did. Jacques wanted to reinforce that the political/religious leaders and the protective force were separate entities, and only one of them watched over the people of Mont St. Michel. It was political showmanship at its worst because each of the men who stood opposite Jacques and the Bishop had given far more to defend this city than the other two ever would.

Haneef had led one of the two minigun teams into Paris and was the only team leader besides Jason to come back alive. His five-feet-seven-inch stature, muscular body, and battle-weary face belied the man's calm and personable demeanor. A devout Muslim from Sudan, Haneef had never adopted the extremist views that so many of his religious counterparts had, opting instead to study international law in Paris. He had been in his third semester of college when the portal opened, and barely escaped the city with his life before making his way to

Mont St. Michel. Haneef had lost more than half his team in Paris. Upon arriving back at the island city, Jason absorbed the rest of Haneef's people under his own command and Haneef took on the responsibility of training new personnel. Despite everything, Haneef remained devout in his faith. He prayed to Mecca whenever possible yet shaved his head and forewent facial hair to show his disdain for Islamic fundamentalism. He viewed the portal as Allah's punishment for the extremism that had taken hold of Islam, Christianity, and Judaism and believed he would survive the apocalypse if he could follow the Koran the way Allah had originally intended.

Gruber stood to Haneef's right. He was six feet in height with blonde hair, blue eyes, and an angular face. No one knew Gruber's story other than he had graduated from college in Bonn and had been vacationing in southern France when the world came to an end. Jacques had given Gruber's team responsibility for defending Mont St. Michel while the others went on search and destroy missions. The only time Gruber's team had seen action was when Jacques had sent them to Geneva to report on the original portal generated at CERN. Half of them died, and Gruber never recovered from the loss. When Jacques sent a second team to check on CERN following the closure of the Paris portal, he had selected Ryan, another member of the protective force, to lead the mission. Jacques had retained Gruber as the leader of a reconstituted city defense team which, now that Demon Spawn no longer roamed the countryside, made him little more than the town constabulary.

Neal Branagan stood at the other end of the table. Although in his early twenties, he still had a boyish face and wavy blonde hair in desperate need of a trim. His eyes seemed older, blue and narrow, mirrors to a soul that had seen and experienced more horrors than someone his age should. Neal was the shortest of the group at five-feet-six inches and had a lean, non-muscular physique. A student at Johns Hopkins University, he had been interning in Paris when the portal opened. Upon arriving at Mont St. Michel, Jacques had assigned him to work with Doc in the infirmary because of his medical background. In time, Neal assisted Doc in developing the anti-matter devices. When Doc died, by default Neal assumed the post of chief physician and anti-matter expert. Jacques kept Neal on the other side of the table along with the protective force leaders so the young man would remember his place in the town's hierarchical structure.

Jacques looked up at Jason as he approached. Jason assumed him to be in his early to mid-sixties, although the burdens of trying to keep Mont St. Michel safe had prematurely aged him. Long, scraggily white hair framed a face creased by wrinkles and highlighted by dark circles under the eyes. Since Paris, Jacques seemed happier and more at ease. Bishop Fiorello stepped back from the table to observe Jason. No one in the city liked the Bishop, least of all the protective force personnel, and not because of the cleric's perpetually stern visage or his "God is punishing us for our sins" attitude. The disdain came from the fact that, in a city where the food supply hovered near starvation levels, his paunch strained against the fabric of his black cassock.

"My boy, it's good to see you again. Come join us." Jacques extended his right hand. As Jason shook it, Jacques said, "I have some excellent news for you. Ryan's group got back from Geneva this morning."

"What did they find?"

"As you expected, the CERN portal was no longer open. When you detonated the device that shut down the exit portal, you must have closed the entry one as well."

"That *is* excellent news."

"I thought you'd be pleased. That makes the other news I have even more relevant." Jacques placed his left hand on the boy's shoulders and steered him toward the table. "I want you to see this."

A map of Mont St. Michel and the surrounding area was spread out across the table, held down in the corners by stones. Jacques always displayed a map like this, only in the past it had been used to plot the locations of approaching Demon Spawn to determine when the city would be overwhelmed. They had called it the Death Map. The closing of the portal killed off every demon that had spilled forth from it, making the Death Map unnecessary. This one marked the towns nearest to Mont St. Michel and delineated large swaths of land, both high-lighted in yellow.

"Now that we're no longer in danger, I plan on rebuilding civilization," Jacques explained. "We're going to move all the survivors camped outside the walls into abandoned towns along the coast. Gruber's team has been surveying the countryside and says there is plenty of fallow land that can be farmed. Those with special skills can work here in Mont St. Michel and produce the items we need to survive. The rest will each be given five acres of land and will provide food for themselves and for those of us in town."

"Like serfs," said Jason, making little attempt to hide the derision is his voice.

Bishop Fiorello bristled. "Like citizens of a new France."

Jacques was more diplomatic. "We're not going to take food from the farmers without making some type of trade. It'll be a barter society. Those in the countryside will offer food for the goods and services the town provides. I know it's a far cry from where we were, but it's a new beginning. And we owe it all to you."

"No, you don't."

Jacques tried not to appear offended. "No need to be modest."

"It has nothing to do with modesty. People like Haneef and Neal, and a lot of good men and women who died, paid for this new beginning. I only led them."

"I used you as a representation of all the Demon Hunters,"

said Jacques trying to recover from his *faux pas*. He gestured to the others standing across from him. "Trust me when I say everyone in Mont St. Michel is grateful for all that you've done for us, especially me."

"And me," added Bishop Fiorello.

Haneef and Gruber nodded with the self-assuredness of combat veterans who have been slighted by civilians. Neal grew self-conscious and averted his eyes. Jason had made his point and decided not to pursue the matter any further, especially since he needed Jacques' support.

"We know that, and we appreciate it. The Demon Hunters would never have been able to succeed if we didn't have the town council behind us."

Jacques accepted his victory graciously. He clapped his hands together once, signifying a change in topic. "So, you wanted to see me because you have a favor to ask?"

"More like a request."

Bishop Fiorello frowned. "I don't see the diff—"

Jacques held up a hand, cutting off the cleric. "Go ahead."

Jason took one step toward the table. "I want your permission to rebuild the search and destroy team and close down the other portals."

CHAPTER FOUR

HANEEF AND GRUBER seemed confused. Neal raised his head, his eyes wide with surprise. Bishop Fiorello huffed. Jacques studied Jason, his expression stoic. He remained silent for several seconds before saying, "Go on."

"According to information Reno gathered talking to other survivors, the creation of an entry portal at each of the super colliders involved in my mother's experiment generated a corresponding exit portal nearby. That means there are still four more portals in Russia, China, Japan, and the United States. We stand a good chance of closing those down like we did the one in Paris."

"How are they our concern?" asked Bishop Fiorello.

"Have you already forgotten the fear we all faced as the Demon Spawn drew near?" Haneef responded. "I'm sure the people living around those portals are experiencing the same thing. If we can close the gates and eliminate the threat, we have an obligation to do so. Or does the church in your new France no longer feel compassion toward their fellow man?"

"It has nothing to do with compassion but with logistics," said Jacques. "I would hate to expend resources desperately needed here to send you around the globe to find that the other countries have already solved their problem."

"I doubt that'll happen," said Jason. "The anti-matter devices Doc created are the only things that will work."

"Could someone at one of the other labs create a device of their own?"

"Unlikely. As far as we know, only CERN could create

solidified anti-matter. Besides, all electronic records were lost when the EMP pulses fried the computers. We were fortunate that Doc remembered the frequency of the Geneva portal when it opened, which allowed him to create the devices."

"Will they survive a long journey?" asked Jacques.

All eyes fell upon Neal. "I guess so," he said hesitantly.

"You guess?" asked Jacques.

"The device we used in Paris survived the trip and worked when we deployed it, so theoretically they should all make it. But Russia is a lot farther away than Paris, let alone Asia and the States. God knows what type of Demon Spawn we'll run into along the way."

"How many devices did Doc create before he... before Paris?" Jason asked.

"Five, in addition to the one already deployed."

"And there are four more portals," said Jason.

Jacques paused while he took in the information. "Neal, what are the odds of four of the devices making such a trip and still working?"

"That depends on whether the team survives."

"Assuming the team makes it to the portals, what are the odds of the devices working?"

"Structurally, they're sound. Time and normal wear and tear shouldn't affect them. As long as they don't get kicked around like footballs, they'll survive the trip."

"We can build special carry cases," Jason added. "We can line the cases with metal to strengthen them and add extra padding if necessary."

"Will that work?" Jacques asked Neal.

"It'll increase the odds but I wouldn't want to bet my life on it."

"That's a shame," said Jason, "since you'll be going with us."

"What?"

"This mission doesn't have a chance of succeeding without

you. You're the only one who knows how the devices work."

"Doc built them before I arrived. I only helped maintain them."

"That still makes you more qualified to handle them than anyone else."

"Enough." Jacques contemplated what Jason had proposed. "Gruber, how many soldiers would Jason need to take with him for this to succeed?"

Gruber mentally crunched the numbers. "Based on Paris, the number of portals to be closed, and the distance that needs to be traveled, I would say at least a hundred, maybe a hundred and fifty people."

"Impossible," snorted Bishop Fiorello.

"You're right," Jason agreed, hoping to quell Jacques' skepticism. "That number is unworkable. It would deprive Mont St. Michel of most of its able-bodied men and women when the city needs them most. Besides, such a group would be logistically impossible to supply from here and could not be sustained on the road."

"That's true," said Gruber.

"What do you recommend?" Jacques asked.

"I want to reconstitute my search and destroy team with those who survived the mission to Paris. I'll put out a call for volunteers to flesh out our numbers. I'm talking twelve, maybe fifteen people at most."

Gruber shook his head. "You don't stand a chance with those numbers."

"We'll supplement our force along the way, getting the locals near the other portals to *ante* up troops that we can train."

Bishop Fiorello chuckled. "If you're going to offer them salvation, they can at least provide the sacrifices?"

"Crudely put, but yes," said Jason.

"Why take all the Demon Hunters?" asked the cleric. "By taking the best people, you leave us vulnerable."

"It makes perfect sense," Jacques interceded. "The Demon Hunters were trained to fight these creatures. To keep them here doing what amounts to police work would be a waste of resources."

Jacques stepped over to the windows, staring mindlessly at his town. Jason kept his gaze focused on Jacques. After several minutes, the latter turned and addressed Jason.

"You have my permission to take up to fifteen people with you and any supplies that you need. When will you be ready to leave?"

"In three days," said Jason.

"That won't give you enough time to train the volunteers," said Gruber.

"We'll train them on the way," Jason responded. "We'll have the time. It'll take us ten weeks to reach Moscow. I want to get on the road as soon as possible."

"Agreed." Jacques clapped his hands together. "That's it, then. I'll issue orders to provide what you need. If you run into resistance, let me know. Are there any questions?"

None.

"That'll be all."

Haneef and Gruber exited. Neal hesitated, casting Jason a disapproving glare on his way out. Jason would talk him down later. Right now, he mentally complimented himself for getting the council to agree. Once the others had left, Jason headed back into town. He had a lot to accomplish in the next three days.

BISHOP FIORELLO WAITED until everyone had departed before speaking. "I would never question you in front of the others, but do you think it's a good idea to send fifteen of our best people off on a wild goose chase?"

"I appreciate your concern." Jacques moved back to the table. "It's far from a wild goose chase, though. It offers us the best of both worlds."

"I'm not following you."

"If I send Jason's team around the world to close the portals and they're successful, then the world will remember who saved them."

Bishop Fiorello raised an eyelid. "And they'll owe us a debt of gratitude."

"Exactly. And if Jason's team is successful, we'll never have to worry about Demon Spawn finding their way to Mont St. Michel. It'll guarantee our survival."

"What if they fail?"

"That would be unfortunate." Jacques shrugged. "But at least we would be rid of anyone here who could pose a challenge to our authority."

CHAPTER FIVE

MOST OF THE tables in the restaurant-turned-dining-hall of *La Mere Poulard*, the hotel outside the main gate of Mont St. Michel that served as the quarters for the protective force, had been stacked against one wall. Two tables stood lengthwise across the center of the floor with eight chairs lined up on one side for Jason and the surviving members of the team that had gone into Paris. The dangers they would face traveling around the world would be undeterminable; Jason assumed that what they had encountered in Paris would pale in comparison to the other Demon Spawn that awaited them. In addition, the chances of any of them surviving the closure of all the portals were slim. Because of this, Jason decided only to recruit volunteers. To his delight, everyone from his original team stepped forward to take on this new adventure. They sat in the dining hall to interview the perspective new members.

Jason and Haneef, his second-in-command, occupied the two center chairs. Off to their right sat Slava. Slava stood five-feet-eleven-inches in height with a muscular build, spiked dark hair, and a goatee. A lot of the wind had been taken out of his sails over the past few months. He and Andre, who used to oversee the search and destroy team, had been street thugs in Moscow prior to the apocalypse. Andre had been the brains and Slava the muscle. Once at Mont St. Michel, they had ruled over the protective force with an iron hand and had taken pleasure in bullying Jason. All that had changed at Falaise when Andre had been killed by man-sized wasps and Jason assumed control. Slava accepted Jason as the new leader and followed him faithfully. His loyalty, toughness, and willingness to engage the Demon Spawn would be critical in the months ahead. Next in line sat Antoine, the most enigmatic member of their team. Born in Casablanca, Antoine had been a member of a Moroccan gang in Lyons when that city had been overrun by demons. In combat, he was callous and violent, one of the best fighters in the entire protective force. In private, he adopted an unassuming demeanor. Several of the team would not be here today if Antoine did not have their backs in Paris. At the end of the table sat Sook-kyoung, the exchange student from the University of Seoul and the one member of the team who seemed most out of place. Tall, slender, attractive, and quiet, she gave the impression of being a college student. However, Sook-kyoung had a black belt in Taekwondo that made her as tough as the others.

Reinhard sat on Jason's left. Bald and lanky, the German never smiled and rarely spoke; when he did, he used short, curt sentences. Not that it mattered. Jason appreciated him for his fighting skills, not his conversation. Jeanette sat two chairs away with Neal at the end, who fidgeted. Neal had argued earlier that he had no business selecting the other team members since he had no combat skills and was being dragged along for the sole purpose of carrying the anti-matter devices. Jason told him that anyone on the team who would place their lives in the hands of other members should have a say as to who joined. Of course, Neal's discomfort could stem from the fact that, so far, the search for new team members had been pitiful.

Jason had put out a call for volunteers that morning. By late afternoon, less than a dozen applicants had lined up out front. The first four had been a waste of time: two brothers, sixteen and seventeen years of age, who wanted to go on the mission because "it sounded fun"; a mousey young woman in her early twenties who was bored and wanted to see "some adventure"; and a middle-aged man from the refugee camp outside the city walls who had lost his family in the first few weeks of the openings and claimed he wanted payback, although Jason knew he wanted to die in combat and join his family.

The man who now sat on the single chair that stood in front of the tables seemed no different than the others. He was five-and-a-half-feet in height, stout, with brown eyes and scraggily dark hair. Jason assumed him to be in his early to mid-thirties. His demeanor exuded confidence, though he displayed nothing that could label him as arrogant or pompous. He bore himself with a sense of sureness, and it didn't concern him whether those across from him realized it or not. Jason intended to find out if he had something to back up that poise.

"What's your name?" Jason asked.

"Gaston Chatelaine. You must be Jason McCreary."

"I am."

"You did an excellent job in Paris."

"You mean closing the portal?"

"That and getting so many of your people out alive." Gaston offered the praise in all honesty and not as someone trying to ingratiate himself.

"Where are you from?"

"Normandy. I was born and lived within ten miles of the coast all my life. I owned a farm near Pont du Hoc until demons overran it, especially those things that spit acid. What do you call them?"

"Soul vampires," Haneef answered.

Gaston shook his head. "Disagreeable little bastards. They killed off all my livestock in minutes. It distracted them long enough to give me a chance to get away."

"And you want revenge for what the Demon Spawn did to your farm?" Jason asked.

"What good would revenge be, other than giving me a sense of satisfaction? They have no soul or conscience. It would be like killing a fox for eating your chickens. The fox didn't do it out of cruelty. He did it because that's what he does. Besides, I still have my farm and can restock it and start over."

"Why don't you resume farming?" Jeanette asked.

Gaston leaned forward and placed his elbows on the ends of the chair rests. "As long as the other portals are open, there's always a chance that the Demon Spawn may come back. You know that, which is why you're going on this expedition. It's going to take you a year, maybe more, to do all this. I can help."

"How?"

"I'm what you Americans call a *suvivaliste.*"

Jason raised an eyebrow. "A survivalist?"

"*Oui.*"

"Can you handle a weapon?" Jason asked.

Gaston chuckled. "A better question would be is there a weapon I *can't* handle."

"Let's put your survivalist skills to the test," said Slava. "How do you purify water?"

"Small amounts or large quantities?"

"Both."

"The quickest way to purify water is to use two drops of bleach for each quart of water, or half a teaspoon for every five gallons." Gaston met Slava's gaze. "If you're trying to purify larger quantities, your best bet is a home-made filter system comprised of layers of rock, sand, and charcoal. Of course, no matter which method you use, I'd boil everything before I drank it."

"How would you heal a large flesh wound?"

"Seal it with crazy glue, if you had any, and then wrap the wounded area in duct tape." Gaston smirked. "Are you going to ask me any difficult questions?"

"No need to." Slava said to Jason, "I say he's in."

The others around the table approved.

"Congratulations," said Jason. "You're on the team."

"I hope I can be of service."

"Trust me, you will be." Jason motioned toward the door. "Please wait for us in the lobby and we'll process you in a bit."

★ ★ ★

JASON WAS PLEASED to see Werner enter the dining hall and take the seat in front of them. Werner had served on Gruber's team. He had gone to Geneva a month ago to check on the entry portal at CERN, a mission which cost Gruber half his men. Jason did not know Werner personally, but knew of his reputation. He had been a corporal in the German Army stationed with an armored brigade in Bavaria when the portals opened. Since mechanized vehicles no longer operated following the world-wide EMP that accompanied the creation of the portals, Werner had been assigned to a contingency unit sent by Berlin to help stem the flow of Demon Spawn coming from Paris. They had been swarmed by soul vampires near Troyes and wiped out. Werner and a handful of others had managed to escape, and he eventually made his way to Mont St. Michel. He still bore scars on his left hand and forearm from where he had been splashed with acid spit from one of the creatures. Werner possessed the bearing of a soldier, with his six-foot-one-inch frame always at attention, his angular face clean shaven, and his blonde hair trimmed into a crew cut.

"It's good to see you," said Jason.

"Thanks." Werner slid into the chair.

"Why are you here?" asked Slava.

Werner seemed hesitant. "I thought you wanted volunteers."

"We do. But you don't have to interview for it. You're one of us. Ask and you're in."

"Many thanks." Werner rose from the chair.

"I have a question," said Jason.

Werner paused and sat back down.

"You've been part of Gruber's team protecting the town for almost six months. You've gone above and beyond by joining the mission to Geneva. I know Gruber could use you. Why do you want to go with us?"

"I'm a soldier," said Werner. "If those things had ever reached here, I would have died defending this place. That's not going to happen now. If I stay behind, I'll be nothing more than a glorified policeman. My place is out there fighting." The German hesitated for a moment as if deciding to speak his mind. When he spoke, his voice had lowered a few octaves. "Besides, I don't like some of the changes that are going on around here."

Jason understood. "We're glad to have you."

JASON HAD NEVER seen this man before, so he assumed him to be one of the thousands of survivors who had sought refuge in the tourist hotels and campgrounds surrounding the town. Jason studied him, attempting to determine what skills he brought to the team. Nothing about him suggested he had military or police training. He was of average height and build, with short cut blonde hair already greying around the brows, and soft facial features. Rather than concentrate on those whom he needed to impress, he checked out the dining hall, taking in all the features.

"We're ready if you are," said Jason.

"I'm ready, mate." The man focused his attention back on those seated at the table. Several seconds passed.

"And you are?" Jason asked.

"Ian Taylor." Another pause.

"Why are you volunteering to go with us?"

"This trip promises to be one of the greatest scientific discoveries in all of history and I want to be a part of it."

"You're a scientist?" Jason asked.

"Yes."

Murmurs of discontent could be heard up and down the table. Neal leaned forward and raised his eyebrows, pleading to give Ian a chance.

"You sound Australian," said Jason.

"I am. Born in the Outback and raised in Sydney."

"You're a long way from home," said Jason.

"Tell me about it. I was supposed to be attending a symposium in Paris. Luckily, I stopped off in London for a few days first to see some old college mates, otherwise I would have been at Ground Zero when those demonic wankers broke onto the scene. When everything went dead, I was on a train in the Chunnel."

"Do you have any military training?"

"Nope."

"Can you handle a weapon?"

"Nope."

"Do you have skills that can be useful on a trip like this?"

"Not unless you count a few years in the Scouts."

"I'm sorry, Ian." Jason leaned back against his chair. "There's nothing we—"

"Wait a minute," interrupted Neal. He sat back and leaned to one side, talking behind Jeanette's and Reinhard's back, speaking soft enough that Jason could hardly hear him. "I could use Ian."

"How?"

"I'm the only one in Mont St. Michel with any scientific background." Neal sat forward and called out to Ian. "What's your field of science?"

"Evolutionary biology."

"Any other training?"

"Well, I had one year of med school before...." Ian thought about the proper words. "They requested I leave."

"What happened?" Neal asked.

At first Ian didn't answer, then he shrugged. "The school caught me stealing Valium. I sold most of it to make a few extra dollars and used the rest to lighten up on the weekend. That ended my career as a doctor, so I went into biology instead."

Neal switched his attention back to Jason. "We need him. He has medical experience as well as knowledge about science. I can train him to help maintain the devices."

"He has no training to go up against Demon Spawn," said Jason. "Someone will have to watch out for him at all times, which could get us killed."

"Doc and I didn't have any training, but you took us along."

"We had to." Jason knew where this line of reasoning was heading. "You were the only two who knew how to handle the devices."

"And now I'm the only one who knows how to do that. If something happens to me, this whole expedition fails." Neal let the words sink in for a few moments before switching to a more conciliatory tone. "I'll train Ian as my backup. That'll double our chances of success. As for his lack of military skills, it'll be several weeks before we encounter any Demon Spawn, which should give you enough time to make him proficient in combat tactics."

Jason conceded. His eyes focused on the others seated at the table. "Does anyone have any objections?"

No one did.

"That settles it," said Jason. "You're part of the team."

"Thanks, mate. Believe it or not, this isn't the worst job interview I've ever had." Ian stood and headed for the door, then stopped and faced the table. "I know you're taking a big chance on bringing me along. I promise I won't let you down."

THE MOMENT THE young woman stepped into the dining hall Jason recognized her as the one who had opened the door for him in Jacques' office. She entered with her head bowed, dropped into the chair, and kept her gaze locked onto the floor.

"Good to see you again," said Jason.

"Thanks." She still did not make eye contact.

"I didn't catch your name earlier."

"It's Victoria. My friends call me Vicky."

"Vicky, please look at me." Jason said it gently, making it sound more like a request than an order. When she did, Jason smiled at her. "You're here to volunteer for our team?"

"Yes," she responded quickly. "I have to... I mean, I want to join."

Jason understood.

"What skills do you have that will be of value?" Haneef asked.

Vicky's eyes focused back on the floor. "None."

"Can you shoot a weapon?"

"I shot a pistol once a few years ago when my brother took me to the range."

"That's not much," said Slava.

"Do you have any survival skills?" Haneef asked.

"No."

"Ever go hunting?"

Vicky shook her head.

"Camping?"

Vicky cried.

"Don't worry," said Jason. "You're on the team."

"Why?" Haneef asked.

"She needs to be on the team for the same reason Werner wants to be on it."

Haneef stared at Jason for a moment and then his eyebrows rose. "Don't worry. I'll train her."

"Do you think Jacques will allow her to go?" asked Jeanette.

"He said I could have whoever I wanted."

"But this is...." Jeanette paused.

"Difficult," Jason agreed. Vicky stared at the floor and cried. "Vicky?"

She sniffed. "What?"

"Look at me."

Vicky raised her head and ran the back of her hand across her nose.

"How did you become Jacques'… assistant?"

"My parents and I lived in Cherbourg when the portal opened. We were lucky. All three of us made it to the refugee camp. While Jacques' people were taking a census of the camp, they realized my folks were older and unable to farm. Jacques agreed to take care of them and set them up in their old business here in Mont St. Michel if I became his… his…."

"Assistant." Jason finished the sentence for her.

"Thanks," said Vicky.

"What did your parents do in Cherbourg?" asked Haneef.

"They ran an apothecary."

Neal leaned forward. "I need Vicky to be my assistant medic on this trip."

"I agree," said Slava. The others around the table concurred.

"Congratulations," said Jason. "You're a Demon Hunter."

CHAPTER SIX

J ASON PICKED UP the hand-held six-barreled GAU-17A minigun and bounced it in his hands, surprised at the weight. "How heavy is this thing?"

"Thirty-five pounds, then add another thirty pounds for the backpack of ammunition." Haneef took the weapon from Jason and swung it from side to side as if firing at a horde of flesh eaters. "Sasha and I pulled our weight on those missions."

Jason's expression momentarily flinched as an image of her face flashed across his mind.

"Sorry," Haneef apologized. "I shouldn't have brought her up."

"It's okay." Jason forced himself to be pleasant. "We've all lost people we've cared about."

Haneef placed the minigun back on the work bench. "Thanks for fixing it."

"Not a problem," said Daniel, the chief gunsmith. "It needed some fine tuning and a good cleaning."

"Were you able to find ammunition for it?"

"Not much." Daniel stepped back, reached under the bench, and pulled out a single ammunition backpack. "I scrounged up about six thousand rounds plus three thousand shell casings that I filled by cannibalizing some smaller caliber rounds. You have almost a full pack. Just to let you know, once your team takes its share, it's going to leave us short on ammunition."

Haneef laughed. "Jacques isn't going to like that."

"I don't plan on telling him," said Daniel. "You guys need

it where you're going. He doesn't need an arsenal to maintain law and order."

"I appreciate that."

"Which weapon do you want me to set you up with?" Daniel asked.

"I'll just be carrying my crossbow."

Haneef shook his head. "That's a bad idea."

"Why do you say that?"

"Have you forgotten what happened in Paris? You fought your way through the subway and Notre Dame with nothing but that crossbow and a machete. Given what we're going to face on our way to Moscow, you might want to be better prepared."

"He makes a good point," added Daniel.

Jason held up his hands. "All right, you win. Fix me up with a FAMAS."

"I can do that."

"Thanks." Jason offered his hand.

Daniel gave it a firm shake. "Tell your guys to take whatever they need. My crew will have it ready for tomorrow morning."

As Daniel headed back to work, Jason and Haneef made their way through the Church of St. Peter, which had been converted into an armory. Slava had recommended that each team member arm themselves with an automatic rifle as their primary weapon, preferably the 5.56mm FAMAS F1 so that all the ammunition they carried would be interchangeable, as well as a secondary weapon such as a machete or hunting knife. The old timers checked out each weapon before selecting one that felt comfortable to them. Daniel's staff assisted the newcomers. Jason knew his people were taking more than their fair share, especially with regards to ammunition. In the early days, anyone seeking sanctuary at Mont St. Michel had to relinquish their weapons, which not only provided the protective force with enough weaponry to defend the town but ensured that no armed insurrections would occur. The arrangement had been acceptable when Mont St. Michel was in imminent danger. In a post-portal world, Jason felt those weapons would be of better use on their expedition and had told his team to take whatever they needed. He rationalized that they did this for the greater good, although he knew he overstepped his boundaries. That's why, even though he had promised Jacques that he would provide a list of everything they requested so the town council could track their inventory, Daniel would not forward the list until after they left.

A part of Jason felt bad for the deception because so far Jacques had been straight up with him. As promised, he had provided eighteen horses for the trip, twelve for the team members and six to carry supplies. Their supplies were limited not by any decision of the town council but by the team's ability to carry them. Most of the allowable weight would be taken up by the five anti-matter devices and their personal weapons. Next came enough food and water to last the team and the horses seven days. Rounding out their stocks were two medical kits, a limited supply of antibiotics and pain killers, maps, and other necessities. Everything beyond that would have to be scavenged along the way. Luxuries such as a change of clothes or personal belongings were foregone all together.

The door to the church opened. Haneef looked in that direction and huffed. "This can't be good."

Bishop Fiorello entered. Jason grimaced. He despised dealing with the cleric. At least Jacques cared about those over whom he ruled, even if that concern selfishly centered on making sure his people were happy and productive to maintain the town council's lavish lifestyle. The cleric lacked even that modicum of empathy. The only thing that matched Bishop Fiorello's pretention about his vaulted position in the city's hierarchy was the pomposity of his supposed faith. Jason fantasized about feeding him to flesh eaters but felt guilty about subjecting the demons to that.

Bishop Fiorello scanned the interior. Upon seeing Jason, he broke into a huge grin. "I'm glad I found you."

"Is anything wrong?" Jason asked, forcing himself to be pleasant.

"No." The Bishop made his way across the rectory to Jason and Haneef. "Jacques asked me to make sure you had everything you needed and to expedite things if there were any problems."

"Pass along my thanks to Jacques. Everything is coming together nicely. We'll be set to depart tomorrow morning."

"Excellent." Bishop Fiorello clapped his hands together and held them as if in prayer. His demeanor abruptly changed to one of concern. His voice grew quiet so no one else could hear. "There is one thing I wanted to bring up. Is it true you chose Victoria for your team?"

Vicky stood ten feet behind the Bishop. At the mention of her name, her eyes widened. Jason answered Fiorello with a non-committal, "Yes."

The Bishop inhaled through his teeth. "The problem is that Victoria has been quite useful around the office and Jacques has grown fond of her. We'd hate to lose her. I hope you understand."

"I do."

Vicky went pale and trembled. Jeanette wrapped an arm around the young woman.

Bishop Fiorello clapped his hands together again. "Excellent. Then you'll have her report back to—"

"The problem is *I* need her on my team," interrupted Jason, speaking loud enough to be heard throughout the rectory. "Victoria has pharmaceutical skills that are vital for the success of our mission."

"You already have Neal and Ian."

"They have medical expertise but know nothing about prescription drugs. Victoria worked in an apothecary. If we're going to have to fend for ourselves for a year, I need her to make drugs."

"But…."

Jason's tone became conciliatory. "I know it's irresponsible of me to take a young girl such as Victoria into harm's way, but I have no choice. Like Jacques said, we all must make sacrifices. I'll take good care of her. I know the town council will repay Victoria's service by taking good care of her parents."

All eyes fell upon Bishop Fiorello, who squirmed in discomfort. Finally, he admitted defeat and attempted to save face. "Of course, you're right. I didn't realize what value she brought to your team."

Vicky's expression lit up.

"Thank you for being so understanding," said Jason.

"It's my pleasure." Bishop Fiorello walked over to Vicky, took her hands in his, and squeezed them gently. "Go with God. We'll provide for your parents while you carry on His work."

"Thank you," said Vicky, a tinge of nervousness in her voice.

"Think nothing of it. And don't worry. We'll find someone one else to fill your position."

Vicky's expression crumbled and tears rolled down her cheeks. If Bishop Fiorello noticed, he said nothing. Instead, he exited the church.

"Allah has reserved a special place in Hell for people like him," snarled Haneef.

Jason shook his head in disagreement. "A bastard like that would just cross through one of the portals and make his way back here."

CHAPTER SEVEN

THE STAFF OF *La Mere Poulard* prepared a huge banquet for the team's last dinner at Mont St. Michel, realizing it may be weeks before the members ate this well again. Jason appreciated the gesture. With everyone in town treating the Demon Hunters like celebrities, Jason had been tempering that image among his team, not wanting them to become cocky or develop a sense of entitlement. Tonight was an exception, so he allowed them their place in the spotlight. His team laughed and joked amongst themselves and with the hotel staff. Some of the young women serving food flirted with the men in his group. Even Antoine chatted amiably with Reinhard. The banquet boosted their morale. They would need to keep their spirits high in the long months that faced them.

Jason watched his team interact with those around them, trying to get a sense for what they felt. He had begun to hone his sixth sense to detect emotions rather than merely physical presence, with varying success. He picked up a mixture of sentiments emanating from his team, mostly excitement and uncertainty about the journey ahead. He identified some anxiety and outright fear, and even a vibe of depression, which he knew came from Vicky. He saw it in her face. She had been sullen all night. Confidence dominated all other emotions, especially from those who had been to Paris. They had survived and felt assured they would do so on this trip. It would be up to Jason to maintain that confidence. He knew that would be the hardest task ahead of him, even more so than keeping them all alive.

Jason stood, picked up a fork, and tapped it against his drinking glass several times until the clinking attracted his team's attention. When all eyes were on him, Jason put down the utensil.

"I'm not good at pep talks, so I'm not going to give one. The truth is, I don't need to. You're all here because you're the best and you believe in this as much as I do. We all know we have a long haul ahead of us. We're going to be on the road for a year or more, and we have no idea who or what we're going to encounter. What I do know is that we're going to be successful. God, or fate, or whatever it is you believe in has given us the means to close the portals. Has given us the opportunity to do something few people have ever had the chance to do—to set things right with the world. We *will* succeed. We *will* close those portals. And we *will* rid the world of the Demon Spawn." Jason picked up his wine glass and held it out in front of him. Everyone around the table picked up their glasses and held them aloft. "To the Demon Hunters!"

"To the Demon Hunters!" The team took a swig of wine and followed that up with a chorus of back slapping, table slamming, and victory yells.

JASON EXCUSED HIMSELF from the dinner around ten o'clock. Most of the team had already gone to bed since they were leaving at 0800, although a few diehards hung around to enjoy their last night of civilization for a while. Jason opted not to go straight back to his room. He wanted to tour Mont St. Michel one final time. For over an hour, he strolled through the back streets and alleys, committing the town to memory, before emerging back onto Grande Rue. Making his way to the Abbey's main entrance, Jason crossed the courtyard to his favorite spot, the terrace overlooking the bay. Sitting on the edge of the wall, he admired the surroundings. The tide rolled in, bringing it with it that salty-briny smell he had grown fond of and the sound of the surf smashing onto the island's rocks. A full moon hung high in a cloudless sky, bathing the area in soft light and leaving a reflection across the water's surface that shimmered with the waves. He savored every moment, knowing it would be a long time before he got to see the ocean again.

A familiar aura excited Jason's sense. "Hello, Jeanette."

"How did you know it was me?" she asked from halfway across the courtyard.

"You forget I have the ability to sense people and Demon Spawn."

"How could I forget? It makes it impossible to sneak up on you." Jeanette entered the alcove. "Am I bothering you?"

"I'm glad you're here."

"Good." She sidled up beside Jason, slipping her left arm under his jacket and around his waist. "Hold me. I'm cold."

Jason wrapped his right arm around Jeanette's shoulder and held her tight. She felt soft and warm against his body. Jason wished he could hold her like this forever. They watched the ocean together in silence for several minutes.

"Can you sense anything out there?" Jeanette asked.

"You mean Demon Spawn?"

"Yes."

"I can only sense an aura when it's within a mile or so. There's no Demon Spawn within several hundred miles."

"Why do you say that?"

"The pulse that shut down the portal also killed every demons generated by that portal. I doubt we'll run into any demons until we get near Russia."

"Good." Jeanette paused. "How long will it take us to reach Moscow?"

"I figure about two and a half months."

"Are you serious?"

"It's over nineteen hundred miles to Moscow and the horses can only travel twenty-five miles a day. I need to make a stop along the way but, once we're on the road, I plan on sticking to the highways since we don't have to worry about Demon Spawn. Hopefully by doing that we'll save time."

"What's the detour?"

"We're going to see your uncle."

Jeanette pulled away from him. "You're not planning on leaving me behind, are you?"

"I wouldn't even think of it."

"You'd better not."

"I want… I need you on this expedition."

Jeanette beamed and wrapped her arm around Jason's waist again, this time placing her head against his shoulder. "Why are we stopping by Uncle Reno's?"

"First, I want you to see him one more time before we begin this trip."

"And the second reason?"

Jason leaned his cheek on top of her head. "I need to ask a favor of him."

CHAPTER EIGHT

THE SEARCH AND destroy team had gathered in front of *La Mere Poulard* a little after seven the next morning to prepare for departure. They each wore new green flightsuits, the typical uniform of the protective force. The girls who tended the stables had brought up their horses and helped mount the saddle bags, ensuring they were tied down properly and the weight evenly distributed. Neal took responsibility for securing the anti-matter devices, which were packed in specially designed saddle bags. He loaded two of the devices on his horse. Jason, Slava, and Sook-kyoung would carry the remaining three. As the others finished readying their horses, they chatted with each other or with the well-wishers who had gathered to see them off.

Jason had already attached his crossbow and FAMAS to his horse's saddle and had strapped the machete to his right leg. He now stood to one side watching his team, with Lucifer and Lilith curled up at his feet. He compared their morale now to the day close to a month ago when they had set out for Paris. Back then, they all had been sullen and morose, believing they were embarking on a desperate mission with little hope for success, and viewing their effort as a suicide attempt. This time, his people possessed a sense of hope and optimism because each of them thought… no, each of them *knew* they had a good chance to save the world. None of them accepted this undertaking with visions of wealth, fame, or glory. They knew closing the remaining portals was the right thing to do. The best word Jason could find to describe what they were about to undertake was quest. It sounded melodramatic, but somehow it fit.

Jason stepped forward. Lucifer and Lilith got to their feet and followed. As he made his way through his group he called out, "All right, ladies and gentlemen. It's time to mount up and move out."

His team said their final goodbyes and climbed into their saddles. Jason mounted his horse and, after ensuring the others were ready, spurred it forward. One by one they exited through Boulevard Gate in the outer wall, passed by the Guard House, and descended into the bay. The tide would not flow back in for several hours, giving the team plenty of time to cross. Lucifer and Lilith raced ahead, chasing each other along the sand and splashing through puddles. When the team reached land, they maneuvered their horses up the embankment and onto the road leading inland. Up ahead lay the refugee encampment that had developed around the motels once used by tourists. Half as many displaced persons lived here as compared to a month ago, most having moved to nearby farms to begin their new lives; the rest would join them in the coming weeks. As they passed, several scores of people came out to wave, applaud, and cheer them on. Jason felt self-conscious but gestured back out of politeness.

Slava pulled up on his right side and Haneef on his left. Slava waved to the crowd. "It seems we're popular."

"They're grateful," said Haneef. "We made life better for them."

"Do you think we'll get the same treatment when we reach Russia?"

"We'll see when we get there," said Jason. "Keep in mind we're not on a victory tour. Remember the Latin Proverb: Unless what we do is useful, glory is vain."

"Where did you hear that?" Slava asked.

"My mother taught it to me." Only now did Jason understand the full impact of the words.

"Haneef, what does Islam say about glory?"

Haneef leaned forward so Slava could hear. "The Koran says that anyone who seeks glory should do so for the glorification of Islam."

"All right, I get it." Slava chuckled. "You're both telling me more guts, less glory."

Jason reached out and tapped his friend on the shoulder. "We're all going to need more guts before this is over."

At the crossroad in front of the encampment, the team veered left. Lucifer and Lilith scampered up to the head of the column and fell in beside Jason. Lilith shook herself, flinging off water and loose sand. Lucifer wagged the stub of his tail as he trotted alongside his master. As the group entered the tree line, Jason caught a final glimpse of Mont St. Michel, knowing it would be a long time before he ever saw the town again.

CHAPTER NINE

THE FIRST NIGHT, the team set up camp twenty-five miles east of Mont St. Michel in an abandoned farm they stumbled across an hour and a half before sundown. Jason assigned everyone a task. Jeanette, Sook-kyoung, and Vicky led the horses to the stable and made sure they were fed and settled in for the night. Ian and Werner gathered wood and brought it to Gaston, who started a fire and cooked dinner. The rest took their supplies into the farmhouse, with Neal and Jason handling the devices. Lucifer and Lilith stayed near Jason, at least until they got a whiff of baked beans and canned meat being grilled, at which point they switched their attention to Gaston. Lilith curled up on the opposite side of the fire waiting to be fed and Lucifer sat to the cook's right, begging with huge brown eyes.

Dinner was simple but pleasant and the conversation light-hearted. The newcomers chatted excitedly. Being the first time in months that they had been away from the island city, they let their enthusiasm show. When Ian rambled on about how much fun this was, Antoine glanced down at his plate and shook his head, and Reinhard and Haneef made no effort to hide their contempt. Jason understood how Ian felt. Newcomers always had a sense of excitement about combat that dissolved upon encountering an enemy. Jason had felt the same the first time he had gone on a search and destroy sweep with Andre. His giddy anticipation of battling Demon Spawn transformed into sheer terror when a pack of flesh eaters ambushed the team. One of them had pinned Jason to the ground, tearing at his face with decayed fingers and trying to bite off a chunk of flesh. He would have died that day if he had not overcome his fear and fought back. From that moment, Jason knew that combat was not about glory and adventure but about overcoming your fear and struggling to survive. He considered trying to dissuade Ian and the others of their fervor and thought better about it. The best way to temper their eagerness would be to let them take on the Demon Spawn and experience the sobering reality of war. Before that happened, though, he would make certain Reinhard trained them over the next few weeks so that, when the newcomers did encounter their first demons, they would live through the ordeal. Besides, Jason had something more important to discuss with the group.

As the team finished dinner, Jason sent Neal off to get one of the anti-matter devices. "Before we settle down, I want to discuss overnight sentry duties."

"Why do we need sentries?" asked Werner. "I thought there weren't any Demon Spawn out here."

"There aren't, but there are other things we have to be concerned about, like wild animals and looters. We'll be fine with two-man shifts of two hours each. Neal and Sook-kyoung will take the watch until eight, Reinhard and Werner until ten, Slava and Gaston until midnight, Jeanette and Vicky until two, Antoine and Ian until four, and me and Haneef until dawn. We'll keep that schedule every night until we reach Russia or run into demons. Is everyone good with that?"

His people responded in the affirmative.

"Good. There's one other thing before you go. You all know we're going to close the portals. You also need to know how we're going to do it."

Neal opened the flap on the saddle bag and pulled down the sides, revealing a pad of dark gray foam rubber two feet square. Placing his hand on the ends, he wiggled the top half until it slid off, exposing the anti-matter device nestled inside. It had the shape of a football but was twice as large. The outside cladding was stainless steel. A one-inch rim ran along the length of the device which allowed the two halves to be joined with more than a dozen bolts.

"That's what's going to close the portals?" asked Vicky.

"Yes," Neal answered. "The device contains solidified anti-matter. The outer casing disintegrates as it passes through a portal. Once the anti-matter inside the device touches the anti-matter in the portal, they'll cancel each other out and blast the gate shut."

"Not only that," added Jason. "When the portal collapses, it emits a pulse that kills every Demon Spawn that crossed through it into our realm."

"And this works?" asked Werner.

"It should," said Neal. "It's the same as the device we used in Paris."

"Nobody was hurt by the blast?" Gaston asked.

"No," Neal answered. "There are no high explosives involved, so there are no shock waves or shrapnel to worry about. There is a concussive force when the pulse generates that will knock the wind out of you for a few seconds but won't do any permanent damage. We were all within fifty feet of the blast and we're fine."

"You said it contains an anti-matter core." Ian crossed the circle and knelt in front of the device, examining it. "Why doesn't it consume itself?"

Neal shrugged. "Doc knew all the details about that because he and Jason's mom were the ones who invented it. All I can tell you is that they found a way to convert anti-matter into a solid. A chunk of it sits at the center of the device in a vacuum inside a thick glass sphere. It's held in place in the center of the vacuum by magnets surrounding the sphere, which is why the device is so large. They produced six of these. We used one in Paris, so that leaves five more to be used against the other four portals."

"What happens if the magnets fail or the glass sphere breaks?"

"I wouldn't want to be the one carrying the device when that happens." Neal's attempt at humor failed when he realized he carried two of the saddle bags on his horse.

"How do you deploy it?" Ian asked.

"That's the easy part," Jason answered. "Any of us can use it. Just throw it into the portal. Once it hits the surface and disintegrates, it detonates automatically. As long as one of us is alive, we can shut it down."

Jason let that sink in with those joining the team for the first time before continuing. "One more thing you newbies need to know. The reason the devices work is because the portals are all one way. The entry portals into the other dimension are created where the anti-matter experiments occurred. We're not worried about those because nothing can pass through them onto Earth. Our concern is with the exit portals that allow everything from the other side to cross over into our realm. Anything that tries to cross these portals *into* that realm is destroyed, so for God's sake, be careful. If you get close enough to deploy a device, throw it in. If any part of your body touches or passes through the portal, you'll lose it. Understood?"

Jason received four nervous replies. *Good,* he thought. *If they're scared then they'll stay on their toes.*

"Okay, get some rest. We're up at six and move out at eight."

CHAPTER TEN

THE JOURNEY TO Reno's underground bunker an hour south of Notre Dame de la Garenne took five days. Jason's team arrived mid-afternoon, with Jeanette leading the way so as not to alarm the sentries. Because Jason had visited the installation twice before, he knew what to expect. As they crossed the farmland surrounding the site and emerged from the overgrown grass that had enveloped the area, the guards in a pair of well-camouflaged Humvees on either flank of the bunker entrance trained their weapons on the potential threat. After a few seconds, a voice called out from the copse of trees.

"Jeanette, is that you?"

"Yes, Marceau. Jason and the others are with me."

"Come on in." Marceau called over his shoulder to one of the sentries. "Somebody get Reno."

By the time the team had reached the bunker entrance and dismounted, Reno had made it topside. Jason recognized Reno the moment he stepped through the open door. He was in his early fifties, with a well-toned physique, graying hair, and a five o'clock shadow. His brown eyes were serious and intense. This time he seemed less stressed. Reno ran up to his niece and threw his arms around her, hugging her tight. "Jeanette, it's so good to see you again."

The young woman hugged back. "Same here, *oncle*."

"I miss you so."

"I'm in good hands."

"I know you are." Reno broke the hug and stepped over to Jason. Jason offered his hand. Reno took it and pulled the teenager in to him, wrapping his arms around Jason's back. "It's good to see you."

"Thanks." Jason self-consciously returned the embrace. Jeanette enjoyed his discomfort.

Reno stepped away from Jason and waved to the rest of the team. "Everyone, come inside. I'll have the cooks prepare us dinner. I'll even have them whip up something for Lilith and Lucifer."

At the sound of his name, Lucifer wagged his stub of a tail.

"There's no need for that," Jason protested. "I dropped by so we could discuss business."

"We'll discuss business *after* dinner."

"I don't want to be an imposition."

"Far from it." Reno placed his hand on Jason's shoulder and urged him toward the bunker. "Ever since Paris, most of those who used to live in the bunker moved out. Only a handful of us stay here now. I'll enjoy the company."

Jason knew when to admit defeat. "I appreciate it."

"Then it's settled." Reno issued an order in French to Marceau. As Marceau took care of the horses, Reno led the others down into the bunker.

As PROMISED, RENO'S cooks prepared a dinner for the Demon Hunters that was more like a feast. There were not as many people residing in the bunker as the last time Jason passed through, although those who remained made every effort to make his team feel welcome. The cooks had broiled a pair of steaks for the werehounds, who devoured their meal and now sat near Jason gnawing on the bones. Everyone had a good time except for Vicky, who sat at the far end of the table silently picking at her meal.

Jeanette talked about her new life as one of the Demon Hunters and living at Mont St. Michel. Reno asked a lot of questions, happy with the way things had panned out for her. Once they had exhausted that topic of conversation, she asked the question that had been bothering her all night.

"Why did so many people leave?"

"They're setting up new lives in the surrounding farms."

"They didn't abandon you?"

"Not at all," Reno chuckled. "The bunker still serves as the focal point for the new community we're establishing, sort of an underground town square. The hospital stayed here as did the armory. The locals gather outside the ground entrance at noon every day to trade goods and barter services. And everyone knows to come back here for shelter if there's trouble."

Jason grew concerned. "Are there still Demon Spawn in the area?"

"No. Even though that threat is gone, there's still the possibility there may be others out there who want to take what we've worked so hard to rebuild. I'd rather be safe than sorry."

"I can't argue with you there, sir."

"Jason, you don't have to call me sir. You're the one we should be honoring."

"Thanks."

"Don't mention it." Reno reached out, placed his right hand on Jason's shoulder, and squeezed. "You said you wanted to talk business."

"I do. I've reconstituted the search and destroy team. We're on our way to close Moscow's portal and then will continue on to the others."

Reno sat back in his chair. "That's ambitious."

"It's very ambitious. It's also necessary. As long as the other portals remain open, we're still at risk from Demon Spawn. Maybe not in the next few months, but eventually they'll make their way here. I want to close them now to prevent that from happening."

"Makes sense."

"I need two things. You mentioned earlier that you had a

two-way radio you use to monitor events following the opening of the portals. Do you know the locations where they opened?"

"If you mean the exact coordinates, I don't. I know the Russian portal opened in Red Square. The Chinese gate is somewhere in the northeast in Manchuria. The initial Japanese reports placed theirs in the vicinity of Tokyo, but I can't confirm that since it's been months since any news has come out of Japan. There's been a lot on conflicting reports on what happened in the United States. All I know for certain is that the portal is located somewhere along the east coast between Washington and New York City." Reno paused. "What's the other thing you need?"

"Does your radio still work?"

"Yes."

Jason leaned forward and rested his arms on the table, his attention drawn to the others seated around him. "I have twelve people on my team, including myself. There is no way I can travel around the world without help. Once we leave here, I want you to get on the radio and try to find groups of survivors who can meet up with us and help."

"There's not much talk out there anymore. Most people have either lost power or been killed. It's not going to be easy."

Jeanette reached out and clasped his hand. "Neither is closing four more portals."

Reno placed his other hand on top of hers and squeezed. "I'll do what I can."

"I appreciate it," said Jason.

"If I find anyone out there who's trustworthy and willing to help, how will they find you?"

"I brought you this." Jason unzipped one of the pockets on the right leg of his flightsuit and withdrew a map that he unfolded across the table. It showed Europe from Spain to the Ural Mountains. A yellow highlighted line stretched from Paris to Moscow. "This is the route I plan on taking to Russia. We won't run into any Demon Spawn until we reach Belarus, so

I'll take main highways to save time. I've marked them on this map. If you find anyone who wants to join us, have them meet us along this route."

Reno slid the map in front of him. "Is this mine to keep?"

"Yes."

"Thanks." Reno studied it for a few seconds. "How do you plan to get to China?"

"I'm not thinking that far ahead right now. Hopefully whoever helps us will have a two-way radio we can use to contact you and radio our plans."

"*If* we find someone willing to help us," said Jeanette.

"What have I told you about being negative?" Reno gently admonished her, eliciting a grin. He studied the map for another minute. "I can do this."

"Are you sure?" Jason asked, not wanting to get his hopes up.

"You're about to travel around the world to save mankind. The least I can do is find you some help."

"*Merci*," said Jeanette.

"Anything for you. That goes for you, too, Jason." Reno paused. "When are you leaving for Moscow?"

"First thing in the morning."

"Good. Then we have enough time for another round of drinks to toast your success." Reno raised his hand to get the attention of one of his kitchen staff. "Bring us five more bottles of wine."

CHAPTER ELEVEN

THE FEAST LASTED another hour before the Demon Hunters
called it a night and headed for their bunks. Each wanted to
get one last good rest since no one had an idea how long it
might be before they slept in a bed again. Jeanette stayed
behind with Reno, the two continuing the conversation long
after the others had left. They chatted about how things had
changed after the closure of the portal as well as life at Mont St.
Michel. Reno steered the conversation onto his main concern.

"Is everything going well with Jason?"

The way her uncle phrased the question caught Jeanette off
guard. "What do you mean?"

"He seems different."

Jeanette thought for a moment and arched her eyebrows.
"He *is* different. Paris made him confident. Now he's more
assertive."

"I don't see that."

"*You* won't. Jason likes and respects you. But he stood up to
the town council at Mont St. Michel because he thinks they're
assholes."

"Are they?"

"Big time." Jeanette laughed. "Before we left, Jason dressed
down Bishop Fiorello, this pompous jerk who acts like he's the
Pope, in front of the whole team."

"Why did he do that?"

"Do you remember Vicky, the girl who sat by herself at the
end of the table?"

"The sullen one?"

"She was Jacques' assistant until Jason put her on the team to get her away from there. Fiorello tried to persuade Jason to leave her behind."

"How did that work out?"

"Vicky's with us." The grin on Jeanette's face showed admiration and affection. Then it faded. "Unfortunately, his newfound confidence also brought with it a darker side."

Reno frowned.

"Nothing bad," said Jeanette. "He sees the world differently. He's still optimistic about the future and about closing the other portals. But he's more aware of the bad that goes on, like what Jacques is doing at Mont St. Michel, and fights against it."

"It's called being mature. Jason is becoming a man. Soon you'll appreciate it."

"I appreciate it now."

"How does he treat you?"

"He's wonderful to me."

"Have you...?"

"No." Jeanette felt her face flush with embarrassment. "I'm not ready yet and he understands. It's one of the many reasons I like him."

"I'm glad. Let me ask you a question. Do you really think this mission has a chance of success or are you following Jason because you like him?"

"Jason knows it's dangerous and that for most of us it'll be a suicide mission. It's why he asked for volunteers."

"You like Jason that much to follow him?"

"This has nothing to do with Jason. This has to do with me. I know how dangerous it is. But if we don't do it, who will? Besides, how often does someone get a chance to change the world for the better?"

Reno leaned back in his chair, studying Jeanette.

"What is it?" she asked.

"I'm just admiring what a young lady you've become."

"Then you approve of my going?"

"Of course." Reno cocked an eyebrow. "Would it have mattered if I didn't?"

"I still would have gone, but I would have felt bad about it."

Reno laughed and slapped a hand against the table. He stood and motioned for Jeanette to do the same. When she did, he hugged her tight, cradling her head against his shoulder. "I'm proud of you. I know your parents would be too."

Jeanette hugged him back and bowed her head, trying to hide the tears of joy that ran down her cheeks.

JASON STOOD OUTSIDE the dining room talking with Haneef and Slava when he spotted Vicky exiting the showers at the end of the corridor. He excused himself and followed, catching up with the young woman in front of her room. Vicky had the door halfway open when Jason called to her. "Wait."

She stopped. "What's up?"

"I wanted to talk with you. Why are you so morose?"

Vicky averted her gaze. "I don't know what you mean."

"Six days ago, when we chose you for the team, you were ecstatic. Since then you've done nothing but mope and act like you don't want to be here."

Vicky's head shot up. "That's not true! I desperately want to be here!"

"Then what's wrong?"

She sighed. "I'd rather not say."

Jason knew what bothered Vicky. He wanted her to admit it. "You don't have that option. I need my team focused on battling Demon Spawn and closing the portals. If you're distracted, you're going to get yourself killed. Or worse, you're going to get some of us killed. If you can't deal with this problem, let me know now and I'll have Reno's people escort you back to Mont St. Michel."

Vicky's eyes widened and her lips trembled. For a moment, Jason thought she might have an emotional breakdown. Then the expression of fear morphed into one of resignation. She took a deep breath. "It's what Bishop Fiorello said at the church the day before we left, when he said Jacques will find someone to replace me. I got out of a terrible situation by letting someone else take my place."

"You're here because I wanted you on the team," Jason tried to comfort her.

"I could have backed out, but I didn't."

"You did what any person would in a situation like that."

"I saved myself at someone else's expense." Vicky lowered her head and cried. "I'm selfish and horrible."

Jason cupped her chin and lifted her head until their eyes met. "You can't save everyone. Trust me, I know."

Vicky sniffed. "How?"

"In Paris, as we were about to deploy the device, my mother appeared on the other side trying to escape." The memories of that incident flooded his mind, stirring up the rage he had tampered down. "Several Golem were between her and the opening, getting ready to attack, and my team was about to be overrun by flesh eaters. It would have taken a few seconds to allow her to get out, but I couldn't risk the lives of six other people, couldn't risk letting the Golem get between me and the portal, which would have meant we failed. I deployed the device."

"You killed your own mother to close the portal?"

"I don't know if she's dead or still trapped in the other dimension. The point is, saving my mother would have resulted in us failing. I had no other choice. Being trapped is my mother's punishment for irresponsibly opening the portals in the first place. Yet not a day goes by that I'm not angry at my mother for the position she put me in, and at myself for not feeling guilty about what I did."

Vicky wiped the back of her hand across her nose. "That's exactly how I feel about the situation with Jacques."

"It's natural but you can't dwell on that. Nothing you could have done would have changed the situation, so don't beat yourself up over it. If it makes you feel any better, I really do need you on this trip because of your apothecary experience."

"You're not just saying that?"

"You'll be more use to me out here in the field than you ever could be back in the Abbey."

"Thanks." Vicky ran her fingers across her eyes and down her cheeks. "Do you think my parents will be okay?"

"I made it clear to Bishop Fiorello that they deserve special treatment because you're now a Demon Hunter. I don't think him or Jacques would risk the bad publicity they would get taking it out on your folks because I brought you onto my team. I take care of my people."

"I won't let you down."

"I'm counting on that."

Vicky opened the door again and stepped into her room when Jason said, "Vicky, remember one thing."

"What's that?"

"We can't stop all the evil in this world. We can only be the best people we can. Once this is all over, and once we have clout from closing the portals, maybe then we can use that influence to change things for the better."

"You're a hopeless optimist." Vicky winked at him playfully. "That's why we might succeed. Good night."

CHAPTER TWELVE

J ASON'S TEAM GATHERED in the dining hall at seven the next morning. Reno had arranged a farewell breakfast for them and, as a surprise, had restocked their supplies from his own coffers. He had even filled a special request of Gaston's for five cloves of garlic and a jar of local honey. As each member finished eating, they made their way topside where Reno's people had gathered the horses by the bunker entrance. Jason, Neal, Slava, and Sook-kyoung were the last to leave, bringing the saddle bags with the five anti-matter devices. As the group made the final preparations to depart, Reno waited by the entrance. When everything had been loaded, they mounted their horses. Lilith and Lucifer hovered around the lead, waiting for their master. Jason and Jeanette walked over to say goodbye to Reno.

"Thank you for everything." Jeanette threw her arms around Reno's neck and hugged him.

"Yes," said Jason, who stood a few feet away.

"It's my pleasure. It's the least I can do considering what you're about to undertake." Reno broke the hug with Jeanette, tapped her on the shoulder, and crossed over to Jason. He shook the teenager's hand. "I haven't forgotten our arrangement. I'll get on the radio today and see if I can find any survivors who can help you."

"We're going to need them, especially when we get to Asia and the States."

Reno removed a folded piece of paper from his pocket and handed it to Jason. "Starting a month from today, I'll go on the radio every night at 2000 GMT and will stay on for thirty minutes. My call sign is MARQUIS. That's the frequency I use. Reach out to me if you get a chance so we can coordinate our efforts."

"You don't have to do all this."

"I want to." An awkward silence passed. Reno said, "Well, it's time."

"I guess."

Jeanette stepped up beside Reno. "I love you."

"I love you, too." Reno wrapped his right arm around Jeanette's shoulder. His eyes met Jason's. "Take good care of her."

"I will."

"She means a lot to me."

"She means a lot to me, too."

"That's why I don't mind letting her go with you. Take care of yourself. You're family now."

Jason and Jeanette mounted their horses. Jason ordered them to move out and the team set off in a line, circling around behind the bunker and corral before heading east. The werehounds took up their usual position on either side of Jason. Reno watched them cross the field until the last horse disappeared into the distant tree line and, even then, stared in that direction for another few minutes. He harbored no illusions as to the dangers Jason's people faced in the months ahead, and he knew the odds of his seeing his niece again were slim. Yet that didn't prevent him from wanting to help any way he could. If he could find survivors who thought like Jason, who were willing to make sacrifices to set things right in the world, then maybe he could better the odds of seeing his niece and Jason again.

Reno made his way back to the bunker and headed downstairs. He would be spending a lot of time on his two-way radio over the next few months.

BOOK TWO

CHAPTER THIRTEEN

Minsk, fifty-seven days after leaving Mont St. Michel

REINHARD SAT IN the shade of the pine tree, leaning against the trunk. He used his bayonet to cut a slice off an apple. "Werner, remember vat I said a month ago about being thankful that ve hadn't run into any Demon Spawn?"

"Yeah?"

"I vas wrong." Reinhard popped the slice into his mouth and chewed. "I'd give anything right now to take on a horde of flesh eaters or a few soul vampires."

"You can't mean that," said Sook-kyoung taken aback by the statement. "Most of us would be dead if we had to fight our way across Europe."

"I'm bored," he grunted. "Ve've been on the road two months *und* it's the same thing every day. Travel for eight hours, set up camp, eat, sleep, repeat."

"It's just another of the ABCs of traveling Europe, mate" said Ian.

"Vat's that?"

"Another bloody campsite."

"Another bloody cathedral," said Gaston.

"Another bloody church," Slava joked.

"Another bloody castle," added Vicky.

"Another bloody city of the dead," said Antoine, bringing an abrupt end to the attempt at levity. The mood became dour.

Jason could not blame them for feeling this way. When planning this trip, he had tried to take into consideration every possible aspect but had not factored in morale. Sook-kyoung was right. Most of them would never have made it this far if they had encountered Demon Spawn every step along the way. However, the monotony of the past two months threatened the team's cohesion almost as much as if they had endured constant attacks by demons.

After leaving Reno's bunker, they headed to Paris, picked up one of the highways circling south of the city, and continued northeast past Reims and toward Frankfurt. Every day they stumbled upon a mass of dead Demon Spawn, the bodies already in an advanced state of decay. Most had been flesh eaters, although occasionally they came upon packs of soul vampires or pus zombies. Not until after the team had crossed the border into Germany had they stopped seeing signs of the creatures, which delineated their farthest line of advance. Then his people had to face a different kind of nightmare—an industrialized world that had become feudal overnight because of the EMP. The team traveled through Germany for days without seeing any signs of life. Jason reasoned that everyone in the path of the approaching Demon Spawn had evacuated the area and either never bothered to return or perished during the harsh winter. It was not until the team reached central Germany that they came across small agrarian communities that had sprung up near the highway, occupied by haggard-looking people who watched them with a wary eye and made no attempt at contact. Jason had reasoned the farmers' paranoia came from a series of hand-painted signs they discovered earlier on the approaches to Frankfurt warning that travelers were not welcome.

Outside of Potsdam, a few miles south of Berlin, the team picked up the E30, which they followed through Poland, passing Poznan and Warsaw, and then switched to a northern route that led them past Bialystok and through more rural areas. Here in the east, the Demon Hunters encountered pretty much the same as they had experienced in the west—desolated towns and villages, isolated pockets of agrarian societies, and warnings around some cities that outsiders were not welcome. The worst experience had been near Warsaw where the team came across a mass graveyard. The section closest to the city consisted of hundreds of make-shift white crosses lined up in rows, followed by a section comprised of mass graves covered with dirt, while the one farthest from the city contained corpses stacked like wood in massive piles of the dead. That had been almost a week ago and morale was slumping ever since.

The one good thing that came out of this trip was the ample opportunity to bring the newcomers up to speed in shooting and hand-to-hand combat. Reinhard had provided forty-five minutes of training every night prior to dinner and it paid off. Target practice had been limited to two rounds a day to conserve ammunition. However, Jason noticed that the newcomers handled their weapons more confidently and had significantly improved their combat skills. Three weeks after leaving the bunker, Jason made the rest of his team join the newcomers' training as a refresher course, partly to integrate the team and partly to prevent his people from going insane with boredom.

Jason pulled the map out of his leg pocket and opened it in his lap, not so much to check on their location as for something to do.

"How much farther until we get to Belarus?" Slava asked.

"We're already there," said Jason. "We crossed the border three days ago."

"Why didn't you say anything?"

"Would it have mattered?"

Slava shrugged. "I guess not."

"Where are we exactly?" Jeanette asked.

Jason studied the map in earnest. "As far as I can tell, we're near Nalboki State Park, and four or five days from Minsk."

"How far to Moscow?" Haneef asked.

"Another two weeks beyond Minsk."

Everyone on the team groaned or sighed. Jason brought

them back to reality. "Look on the bright side."

"What bright side, mate?" Ian asked.

"Based on how far the Demon Spawn traveled from Paris, plus the three months that have passed since we closed the portal, I figure we should be running into our first ones from Moscow any day now."

The wise ass remark had the desired effect. The team switched from bored and cranky to professional and guarded, even the newcomers.

"What type of demons do you think we'll encounter?" Vicky asked.

"If we're lucky, flesh eaters and soul vampires."

"'If we're lucky'?" Vicky glanced at the others seated around her.

"Trust me," said Antoine. "There is some bad-ass shit that can come out of those portals. Flesh eaters and soul vampires are the least of your concerns."

For a moment, Jason thought the newbies might wet themselves. Before boredom could morph into fear, he refolded the map, slipped it back into his pocket, and stood up. "Lunch time's over. Let's move out."

CHAPTER FOURTEEN

JASON BROUGHT HIS horse to a stop in the middle of the intersection where the main road veered right and a secondary road continued straight. A rusted sign thirty feet farther down the latter read LIDA 3 KM. Lucifer and Lilith moved in on either side of him, scanning his flanks for danger. As the rest of the team came to a halt, Haneef and Slava joined Jason.

"Is everything okay?" Haneef asked.

Unzipping the leg pocket on his flight suit, Jason removed the map and unfolded it. "I want to make sure we're still going in the right direction."

"Do you want me to have everyone take five?" Slava asked.

"This will only take a few seconds."

Jason found the check mark he had made last night and followed the road to this intersection. The small village of Lida was less than two miles ahead of them. The main road that dog-legged east would take them to Minsk and Moscow. He refolded the map, slid it into his pocket, and motioned to the right.

"We need to go in that direction. Tell the—"

Jason detected multiple auras in the vicinity. Lucifer and Lilith felt it at the same time. The fur on both werehounds bristled and their ears cocked forward.

"What's wrong?" Haneef asked.

"I'm picking up Demon Spawn in the area, probably flesh eaters because the auras are weak."

"How many?" Haneef asked.

"It's hard to tell but I'm guessing a few hundred."

"Where are they?"

"I don't know yet."

"Shit," mumbled Slava. He lifted the binoculars and scanned the countryside.

Lilith detected them first. She stepped forward a few feet and stared down the road toward Lida, her ears arched forward and a growl coming from deep in her throat. Slava shifted his gaze in that direction.

"We have company." He handed the binoculars to Jason. "And plenty of it."

Jason raised them. Less than a mile down the road between two and three hundred flesh eaters staggered toward the intersection, moving in one giant horde. They were aware of Jason's team and were hungry.

Slava leaned closer to Jason. "If we double time, we could be out of the area before they get here."

"They'll just follow us and catch up with us tonight while we're sleeping. I don't want to take the chance."

"I'll have everyone dismount and prepare to engage."

"Don't do that either. We passed a crossroads about two miles back that swings around and comes out a few miles ahead of here. Double time the others that way and wait for me."

"Where are you going?"

"I'm going to lead them on a wild goose chase."

"Copy that."

As Slava and Haneef left, Jason called out, "Have Reinhard and the newbies join me."

By the time Reinhard and the others reached Jason, the flesh eaters had approached to within two thousand feet of the intersection. Lilith and Lucifer took up position on Jason's flanks. The German brought his horse alongside Jason's.

"Vat's up? Are ve going to fight a rear-guard action with the expendables?"

Jason shook his head. "It's time for Demonology 101. I want the recruits to get up close and personal with what they're

74

going to be fighting."

Ian joined them and spotted the approaching horde. "Bloody Hell, what are those things?"

"Flesh eaters," said Jason loud enough so they could all hear.

"You mean zombies?" asked Gaston.

"A bite from one of those won't transform you but you'll get one nasty infection." Jason's left shoulder involuntarily twitched from the memory of the bite he had received in St. Mere Eglise.

"Why are they naked and... and...." Vicky couldn't find the right word.

"Cooked," Werner finished her sentence.

"They're humans that have been condemned to the other dimension."

"Are you serious, mate?" Ian asked.

Jason motioned to Reinhard. The German rode ahead until he was two hundred feet from the horde. He raised his FAMAS, took aim on the nearest flesh eater, and fired a three-round burst. One bullet struck the demon between its eyes. The creature's head exploded. As the corpse dropped to the pavement, a blue eddy of light escaped from the body and spiraled skyward.

"That's its lifeforce," said Jason.

"Fascinating." Ian spurred his horse forward a few feet to get a better view.

"Don't get too close," warned Jason. "They're not strong, fast, or fierce, but if you're careless they can overwhelm you. We've run into thousands of these things since the portals opened. They're the most common of the Demon Spawn."

The flesh eaters had approached to within a thousand feet of the intersection. Reinhard rejoined the group.

"We've seen enough," Gaston prodded. "Let's go."

"Stay where you are."

"Are you nuts?" Gaston asked.

Jason maneuvered his horse so he stood in front of the others. "These are the least dangerous demons you're going to encounter. If you can't handle this test, then you're useless to me."

"Test?" Werner asked.

"Each of you has to shoot a flesh eater through the head before you fall back."

The four newcomers stared at him dumbfounded.

Jason maneuvered his horse beside Reinhard's. Lilith and Lucifer tagged along. "Do you think they're up to it?" he chided.

"They'd better be, othervise there's some major ass kicking in store for them tonight." The German spun his horse around and backtracked along the road they had just traveled. "I'll be vaiting at the detour. Hurry up unless you vant to be left behind."

Werner unslung his FAMAS and positioned his horse so he could get a better shot. He sighted on a flesh eater less than five hundred feet distant and slowly squeezed the trigger. The bullet punched into the demon's throat. Werner aimed again. This time he took a deep breath and held it. The round ripped into its head, dropping the body to the ground and freeing its lifeforce. He spurred his horse and followed Reinhard.

Vicky went next. She aimed at a demon to the right of center. Her first two shots were high, the rounds punching into the horde behind it.

"You're jerking the trigger," said Jason. "That's causing you to pull the weapon up as you fire. Try it again, but this time squeeze with a slow, gentle motion."

Vicky inhaled and followed his advice and brought down the flesh eater with a shot to the forehead. She rode off after Reinhard.

The horde was three hundred feet away.

"What are you two waiting for?" Jason asked.

"I'm fascinated by them," Ian answered. "From a biological aspect, they're amazing."

"If you want, I'll leave you here so you can study them."

"No thanks." Ian moved his horse forward a few yards, unslung his FAMAS, and took down a demon with a single shot. As he passed by Jason, he offered a mock salute and trotted off after the others.

That left him, Gaston, and a horde of flesh eaters less than two hundred feet away. Lucifer and Lilith moved nearer to Jason, their eyes begging to retreat.

"Any time now would be helpful," said Jason.

"I'm scared." Gaston's voice trembled.

"If you think you're scared now, wait until we're charged by soul vampires."

"I can't do this."

"You can and you will"

The horde was one hundred and fifty feet away. Lilith whined to get her master's attention.

"I c-can't. Don't make me."

"Fine."

Jason whistled for the two werehounds and left. Gaston fell in behind him. After they had gone five hundred feet, Jason reached out, grabbed the reins to Gaston's horse, and stopped.

"Get off," Jason ordered.

"What?"

"You heard me. If you can't fight, you're of no use to me. You can stay here, but the horse and supplies belong to the team." When Gaston hesitated, Jason yelled. "Now!"

Gaston dismounted. The terror in his eyes bordered on panic. "What'll happen to me?"

"You'll either run fast or be eaten."

"You can't leave me like this!"

"Then show me I can rely on you in combat, otherwise I'm out of here."

Gaston alternated his focus between Jason and the flesh eaters. The Frenchman slid the FAMAS off his shoulder and clasped it in front of him, his eyes fixed on Jason. For a second, Jason thought Gaston might use it on him. Instead, he advanced down the road toward the approaching horde, stopping three hundred feet away. Raising his weapon, he aimed at a one of the demons in the front and fired three rounds. The first two punched into its chest and the third overshot its shoulder. Gaston lowered his weapon and stepped back, his body shuddering. Suddenly, the trembling stopped. Gaston aimed again, carefully lining up the shot. He fired a single round that caught a flesh eater in the forehead, shattering its skull. With his one kill scored, Jason expected him to retreat. Instead, Gaston stood his ground, taking down several more using less than two bullets per demon until the magazine ran out of ammunition. Gaston replaced it and continued his assault. By the time he emptied his second magazine, he could take down a flesh eater with a single shot to the head. The horde had made it to within fifty feet of Gaston. The Frenchman fell back, reloading as he did so. Once he reached Jason, he slung his FAMAS over his shoulder and climbed up onto his horse without saying a word.

The two set off after the others, with Lucifer and Lilith following by their master's side.

IT TOOK SEVERAL hours for Jason and Gaston to catch up with the rest of the team. They had maintained a slow pace to make certain the flesh eaters continued to pursue them. A mile from the crossroads, they raced ahead out of the horde's sight and picked up the detour. After pausing at a bend in the road and waiting half an hour to see if any of the creatures followed, which none did, they proceeded to the rendezvous point. The two groups linked up at a second crossroad two miles to the east of the Lida intersection and set out toward Minsk.

CHAPTER FIFTEEN

THE TEAM TRAVELED until half an hour before dusk to put as much distance as possible between themselves and the flesh eaters before settling in for the night. For their camp, Jason chose a small hill covered in trees that sat in a field half a mile from the main road. The location offered a good defensive position and provided a clear view of the road in case any Demon Spawn caught up with them. Jeanette and Sook-kyoung tied the horses to trees on the opposite slope farthest away from the road while Gaston set up a smokeless fire using dried twigs. Reinhard and Slava agreed to keep watch while the others ate dinner.

As everyone finished eating, but before they could wander off, Jason stood and asked for their attention.

"Running into those things this afternoon means we're now in demon territory, so we're going to change the sentry schedule. Antoine, Neal, Sook-kyoung, and Gaston will take the first shift until eleven. Jeanette, Haneef, Ian, and I will replace you. Reinhard, Slava, Werner, and Vicky will take the shift from three in the morning until dawn. Be alert for anything, not just flesh eaters and soul vampires. God knows what new demons we'll run into out here. Any questions?"

There were none.

"Good. Somebody relieve Slava and Reinhard so they can eat."

"I will," answered Antoine.

"Me too," said Sook-kyoung.

"Thanks."

Gaston set aside two plates of food as the others wandered off. When Jason passed by, Gaston asked, "Sir, can I talk to you?"

"You can," said Jason as he approached the campfire. "Only if you stop calling me sir. What's up?"

"I want to thank you for earlier today."

"You know I wouldn't have left you out here."

"That's good to know, but I meant thank you for making me confront my fears."

"You seemed to get over them quick enough."

"I had to otherwise I would have gotten myself killed." Gaston sighed.

Jason stepped closer so no one else would hear him. "We were all scared our first time encountering Demon Spawn. I still want to piss myself when we run across them. I'd be more concerned if you weren't scared."

"Why?"

"Because it'd mean you're cocky and overconfident, which is more dangerous."

Gaston nodded his understanding. "I won't let you down again."

"I know." Jason patted Gaston on the arm. "Now finish cleaning up and get some rest. You have a long night ahead of you."

CHAPTER SIXTEEN

*S*ASHA FACED THE *stairwell that led to the roof of the Notre Dame bell tower and aimed her minigun at the opening. The first four flesh eaters exited the stairwell. She sighted in on the lead demon and squeezed the trigger. It blew apart, showering those behind it with chunks of decayed flesh and gore. She lifted her finger off the trigger, switched her aim to another flesh eater, and fired again, decimating it. Beside her, the rest of her team lined up their shots before firing. At first the tactic worked fine, bringing down ten demons in the first few seconds. Soon the mass pushing its way up the stairwell became too heavy and an increasing number made their way onto the roof. Some stumbled over the remains, spoiling the humans' aim. Others staggered to the sides, spreading out and threatening to swarm the team. Sasha and the others increased their rate of fire. They took down every demon that reached the roof but were going through ammunition at an alarming rate.*

And the flood of flesh eaters continued.

Sasha kept up the assault, swinging the minigun from side to side. There were too many to stop them all. Eventually, she used up her last round. The only sounds were the whir of the spinning barrel mount and the moans of the remaining flesh eaters. Close to two dozen had survived. They moved across the roof, circling the humans. Sasha unbuckled the chest straps to her minigun and slid the weapon and backpack off her shoulders. Removing her machete from its sheath, she held it in front of her, her knuckles tightening around the grip. She slashed her way into the approaching horde as if her life depended on it because, in fact, it did. She plunged her machete into the face of the nearest demon. It stiffened as the blade sliced into its brain. Placing her foot on its chest, Sasha pushed. The flesh eater slid off and tumbled into another demon, knocking it to the ground.

The horde swarmed Sasha. They moved in around her, pinning her arms by her side and pushing against her. A set of teeth dug into her shoulder, biting through the flightsuit and piercing the skin. A decayed hand clawed at her face, the fingers gouging at her eyes. Rather than be eaten alive, Sasha tumbled backward over the edge of the wall, plummeting three hundred feet to the ground below, and taking three of the demons with her. Her eyes stared up, locking on Jason's.

"I'm coming back for you."

Jason woke with a start. He sat upright, his heart pounding, his body damp from sweat. He must have cried out because Lucifer and Lilith were also awake, both werehounds staring at him. Lilith lay back down and curled up. Lucifer stood, crossed over to Jason, and licked his face.

"Are you okay?" Jeanette whispered on his left.

"Yes."

"Are you sure?" She reached out and held his hand.

Jason squeezed it. "I had a nightmare."

"Was it about Sasha?"

"How did you know?"

"Because you called out her name before you woke up."

Jason sighed and moved beside Jeanette so they could talk without disturbing the others. "I dreamed about how she died."

"That's natural."

"It seemed so real, so vivid."

"You're purging a traumatic event."

"The strange thing is, I never saw Sasha die. Yet it felt as if I was there."

"I wish I could help," Jeanette said with a tinge of sadness in her voice.

"You can." Jason spooned her and wrapped his left arm around her shoulder. Jeanette placed her hands on his arm and hugged, sighing in contentment. Jason usually experienced excitement being this close to Jeanette, but not tonight. He enjoyed the softness and warmth of her body against him, only now it had more of a comforting effect than anything else, which he needed. The nightmare bothered him more than he admitted. Sure, he had experienced them many times since the opening of the portals. Everyone had. But this one was too vivid, too personal, and too real. It felt more like a vision than anything else and it left him with an unsettling vibe.

CHAPTER SEVENTEEN

DAWN BROKE AT camp. The sun had not yet climbed above the tree line, leaving the area in shadows and the surrounding fields covered in a layer of ground fog. One by one, the team woke and sauntered over for breakfast. Gaston stoked the fire. Some of them sat around waiting for their meal while the majority packed up or moved to the outer edge of the woods to relieve themselves. Jason recalled the sentries. When they arrived at the campfire, he asked how their shift went.

"I didn't see a single Demon Spawn all night," said Reinhard.

"Same here," added Werner.

"I didn't see *anything*," added Slava. "Not even wildlife."

"Is that bad?" Vicky asked.

"It could mean there's something nearby that scared them away," said Slava.

"Or maybe the flesh eaters passed through earlier," added Reinhard.

Jason wondered if his dream was in any way related to this anomaly. "We'll be extra cautious when we move out. Relax for a while. We'll break camp after breakfast."

As Reinhard and the others left, Jeanette came over. "Sookkyoung and I are going to check on the horses."

"All right. I'll call you when breakfast is ready."

"You'd better." Jeanette's eyes scanned the campsite. Since no one paid any attention to her, she leaned forward and kissed Jason, and then rushed off.

ANTOINE STROLLED FAR enough away so that no one could see him. He stood behind a tree and unzipped his pants. A rustling in the bushes distracted him. Grabbing the hilt of his machete, he spun around, ready to attack. Neal stood by the next tree. Upon seeing Antoine exposed, Neal covered his eyes with his hand.

"I'm sorry, man."

"Do you mind doing that somewhere else? I'm taking a piss here."

"Of course." Neal zipped up, nearly catching himself in the process. He pointed to a large bush twenty feet away. "I'll go over there."

Antoine glared at him. Neal shut up and ran off. Antoine went back to business, shaking his head and mumbling under his breath.

HANEEF ATTEMPTED TO determine the direction of Mecca. Once he it figured out, he dropped to his knees and placed his forehead against the dirt, initiating his morning prayers.

THE HORSES STOMPED their hoofs and moved away from Jeanette and Sook-kyoung as they approached, although they quieted down a little once they recognized the women.

Jeanette stroked her hand along the bridge of her horse's nose. "What's the matter, girl?"

"They seem spooked." Sook-kyoung went to pet one of the horses, which backed away.

Jeanette's horse jerked its head to the side, pushed her away, and pulled until it strained to break the rope securing it to the tree. The horse grew frantic and neighed in fright. Within seconds, all the horses were acting the same way. Jeanette stepped back a few paces and slid the FAMAS off her shoulder. Sook-kyoung had already done the same. The two women moved against the nearest trees, their eyes scanning the fog for movement, their guns held in the high ready position.

JASON SPREAD THE map on the dirt to check their current position and plan the day's trek.

Ian crouched beside him. "Do you know where we are?"

Jason pointed to their location on the map. "We're here, west of Naliboki State Park. I'm hoping by the end of the day we'll be—"

Jason detected multiple auras. One moment he distinguished nothing and the next they overwhelmed his sixth sense, causing him to momentarily lose concentration. He had never experienced anything so powerful before. These auras were dominant and malevolent.

Ian placed a hand on Jason's shoulder, causing him to jump. "Is everything okay?"

"No." Jason struggled to his feet and swayed. The auras made him dizzy. "We have a shitload of trouble heading our way."

ANTOINE HAD ZIPPED up his pants when the noise cut through the silence. It came from an animal but sounded more terrifying than anything he had heard before. It was a clicking from within the throat, deep, guttural, and vicious. He detected movement to his right. By its size and gray, leathery skin, it reminded him of a soul vampire, although it had more of a human form. Crimson eyes glowed from a featureless face and honed in on Antoine. It raised a hand and Antoine's blood ran cold. Foot-long talons extended from the ends of its fingers. A slit formed across the lower part of its face and opened, revealing a row of brown-stained, jagged teeth. The demon lowered its hand back to the dirt and poised to strike.

Antoine reached for his FAMAS as the Demon Spawn lunged.

CHAPTER EIGHTEEN

ANTOINE RAN BACKWARDS, trying to give him enough space to raise his weapon. The demon decreased the distance faster than he anticipated. "Neal, we have company!"

Neal emerged from behind the bush. "What did you.... Holy Shit!"

The exclamation caught it off guard, giving Antoine time to aim and pull the trigger. The demon stopped and raised its hands in front of its chin, the fingers closed to protect its face. The first ten rounds slammed into the talons and ricocheted off as if striking armor. Antoine lowered the barrel and emptied the last twenty rounds into its abdomen. The bullets thudded into dead flesh with no effect; the Demon Spawn did not even flinch. Antoine popped out the magazine and reached for a full one.

It dropped its hands, snarled, and sprang.

A TRIO OF Demon Spawn descended on the horses. In their panicked state, the animals nearly crushed Jeanette and Sook-kyoung. The women retreated to the safety of the nearby trees and readied their weapons. They could hear the clicking of the approaching demons but, because of the horses, they could not tell from which direction or how near they were.

The first Demon Spawn jumped, leaping over the animals at the edge of the band and landing on the back of one horse in the center. The animal neighed and bucked, trying to throw off its attacker. The demon drove its left hand into the front of the horse's neck, the talons puncturing the trachea. Stunned by the pain and violence, the animal froze. With its right palm facing down, the Demon Spawn leaned back, plunged its hand into the horse's lower abdomen, and flicked downward. The talons sliced through the horse's colon and intestines before ripping through the skin, eviscerating the animal. Collapsing onto the dirt, the horse cried out and thrashed around in its own viscera. The demon slid to the ground to feed, its back to the two women. Two more attacked a pair of horses in the same manner.

Jeanette pointed to Sook-kyoung and then to the first Demon Spawn. Sook-kyoung aimed her FAMAS. Jeanette selected the one nearest to her. The women fired simultaneously. Jeanette pumped eleven rounds into its head. It flopped onto its back, flailing and kicking, an anguished mewl escaping from its mouth.

Sook-kyoung fired half a dozen rounds into the back of her demon, which only pissed it off. It spun around to face her. She adjusted her aim and squeezed the trigger, releasing a ten-round burst. This time, it raised its talons in front of its face and deflected the bullets. Sook-kyoung waited. After a moment, it lowered its hands and clicked. Sook-kyoung emptied the remainder of the magazine into its face. The demon cried out as its head was pulverized into a bloody pulp and its body flung back onto the horse's corpse.

Jeanette didn't see the third demon abandon its meal, duck behind the horses, and circle around the exterior of the band. It leapt out from the right, slamming Jeanette to the ground and knocking the wind out of her. Sitting on top of her chest, it clutched Jeanette by the throat with its left hand. She felt the razor-sharp edges scraping against her skin. The demon raised its right hand and dangled its talons over her face, ready to strike.

THE SCREAMING AND gunfire interrupted Haneef's prayers. Jumping to his feet, he scurried over to his minigun. A clicking came from his right. Three Demon Spawn raced through the trees. He had never seen this type before. Two broke to the left and headed for the center of the camp while the other charged him. He screamed "Incoming!" to warn the others about the approaching danger.

Haneef did not have time to mount the weapon system on his back. Instead, he picked up the minigun and swung it toward the demon.

JASON AND THE others grabbed their weapons, although they didn't know where to train them. Lucifer and Lilith morphed. The fur on Lucifer's back and legs receded, allowing the skin to harden into scales. Three-inch spikes tore through the muscles around his shoulders, and horns extended from behind his ears, giving his head the appearance of a bull. His paws lengthened several inches and his nails became talons. Lilith howled as she changed into her demonic form. The shiny black fur stiffened like the spikes of a porcupine. The tail elongated into a five-foot appendage with a stinger on the end, much like a scorpion. They took up a protective stance on either side of Jason. When Haneef screamed his warning, the group turned in that direction in time to see a pair of Demon Spawn rushing through the trees toward them. All seven opened fire at once. Over a hundred rounds of ammunition slammed into them, both of which broke to the right and disappeared back into the woods.

Gunfire erupted from where the horses were tied up. Jason tapped Reinhard on the shoulder. "You and Ian help the girls. Slava and Vicky, find Haneef and make sure he's all right."

As the four raced off to help their comrades, Jason glanced around the camp. "Shit! Where are Antoine and Neal?"

Werner pointed toward the woods. "They went off to take a

leak a few——"

Lucifer growled and stepped toward the trees behind Werner.

"Watch out!" Jason shoved Werner out of the way as one of the demons, which had doubled back on them, emerged from the trees and charged.

ANTOINE RACED FORWARD, raised the butt of his FAMAS, and drove it into the demon's face. He had done that to flesh eaters and soul vampires in the past and had knocked them off their feet. The blow didn't even phase this one. The demon slammed into Antoine, pushing him against a tree. It swung at him with its right hand, its talons extended.

JEANETTE COULD NOT avert her eyes from the talons dangling over her face. *Damn it*, she thought. *Just get it over with.*

The Demon Spawn snarled and stiffened its arm. A moment later, a dozen rounds tore into its head. It grabbed its shattered skull and moaned, loosening its grip on Jeanette. Sook-kyoung rammed the butt of her FAMAS into the wound, pushing it into the dirt. Reaching down, Sook-kyoung yanked Jeanette to her feet.

"Thanks," said Jeanette.

"Save it." Sook-kyoung pointed to the other two. Their head wounds had almost healed. "We need to get out of here."

The first demon stood up. Its eyes focused on the two women. It clicked and lowered itself on its haunches, ready to strike.

Sook-kyoung took Jeanette by the arm and headed back into the band of horses.

THE DEMON SPAWN swung its talons at Haneef's face and would have sliced it off had Haneef not blocked the blow with his minigun. When he attempted to pull the weapon back to get off a shot, the demon clutched the barrel in both hands. The two struggled. Haneef hung on tight, knowing he would be slaughtered if he released his grip.

"Hang on, buddy." Slava approached from the left, with Vicky on the right.

Upon spotting the new threat, the demon flung Haneef to the side. He dropped the minigun as he tripped over a rock and tumbled onto his back. Slava and Vicky opened fire. The demon placed its taloned hands across its face, blocking the fusillade. When the two ran out of ammunition and replaced their magazines, it lowered its hands and attacked.

ANTOINE DUCKED AT the last moment. The demon's talons missed him by inches, imbedding in the tree instead.

"Stay down!" Neal raced up on the right, his machete raised above his head. He brought it down on the Demon Spawn's neck. The angle was off, so instead of decapitating it, he lodged the blade deep into its shoulder. Antoine removed his machete from its sheath. He pointed the blade up and drove it into the demon's abdomen, slicing up under the ribcage. It convulsed so violently it snapped off two of its talons, leaving them stuck in the tree. Antoine twisted the blade one hundred and eight degrees, gutting the demon. He tried to remove the machete, but it would not slide free. Standing up, Antoine pushed Neal aside, removed the latter's machete from the demon's shoulder, and, brandishing the weapon like a baseball bat, swung it against the back of its neck. The blade sliced half-way through skin and muscle. He had to hack three more times before the head separated from its body and dropped to the dirt.

Falling back against the tree, Antoine inhaled several times to catch his breath. As he did, Neal placed his right foot on the demon's body for leverage and yanked at the machete lodged in it its abdomen. The blade pulled free with a sickening slurp.

"Are you ready to help out the others?"

"Let's go." Antoine pushed himself off the tree and followed Neal back into camp.

JEANETTE AND SOOK-KYOUNG exited the band as the two regenerated Demon Spawn jumped to their feet and gave chase. They shoved the animals aside, desperate to find their attackers. Jeanette needed to figure out a plan to get out of this, and quickly. They had, at best, a few seconds before the demons tracked them down.

IF JASON HAD not shoved Werner out of the way, the Demon Spawn would have slashed him across the back of his neck, decapitating him. Instead, it tripped on Werner's hunched over body and crashed face first into the dirt. The force of the contact flipped Werner over. He landed on his side, rocking back and forth, crying out and clutching his abdomen. Gaston went to help.

The second one, which had circled around behind Jason, leapt at him. Lucifer and Lilith jumped in front of their master, catching it in mid-flight and driving it into the ground. Lucifer sat on its chest, resting his weight on his front paws and pinning down the creature. It lashed at him with its talons, which scraped harmlessly against Lucifer's scales. The Demon Spawn became frantic, clicking and thrashing, threatening to throw off Lucifer. Lilith circled around to its head. Raising her tail, she plunged the stinger between its crimson eyes. It convulsed underneath Lucifer. Lilith kept her stinger in its skull, injecting paralyzing fluid and preventing the demon from regenerating.

Jason ignored the battle playing out behind him, concentrating instead on the first Demon Spawn. Jason raised his crossbow and aimed. When it jumped to its feet and spun around to face him, Jason fired an arrow into its left eye. The orb ruptured. Fluid and blood flowed out of the socket and down its face. The demon swiped its hand, breaking off the extended bolt. The wound healed instantly. It surged forward, its arm above its head, ready to slash Jason open.

JEANETTE HEADED FOR the field beyond the horses. She knew it would not save her, but what choice did she have? She and Sook-kyoung ran as fast as they could, waiting for death to catch up to them.

A scuffle broke out behind them, accompanied by intense clicking from the Demon Spawn and the sound of blades slashing into flesh. The noise died out and things grew quiet except for the disturbed neighing and shuffling of the horses. Sook-kyoung looked over her shoulder and stopped running.

"What in God's name is that?"

Jeanette spun around. The two Demon Spawn lay scattered across the ground, beheaded. Three figures stood above the corpses. They each wore long, black cloaks with the hoods pulled up over their heads, which cast their faces in shadows. Two of them brandished broad swords which they held in front of them, the tips of the blades resting on the ground, gloved hands clasping the hilts. The third knelt and picked up the severed head of one of the demons. The figure examined it before dropping it back into the dirt.

"It's safe to come back, ladies," said a deep, low voice from under the hood. "They're dead."

THE DEMON CHARGED straight at Haneef, its arms extended and its talons pointed at him. Haneef prayed to Allah that the end would be swift and painless and that he would be deemed worthy enough to ascend into Heaven. He stood straight and prepared to meet his death with dignity. Instead of attacking, the demon jerked to a halt. The blade of a broadsword pierced its abdomen from behind. It stared down at the protrusion. The blade flicked up, slicing its way through the demon's chest and neck, cleaving its head into two separate halves. A moment later, a horizontal slash of the blade lobbed off the two sections of the demon's head. The carcass fell to the ground. Behind it stood a figure dressed in a long, black cloak.

JASON REACHED FOR his machete to fend off the approaching Demon Spawn, a gesture he knew would be futile. A figure in a red hooded cloak stepped between him and the demon. It lashed out with its right hand. The cloaked figure used the trident-shaped dagger in its left hand to hook the demon's wrist in mid-swing, catching it on the sharpened *quillion* and blocking the slash. Then figure's right hand emerged from under the cloak holding a saber which the figure thrust through the demon's chin up into its skull, stunning it. The figure spun to its right and flipped its left arm down, the dagger still hooked around the demon's wrist, which forced it to bend at the waist. As the figure completed its spin, it slashed down with the saber. The blade cut through the demon's neck, slicing off its head in one clean stroke. The cloaked figure jiggled the dagger, releasing the Demon Spawn, and then slid the twin weapons back into their scabbards. The carcass flopped into the dirt.

Lucifer growled. A second figure in a dark gray cloak had stepped up to the Demon Spawn the werehound had pinned to the ground. Lucifer and Lilith backed away from the hooded figure, not sure how to respond. The figure placed one foot on the demon's chest to hold it in place and lifted a broadsword above its neck. Clasping the hilt in both hands, the figure drove the tip of the blade into its throat and moved it from side to side, severing muscles and tendons and shattering its spine. After a few seconds, the demon's head popped off and rolled a few inches from the body. The two werehounds retreated to

Jason.

Jason focused on the mysterious figure that had saved his life. It faced him. Silver armor shielded the front of its fore and upper arms. A larger plate protected the chest from the neck to the waist. Emblazoned in the center of the chest plate was a circle surrounding a raised R in the upper left quadrant and a raised A in the lower right. A brass crucifix centered between the two letters glistened in the morning light. Gloved hands extended from under the cloak, the tops of each finger covered in small silver armor plates. The hands reached up, clasped the edges of the hood, and pulled back the cloth to reveal strands of long red hair.

"Oh my God," Jason exclaimed.

Sasha smiled. "Are you surprised to see me?"

CHAPTER NINETEEN

"**B**UT YOU'RE...." JASON struggled to find the words. "I mean, I thought you were... were...."

"Dead." Antoine finished the sentence as he joined the conversation. He stepped up to Sasha, his eyes locking on hers. "I saw a horde of flesh eaters push you off the bell tower of Notre Dame Cathedral."

Sasha sighed. "Technically, I am dead."

Lucifer and Lilith raced up to greet Sasha. When she reached down to pet them, Lucifer backed away and whined. Lilith ran over to Jason and stood behind his legs. By now, the rest of Jason's team had joined them, each staring in disbelief.

Jason focused on her aura. It belonged to Sasha but not the young woman he had known before Paris. This aura seemed like a hybrid between a human and a Demon Spawn, although without the malevolence. He shook his head, unable to grasp the situation. "How can you be here if you're dead?"

"Jason, I came back to help you."

"*We* came back to help you." The figure in the dark gray cloak moved up beside Sasha and pulled the cowl off his head. He stood six feet in height with a lean yet muscular figure. The man was older than the rest of Jason's team, probably in his late thirties or early forties. He possessed hard features, most notably the cold, brown eyes as well as lips locked in a perpetual scowl.

"Who are you?" Jason asked, not attempting to hide his suspicion.

"Father Belsario. And while you have legitimate questions

to ask, may I suggest that you save them for later? Right now, we need to take care of your friend and get out of here while we have the chance."

"Are there more of these things in the area?" Jason asked. "I don't sense any?"

Jeanette reached out and clasped his hand at the thought of having to fight more of those demons. Sasha flinched at the gesture.

"There are none nearby but I'd rather err on the side of caution."

"Agreed."

Jason stepped around Father Belsario and moved beside Werner. Neal knelt by the German, checking his vitals. The other members of the team gathered around their friend. Jason patted Werner's leg. "How are you doing?"

"He's lucky," answered Neal, pressing his fingers along Werner's right side. "He's only cracked two ribs."

Werner grimaced when Neal touched a bruised area. "How is that lucky?"

"You could have broken one, which would have been excruciating. Or worse, you could have punctured a lung, in which case we'd be digging your grave right now."

"Your bedside manner leaves much to be desired," Werner joked, wincing when he chuckled.

"Sit up," ordered Neal.

When Werner did, he gasped.

"It's going to hurt for a few weeks. Stay still." Neal waved Vicky over. "Bring me a roll of bandages and some pain killers."

Vicky went off to get the medical bag.

Jason asked, "How long will it take to patch him up?"

"He'll be ready to move in about fifteen minutes, although the horseback ride is going to hurt."

"Something to look forward to." Werner meant it to be humorous but, because of his pain, the joke fell flat.

"Did we lose any of the horses?" Jason asked Sook-kyoung.

"Three. Those things ripped them apart."

"What about you?" Jason asked Father Belsario. "Are your horses tied up nearby?"

"We travel on foot."

"It's over three hundred miles to Moscow. You're going to get tired."

"We don't tire." The cleric's tone hung heavy with exasperation. "If you'll excuse us, we'll set up the perimeter guard while the rest of you get ready to depart."

Father Belsario snapped his fingers and pointed away from the camp. The other four cloaked figures split up and moved to the edge of the woods. As Sasha walked by, she mouthed the words "we'll talk later" to Jason and disappeared amongst the trees. Jason waited for them to leave before addressing his team.

"Pack up and prepare to move out. We hit the road in an hour."

His team responded, all except Ian who crouched in front of the carcass of the creature Sasha had cleaved in half, poking around its insides with his machete. Jason squatted beside him. "What's so fascinating?"

Ian pointed out the various organs with the tip of his machete, occasionally using the blade to push one aside to expose another. "This thing has a heart, liver, two kidneys, two lungs, and large and small intestines."

"Don't most animals?"

"Yes, but I think these things were once human."

"Are you sure?"

Ian slid the machete across the dirt to dislodge the viscera, and then rubbed the blade against the leg of his pants to clean it. "There is a lot more trauma to these organs than I've seen before, but the size and configuration are the same as those belonging to a human. To be certain, I'd need to study it more closely."

"We don't have time. For now, keep this between us. I don't want to spook the others."

Ian nodded and slid the machete back into its sheath.

"Come on. I want to get away from here as soon as possible."

CHAPTER TWENTY

T HE TEAM TRAVELED all day in silence. No one trusted the cloaked figures. Even having Sasha among them did little to dispel the uncertainty. The werehounds, who used to enjoy Sasha's company, stayed as far away from her as possible. Jason felt the same way. These people made him uneasy, especially the four who had yet to pull back their hoods and reveal their faces. He had declined Father Belsario's offer to head the column, fearing his team might be led into an ambush. Putting them at the rear caused as much consternation. Jason lost track of the number of times he checked behind him to see what the cloaked figures were up to. Occasionally, he tried to ping on Sasha's aura, hoping to get a feel for her. Every time he picked up the same sensation, a combination of human and Demon Spawn with a mix of emotions. He detected nothing evil or threatening.

The team set up camp for the night along the northern sector of Nalboki State Park in a garage used for maintenance equipment, most of which sat useless inside the building. When Father Belsario offered to have his people stand watch, several of Jason's team shook their heads. Jason understood their concern because he felt it himself. Yet Sasha's eyes pleaded for him to agree. He did, although with apprehension.

Everyone stared at their plates during dinner, making the meal quiet and awkward. That is, everyone who ate. Sasha and Father Belsario sat together in the circle around the campfire opposite Jason. They did not eat but waited patiently for the others to finish. When the last of Jason's team placed their plate on the floor, Sasha cleared her throat.

"I guess now is a good time to explain what's going on."

Jason gave her his attention.

"Just to be clear, I did die in Paris. However, I was given the opportunity to come back as one of the Purgatoriati."

Jason held up his hand to cut off Sasha. "What do you mean 'come back'? What is the Purgatoriati? Who gave you the opportunity?"

"I did," said Father Belsario. "To answer your other questions, the Purgatoriati were established by Heaven to return to Earth and assist in closing the portals."

Antoine scoffed. "There is no Heaven."

Father Belsario glared at the Moroccan. "Do you believe in Hell?"

"Of course not."

"Where do you think all these demons you've been fighting come from?"

"Another dimension."

"That dimension is Hell." When Antoine did not respond, Father Belsario switched his attention back to Jason. "Millenia ago, Heaven and Hell agreed not to interfere on Earth and allow man to use his free will to choose the path of good or evil. That all changed with the opening of the portals. Although Satan did not plan the destruction of civilization and the disgorging of millions of his demons into our realm, he used the situation to his own advantage. Heaven wants to counter that by providing mankind with help. The problem is no one in Heaven is willing to return to Earth."

"Good religious virtues," scoffed Slava.

"It has nothing to do with religion or virtue," explained Father Belsario. "No one wants to give up paradise to come back, especially since the gates were opened because of man's own arrogance."

Jason bristled at the comment yet remained quiet.

"I had to travel to Purgatory to find volunteers. The only

incentive I had to offer was a promise that anybody who joined would have a five hundred years taken off their banishment. Even then, Heaven only allowed me to recruit five members as a trial run."

"Hence your title?" Jason asked.

"The Purgatoriati," said Father Belsario.

"And you went with him to recruit?" Jason asked Sasha.

Sasha shook her head. "I was in Purgatory when Father Belsario arrived. He tracked me down and asked if I would come back. Of course, I agreed."

Jason wanted to know why Sasha ended up in Purgatory rather than Heaven yet did not want to embarrass her by asking. He pointed to the chest plate with the raised R and A emblazoned in the center of the circle. "What do the letters stand for?"

"Repentance and Atonement," said Sasha. "It's the only way to save our souls. We must be genuinely sorry for whatever sins we committed and must make things right. We can do the latter by returning to Earth and joining the war against the Demon Spawn."

"Don't get me wrong," said Jason. "But there are only six of you."

"The Purgatoriati have been granted increased strength and agility," said Father Belsario. "We don't need to sleep and we don't become tired. In battle, we have the strength of five mortals."

"Can you be killed?" Jeanette asked.

"We're already dead. We feel pain the way you do, but it doesn't impair our ability to fight. When our bodies are destroyed or take enough damage to be rendered useless, our souls leave them and return to Purgatory."

Jason didn't know what to say. Sasha stared at him, her eyes pleading for him to accept that she and the others had returned from the dead. The concept seemed fantastic, yet so did the existence of portals into Hell and demons walking the

Earth. He honed in on the Purgatoriati's auras, hoping to find a clue to their true motivations. Jason picked up nothing from Father Belsario, although he could not determine whether the emotional blank slate came from the cleric concealing something or from his unusual multi-afterlife heritage. The four cloaked figures standing watch along the perimeter gave off an air of darkness, more like sorrow and self-loathing than anything threatening. Sasha's aura, on the other hand, buzzed with a myriad of emotions, with one standing out more than any of the others—sadness. Jason could not detect anything from the newcomers that suggested malice. After listening to Sasha and Father Belsario, he felt more comfortable with accepting the Purgatoriati.

"So?" prodded Sasha.

"Welcome to the team," said Jason.

Sasha took Jason's hand in hers and squeezed. "Thank you for trusting us."

"We can use the extra help."

"More so than you realize," added Father Belsario.

"What do you mean?" asked Haneef, a tone of concern in his voice.

"When you eliminated the portal in Paris, Hell recognized that the gates were vulnerable. Rather than lose access to our realm, Demon Spawn have reinforced the portals to defend against further attacks. When we get to Moscow, it won't be as easy to close that one as it was in Paris."

Jason felt morale around the campfire plummet. Not that he blamed them. The news depressed even him, except that he couldn't show it. Jason put on a false bravado and slapped his hands against his knees. "Then it's a good thing you found us when you did."

CHAPTER TWENTY-ONE

BECAUSE THEY DID not require rest, Father Belsario had volunteered the Purgatoriati to man the watch until dawn, allowing Jason's team to sleep through the night. Although Jason still harbored a few apprehensions about them, he felt comfortable enough to agree. As his team sauntered off to bed down and the Purgatoriati took up their positions, Jason motioned for Slava and Haneef to hang back. Jeanette stayed with them.

"What's up?" Slava asked once they were alone.

"What do you think of our new friends?"

"You want the truth?"

"Yes."

"I know they saved us this morning, but I don't trust them."

"I'm glad I'm not the only one that feels that way," added Jeanette. "It seems convenient that they show up now."

"Haneef?"

"I trust them because of Sasha."

"Are you sure it *is* Sasha?" Jeanette asked Haneef.

"I've known her for a long time, It's her."

"It is," added Jason. "I can sense Sasha's aura."

"What do we do now?" Slava asked.

"Spread the word to the others to stay alert. Have everyone keep their weapons nearby to use on a second's notice. I also want someone to stay awake to keep an eye on the Purgatoriati. I'll take watch until ten. Slava will take it until two, and Haneef will finish off until dawn."

"You want us to check on them?" Haneef asked.

Jason shook his head. "I don't want them to know we're watching them. Just stay awake and keep your eyes and ears open. If you hear anything suspicious, raise the alarm."

"Got that," said Slava.

"Can do," added Haneef.

As the two men walked off, Jason said to Jeanette. "Come with me."

"Where are we going?"

"To talk with Sasha. Maybe she can fill us in more about what's going on."

"You don't need me for that."

"Yes, I do."

"Sasha will be more open with you if I'm not around." When Jason protested, Jeanette placed a finger on his lips to silence him. "I know you had feelings for her."

"That's not why I want to talk Sasha."

"I trust you. But this is something you have to do by yourself." Jeanette kissed him, holding her lips against his a little longer than usual. "Good luck."

JASON FOUND SASHA standing guard two hundred feet from the rear wall of the garage. As he drew near, she placed a hand on the hilt of her saber and spun around. On seeing it was him, she relaxed. "What are you doing up? I thought you'd be getting some rest."

"I couldn't sleep."

"You don't trust us and you're here to pump me for information."

"That's not true."

"Do you really think you can keep anything from me?" chastised Sasha. "It's okay. I don't blame you. Under the circumstances, I'd be suspicious."

In the soft glow of the moon, Jason could barely make out

her eyes. He saw the love and understanding in them, the same emotions that had comforted him so many times before. Jason did not realize until now how much he had missed Sasha.

"What do you want to ask me?"

"What happened?"

"You mean in Paris?"

"No. Antoine told me how you di… what happened at Notre Dame. I mean afterwards."

"Father Belsario covered that. He wanted to put together a force to help you battle the Demon Spawn and came to Purgatory seeking recruits."

"That's not what I'm asking. Why did you wind up in Purgatory?"

A touch of sadness tinged Sasha's eyes. "Despite what you think of me, I'm not perfect. After I fell off the bell tower, I woke up in Purgatory. No one ever explained why I was there. Why does anybody? Lack of faith? Failure to renounce your sins? An unwillingness to accept a divinity? Maybe nobody goes to Hell anymore since it's no longer a one-way trip. I don't know."

"What's Purgatory like?"

"You exist."

"You lost me."

Sasha contemplated how best to describe it. "Do you know that mood you get in when you're depressed, when you have no feelings and are only going through the motions?"

"Yes."

"It's like that, except it lasts for hundreds of years until you've fulfilled your penance and are allowed into Heaven. It's total nothingness."

"No pain of suffering?"

Sasha shook her head.

Jason paused, not certain if he wanted to hear the answer to the next question. "So why did you agree to come back?"

"I came back because of you."

"For me?" Jason asked with more excitement in his tone than he had intended.

"*Because* of you. What you're doing is the most selfless and heroic thing I've seen in my life. No one else is trying to save mankind. I wanted to be part of that. I want to complete what we started in Paris and restore order to the world. And...."

When Sasha didn't finish, Jason prodded her. "And what?"

"I wanted to make amends, to say I'm sorry for not treating you right when I was alive."

Sasha's answer took Jason aback. "You never mistreated me."

"I didn't treat you the way you deserved. You loved me and I knew that. And I lo... I cared for you, but I always kept you at arms' length because of the differences in our age. By the time I realized how foolish I was, you had already found Jeanette."

"You came back to steal me from Jeanette?"

Sasha's eyes became even sadder. "I wouldn't do that to you. You two are happy together. I came back to make sure that all those who lost their lives in Paris didn't die in vain. I also figured if I showed up with the Purgatoriati you might be more inclined to believe that they're here to help."

"You succeeded in that," Jason chuckled. "The reason we trust the Purgatoriati at all is because you're one of them."

"I'm hoping you'll learn to trust them. Father Belsario is dedicated to helping you succeed, as are the other members."

"It'll take time for us to trust them completely, but we'll try."

"Thank you." Sasha took Jason's right hand and squeezed gently. "You won't regret it."

I hope not, Jason thought. Instead, he said, "I better get back to camp and make sure everyone is settled."

Jason walked away, pausing when a few yards distant. "Thanks again for coming back. It means a lot to have you with us for this fight."

"Thank you for accepting us. We won't let you down."
"I know. Good night."

BY THE TIME Jason reached the campfire, most of his team was asleep. He found Jeanette and unfolded his sleeping bag beside her. As he settled in, she rolled over and met his gaze.

"Did you talk with Sasha?" she whispered.

"I did."

"And?"

"I feel more comfortable with the Purgatoriati."

"Good."

As Jason lied down, Jeanette unzipped her sleeping bag and pulled the flap aside. With her free hand, she waved for him to join her.

"Are you sure?" he asked.

"Yes," said Jeanette. "I don't want to be alone tonight."

Crawling over to Jeanette, Jason slid inside the sleeping bag with her.

CHAPTER TWENTY-TWO

THE FIRST FULL day with the Purgatoriati had been uneventful. Even though Jason's team had slept through the night, few of them felt rested in the morning, their sleep having been fitful because they were nervous about allowing the newcomers to stand watch. Making it through the night without incident had helped assuage some of their fears. Jason had tried to reassure his people by having Father Belsario join him and Haneef at the head of the column. That night, they camped a few miles east of Rakaw Pakay, less than twenty miles from downtown Minsk. Once again, the Purgatoriati had kept watch. This time, the group felt more comfortable with them, so everyone got a better sleep. They set out an hour after dawn and continued east.

At mid-morning, they arrived at the Minsk Beltway, which circled the city. Jason paused and signaled for them to stop for a few minutes.

Haneef pulled his horse up on the left. "Where do we go from here?"

"Hang on." Jason consulted the map. "We'll head north around the ring road. It's the quickest way to reach the highway to Moscow, and it bypasses downtown."

"Do you think traffic congestion will be a problem?" Father Belsario asked.

"Not if that's any indication." Jason pointed to the beltway where only a few scores of vehicles were visible. "I'm more concerned about running into Demon Spawn."

Slava brought his horse up alongside Jason's other flank.

"Are you sensing anything?"

Jason shut his eyes and allowed his sixth sense to wander. He detected nothing in the vicinity. "Not a thing. What about you, Father?"

"The Purgatoriati don't have the same abilities as you do. If you want my opinion, it would be safer to avoid Minsk altogether."

"I agree. But to do that, we'd have to backtrack to the next nearest highway, and that would another two days to the trip."

"Shit," muttered Haneef.

Slava huffed. "No way."

"Those are my thoughts," said Jason. "Minsk isn't too big, so we should clear the city in a few hours. Slava, tell the others to move out and to stay alert."

Slava gave a mock salute and went back to advise the team. Jason spurred his horse ahead, followed by Haneef and Father Belsario. Lucifer and Lilith fell in behind their master. Moving up the exit ramp and past a stalled tractor trailer, Jason entered the northbound lanes of the Minsk Beltway. Ahead of him were various abandoned vehicles, each spaced out enough to allow them to pass. Lucifer and Lilith raced on ahead, sniffing around one vehicle before moving on to the next. On both sides of the beltway sat rows of apartment buildings. Numerous balcony doors and windows were open and, from a few, curtains hung out and blew in the wind. In front of each building lay the detritus of a mass exodus—cars parked at awkward angles, discarded bicycles, piles of luggage, and scattered debris. Yet there were no corpses, which indicated the locals had escaped before the Demon Spawn descended upon Minsk. Hopefully without humans around, the demons had moved on.

The group traveled for several miles until the residential district came to an end along the banks of a lake. A small bridge stretched from one bank to the other. On either side, acres of open land overgrown with grass and weeds stretched into the distance. Lucifer's ears perked up. He rushed over to the guardrail, his attention focused on something moving through the growth. Lilith joined him. Jason raised his crossbow and kept his eyes focused on where they stared, his concern becoming relief when a family of deer emerged from the meadow and made its way to the water's edge to drink. Lucifer growled and crouched, ready to give chase. Jason whistled. The werehounds switched their attention between him and the deer before joining their master.

On the other side of the bridge, the Minsk Beltway passed through a heavily wooded area with dense forest on either side. After a few hundred yards, no evidence existed that they were on the border of a large city. Wildlife here was more prevalent, mostly small animals. Jason grinned as he watched Lucifer's head dart back and forth, wanting to chase after each critter that emerged from the trees or darted across the beltway. He would let them have their fun if he thought—

Jason's sixth sense spiked. He jerked upright in his saddle and yanked back on the reins, causing his horse to buck. At the same moment, Lilith whined. Her head moved from one side of the beltway to the other. She moved beside her master and nestled against his horse, seeking guidance. Jason did not notice. An overwhelming mass of auras flooded his senses. They were benign, which indicated flesh eaters. Except there were more than he had ever felt before.

A hand touched Jason's shoulder. The gesture snapped him back to reality. Slava had brought his horse up alongside. "What's wrong?"

Haneef stopped his horse a few yards away. He sat in the saddle, his minigun at the ready, scanning the area for any sign of danger. Behind him, the rest of the team were on alert. The Purgatoriati had spread out, forming a circle around the others, their broadswords drawn and raised.

"Jason." Slava shook him. "What's wrong?"

"Flesh eaters." Jason spoke up loud enough for the others to hear. "We're about to be swarmed."

Three hundred feet ahead of them and to the left, a rustling cut through the silence. Everyone focused their attention in that direction. Animals broke through the tree line, mostly deer, bear, and wild horses. The stampede hurtled the guardrail and darted onto the beltway. Off to the right, a swarm of birds took flight, forming a black mass that circled the road and headed north. The other animals veered and followed the flock. A moment later, flesh eaters broke through the tree line on both sides of the beltway, hundreds stretching along either flank in front of and behind the group. The nearest ones spotted the humans and surged forward.

Jason heard his team unsling their weapons. "Stand down. We're in no immediate danger."

As if to prove his point, the first row of flesh eaters reached the guardrail and tumbled over, creating a small pile of demons. They continued to cascade over, pushed by the surging horde behind them. Those on the pavement struggled to get to their feet.

"We could rush ahead," offered Haneef. "We should be able to push our way through."

"It's too risky. If there are more of those things farther down the road, we'll be swarmed." Jason pointed in the direction they had come from. "We'll backtrack and circle around the city."

Haneef ordered the others to fall back. As they did, Jason remained at the front of the column, keeping a watchful eye on the flesh eaters. Lucifer and Lilith stayed by him, switching their gaze between Jason and the horde. The Demon Spawn swarmed along the guardrails and enough had crossed over that, once they regained their footing, they would seal off the beltway. Lilith whined once.

"Okay," said Jason. "Let's go."

As Jason retreated, more and more flesh eaters moved in on both sides. When he reached the bridge spanning the lake, he found the rest of his people paused. Racing to the rear of the column, he moved up alongside Haneef.

"Why did you stop?"

Haneef motioned to the south. Another three hundred flesh eaters had emerged from the neighborhoods they had passed through and converged on the bridge, blocking their retreat.

"We're screwed," said Slava.

"Not yet." Jason side stepped his horse so everyone could hear. "We're going to set up on both ends of the bridge so they can't outflank us. Neal, take the horses to the center and stay with them. Haneef, set up on the south end and clear a path for us to escape. Slava, Antoine, Jeanette, and Vicky will cover you. The rest of you are with me on the north end. We don't need to kill them all, only keep them from overrunning us."

Jason's team dismounted and made their way to their assigned battle stations.

CHAPTER TWENTY-THREE

JASON TOOK UP position where the road joints separated the bridge from the beltway. On either side of the structure, the ground sloped down twenty feet into the river. It was the perfect place to set up their defense. The rest of the team spread across the four lanes of highway. The Purgatoriati withdrew their edged weapons and clutched them against their chests, the blades pointing up. Lucifer and Lilith morphed into their werehound forms. The flesh eaters were still more than one hundred feet away. His team raised their automatic weapons and aimed. Jason held up his hand. "Hold your fire."

"Are you nuts, mate?" Ian asked.

Jason ignored him. His team kept their weapons in the high ready position, their eyes shifting to him every few seconds, waiting for the order. Behind them, Haneef opened fire with his minigun.

The horde approached to within fifty feet.

"Jason?" prodded Sasha.

He said nothing. The flesh eaters approached to within forty feet.

Lilith whimpered.

When the horde had closed to within thirty feet, Jason called out. "Take them down and make every shot count."

HANEEF UNHOOKED THE GAU-17A minigun from his leg mount and aimed it at the approaching demons. Around him, the others readied their weapons. He waited for them to get closer so he didn't waste ammunition. Once the horde closed to fifty feet, he squeezed the trigger. The minigun whirred to life. A stream of 7.62mm rounds ripped into the Demon Spawn which, along with the automatic weapons fire from the others, decimating the front row of flesh eaters.

AT FIRST, THE flesh eaters continued to surge toward Jason's team. As expected, though, the concentrated fire took its toll. With each volley, half a dozen dropped to the pavement. In a matter of seconds, enough bodies littered the beltway to trip up those behind them, creating a squirming barricade of the undead that held back the horde. Each burst of gunfire added more bodies to the pile, further slowing their advance. When someone paused to reload, one of the Purgatoriati would step forward and slash down a flesh eater with his broadsword, then fall back to let that person resume firing. Jason knew this would only slow the advance, not stop it. The mass of flesh eaters pushing from the rear would crumble this barricade within a few minutes. When that happened, the only thing that would save them would be if Haneef had cleared an escape route.

HANEEF REMAINED CALM and fired short bursts from his minigun to inflict the greatest amount of damage on the horde. The others concentrated on taking out the flesh eaters on the far ends of the horde, dropping them with single shots to the head. The onslaught had brought down numerous demons, the piles of bodies slowing the advance of those behind them. Haneef knew he could not sustain this rate of fire too long. Between the chunks of body parts tossed into the air and eddies of blue light drifting skyward, he could not tell how many of them remained.

THE CENTER OF the mound of corpses bulged, the weight of the encroaching flesh eaters too much for the pile to support. When it finally collapsed, a stream of Demon Spawn poured through the breach like water through a failed levee.

Before Jason could react, Father Belsario rushed forward. He swung his broadsword from right to left, severing the heads of two demons and slicing a chunk of rotted flesh from the chest of a third. The rest of the Purgatoriati joined the melee, cutting down anything that made it through the opening. Sasha stood on top of the mound, slashing away grasping hands with her dagger and driving the blade of her saber into their skulls. Lucifer and Lilith attacked the ones trying to get to Sasha. Lucifer charged into the horde, the spikes on his back impaling a pair of flesh eaters and shoving them back. Others filled the space he had created, swallowing him up in the mass. Lilith spun around and whipped her scorpion-like tail, slicing open the torso of one demon and decapitating another.

Jason and his team switched their fire onto the mass of flesh eaters crushed against the mound on either side of the breach. So many demons surged forward that other breaches began to form. When the team concentrated their fire on those weakening one section, pressure in another began to build. The Demon Spawn were about to tear open seven more breaches that would overwhelm the bridge.

HANEEF'S MINIGUN CLATTERED as it expended the last of its ten thousand rounds of ammunition. He lifted his finger off the trigger. As the rotating barrel whirred to a stop, his heart sank. More than fifty flesh eaters had survived the onslaught and continued converging on them, a few only thirty feet away. Slava, Antoine, Jeanette, and Vicky kept up their fire, yet they would not be able to take down the remainder before they were overrun.

ONE OF THE Purgatoriati stood on top of the mound, hacking away at the flesh eaters pushing through the breach, when a flesh eater grabbed his leg and pulled him into the horde. Dead hands tore away his cloak and clawed at his skin. He howled in agony as they ripped open his abdomen and yanked out his intestines while others chewed away chunks of flesh. Two more Purgatoriati dropped their broadswords and rushed forward to save him, only to be swarmed. Father Belsario and the last Purgatoriati tried to free their comrades, but too many flesh eaters surrounded them. Sasha pushed past the men, slashing at the demons. As she hacked off undead hands and arms, Father Belsario and the last Purgatoriati dragged the others to safety. Sasha fell back and joined them. However, the damage had been done. The melee distracted the Purgatoriati from defending the breach. With nothing to stop them, several flesh eaters pushed through and swarmed the bridge.

Other openings were forced through the mound. Jason's team concentrated their fire in those areas, slowing the advance. At least one hundred and fifty flesh eaters remained. A complete collapse of the line was imminent. Jason checked on Haneef. Even with the minigun, he had not been able to clear an escape route. Jason weighed three options, none of which were good. Stand, fight, and be overwhelmed. Mount up and make a break for it, although he'd lose most of his team trying to push through the horde. Or abandon the horses and supplies and escape by swimming to safety. He had seconds to decide before it would be too—

"What's going on over there?" Ian pointed to the right flank where the sound of gunfire could be heard and eddies of blue light formed a cloud over the horde.

Jason stepped onto the bridge abutment to get a better view. Flesh eaters toward the rear were being blasted apart by a small group of humans two hundred feet to the right that advanced along the shores of the lake. Three mobile machineguns mounted on two-wheel chassis were arranged in a line abreast and fired into the horde. Behind the machineguns stood fifty men and women in camouflaged uniforms, each firing an AK-47 automatic rifle or light machinegun. The combined fire power cut a large swath out of the horde. When one of the mounted machineguns ran out of ammunition, the gunner lifted the weapon by its carriage and rushed forward fifty feet while the loader followed alongside, carrying the watercooler canister and spare ammunition boxes. As they repositioned and reloaded, the other troops moved up. Within ten seconds, the barrage resumed, bringing down more flesh eaters. Two machinegun teams and twenty soldiers advanced along the southern shore of the lake, providing the same support to Haneef.

The attack from the flank caused the bulk of the flesh eaters, especially those not abutting the pile of corpses, to shift in the direction of the new threat. Sasha took advantage of the distraction. Rushing over the mound, she waded into what remained of the horde, slashing with her saber and dagger. Father Belsario joined in, placing his back against hers to bring down any demons that drew near. Lucifer and Lilith emerged from deep within the horde and took up a position on their flanks. The tallest of the Purgatoriati stormed into the breach. He crouched and swung the broadsword above his head, decapitating the surrounding flesh eaters or crushing their skulls. Two others stood ten feet away, cutting down anything that made it past him.

Jason and his team dropped back and resumed firing, taking down those flesh eaters that pushed through the smaller breaches. Because the mass no longer shoved against them, they had more room to maneuver. On the far left, thirty broke through in front of Antoine and Werner. Antoine stood his ground, taking careful aim and putting down the flesh eaters one by one. Werner swung around to the right to catch them in a crossfire. Sook-kyoung rushed over to assist. In less than a minute, the mini-horde had been wiped out, except for five demons that converged on Antoine, too close for Werner or Sook-kyoung to fire at. Antoine aimed his FAMAS at the nearest and fired a single round into its head, knocking it backward and releasing its lifeforce. He switched to another and fired, taking this one down, and expending his last round in the process. With the other three too close for him to reload, Antoine switched to hand-to-hand mode. Raising his FAMAS beside his head, he raced forward and smashed the stock into the nearest demon's face. Bones cracked and teeth shattered, yet the blow barely slowed it. Antoine kept up the assault, bashing the skull four times until it shattered and scrambled the brain, putting the demon out if its misery.

The last two flesh eaters reached Antoine. Each grabbed an arm and knocked him off balance, trying to pull him to the ground. Sook-kyoung rushed forward. When she got within striking distance, she initiated a flying drop kick, catching one of them in the chest and propelling it against the outer guardrail of the bridge. Sook-kyoung side stepped toward the demon, kicked out, and slammed her right foot into its chest, sending it toppling over the rail and into the lake. With only one flesh eater tugging at him, Antoine regained his balance. He brought the elbow of his free arm around and drove it into the demon's face with such force he heard the skull crack. Its grip on his left arm slackened. Antoine yanked himself free. Bending down, he lifted the flesh eater onto his shoulders and tossed it off the bridge.

The battle ended after five minutes. Jason's team wiped out the last flesh eater that hovered around the mound as the three machinegun teams took down the remaining demons. On the other end of the bridge, the twin machinegun teams had cleared away the last of the horde. Haneef and the others had rejoined Jason. Father Belsario and his Purgatoriati searched through the mass of bodies until they found the half-eaten corpse of their friend buried under a pile of flesh eaters. The others stood with their heads bowed as the cleric knelt beside their fallen comrade and prayed. Jason scanned the killing field for Lucifer and Lilith, breathing a sigh of relief when the two werehounds, now back in their dog-like forms, maneuvered through the corpses toward him. He crouched as they hopped the mound and raced over to him, greeting their master with a double face bath.

A hand touched Jason's shoulder. Jeanette motioned toward the opposite end of the killing field. "We have company."

Three figures in camouflage uniforms made their way through the mass of bodies. The first carried no weapon other than a holstered side arm. The other two held AK-47s but were more concerned with keeping an eye on the surrounding corpses to make certain none rose and attacked. Jason faced his own team.

"Stand down and shoulder your weapons."

"Do you think that's a good idea?" Slava asked.

"Just do as I ask." Jason stepped over the mound of undead.

"Do you want me to go with you?" Jeanette asked.

"I'll be fine. You stay here."

Jason made his way across the killing field. As he approached the three figures, the pair with the AK-47s stopped, allowing their comrade to proceed by himself. Jason paused when thirty feet away and studied the approaching figure. He seemed young, probably in his late twenties, with a lean yet toned body. The blue eyes that locked on Jason were friendly, yet they expressed confidence and a hardness born in combat. He had the bearing of a military officer. The figure stopped in front of Jason and offered his hand.

"I'm Captain Vasiliy Melnikov of Moscow Military District's 4th Guards Independent Tank Brigade." The captain spoke with a thick Russian accent. "Are you Jason McCreary?"

"Yes, I am," said Jason, surprised the captain knew his name.

Melnikov yelled something in Russian to the rest of his

group and then spoke to Jason. "We've been searching for you and your team for over a week."

"Thanks for helping us."

"What is it you Americans say? We arrived in nick of time." Melnikov examined the killing field as if he only now appreciated what had happened here. "I have message for you. Reno says to tell you he has arranged help you requested."

CHAPTER TWENTY-FOUR

MELNIKOV RECOMMENDED THEY leave the area before more Demon Spawn were drawn by the noise, a suggestion Jason agreed with. The Russian led them into downtown Minsk, with half of his troops taking point and the other half, including the mounted machineguns, bringing up the rear. When they reached their destination, the Minsk Passazhirsky Railway Station, Jason was taken aback to see their mode of transportation. He had expected a corral of horses. Instead, four city buses modified to sit atop a pair of railroad tender wheels were parked at one of the station platforms. A funnel extended from the roof at the rear of each bus. A dozen soldiers and a sixth mobile machine gun guarded the platform.

"This is how you get around?" Jason asked.

"We make do," Melnikov replied. "After EMP destroyed all electronics, we improvised. Horses were okay for local travel, but Russia much larger than Europe, so we pulled several old steam locomotives out of storage and refurbished them. We did same for our military hardware. Our machine guns are old M1910 Maxims from Great Patriotic War we found in military museum outside of Moscow." Melnikov held up his weapon, which had a bipod mount attached to the barrel and a round ammunition drum on top. "We also found several dozen crates of DP28 light machine guns which we confiscated. What we couldn't scavenge, we adapted. Let me show you."

Melnikov led Jason and his team onto the nearest bus. The seats in the rear portion had been removed and were replaced with a steam engine and a makeshift tender filled with coal. Two men in ash-covered overalls smoked cigarettes, one leaning against the interior wall, the other lying down on top of the coal. Upon seeing the captain, the man against the wall snapped to attention and saluted.

Melnikov saluted back. When the two men went back to smoking, he continued. "After failed attempt to close portal in Moscow, what left of Moscow Military District relocated to rail yard thirty kilometers outside city. To get around, we converted buses into steam engines."

"Ingenious, mate," said Ian.

"It's quite simple. We just replaced diesel engines with smaller steam ones hanging around yard, modified transmission, and converted rear of buses to hold coal. What they lack in comfort, they make up for in efficiency. We should be back in Moscow early tomorrow morning. Which is good thing. General Zhirinovsky has been anxious to meet you ever since he received radio message from Reno."

"I'm glad my uncle reached you," said Jeanette.

"It was miracle he did." Melnikov lowered his voice so the crew couldn't hear. "General has been going into depression for months. One by one, other groups of survivors around world we in contact with dropped off airwaves. Last contact with any one was four months ago. Two months ago, general stopped monitoring radio. Only reason we picked up Reno's message because one of our radio operators still tuned in at night for a couple of hours because he had nothing better to do. Ten days ago, he hear message from Reno that your team on way to Moscow. General ordered me to take unit out to find you and bring you back. When he heard you were on your way, it gave him hope again."

"Why?" asked Sasha.

"Until you, no one had attempted anything against portal. We tried once, a week after first opened, but miserable failure. General abandoned hope of ever saving world and had pretty much sat back and waited for death. Now he's old self again and wants to do everything possible to make certain you succeed."

"Thank you," said Slava.

"You're welcome." Melnikov placed a hand on Slava's shoulder and squeezed. "We don't have enough transport to take your horses, so we'll have to leave them here with some of my men for a few days until we can send buses back for them. Will that be okay?"

"As long as they're safe," said Jason.

"I guarantee it. These buses will get us to Moscow even if we run into any *plot' yedokov*."

"*Plot' yedokov?*" Jason was confused.

"Flesh eaters," said Slava.

"They're most prevalent dead demons out here. Them and ravagers," added Melnikov.

"What are ravagers?" Jeanette asked.

Melnikov shivered. "They're human in form. Blood red eyes. Talons for fingers."

"We ran into a pack of them two days ago," said Jason.

"They rip people apart and eat them. They are worst out here."

"Why do you call them dead demons?" Ian asked.

"I don't," said Melnikov. "Demons are demons, as far as I'm concerned. But Dr. Frankenstein likes labeling them."

Ian's eyes went wide. "Dr. Frankenstein?"

"Forgive me. That nickname we give Dr. Ustagov. He is biologist from University of Volgograd. Has examined every demon we've been able to capture."

"I want to talk with him," Ian said excitedly, reminding Jason of a kid in a toy store.

"You will, once we get to Moscow." The captain clapped his hands to get the attention of his own men. "Let's load up. We head out in ten minutes. I want to be in Domodedovo by noon tomorrow."

CHAPTER TWENTY-FIVE

THEY ARRIVED AT Domodedovo shortly after sunrise the next morning. The Russians had set up camp at a small rail yard halfway between the town and the airport. To secure the compound, the Russians had erected walls comprised of steel sheets twenty feet high, with each sheet held in place by torn-up railroad tracks, one end of which had been dug into the ground and the other welded to the plates. To the north and south, the walls had been anchored to the outer perimeter of warehouses and administrative buildings, and each structure had been walled up and covered in more plates. To the east and west, boxcars had been knocked onto their sides to block all the tracks but one, and the steel wall had been erected around the exterior of this barricade. One hundred feet from the enclosure, a four-foot high, reinforced chain link fence circled the compound. This had been topped with a foot of coiled barbed wire from which the decayed corpses of several flesh eaters still hung. Guard posts had been erected at one-hundred-foot intervals along the wall, each manned by a two-person machine gun crew. When the buses approached, guards slid aside a heavy steel gate, exposing the tracks. Two other teams raced out, unlatched the sections of chain link fence that served as a gate, and opened them. Once the buses had passed through the perimeter and entered the compound, the guards secured the chain link fence and closed the metal gate.

More buses and cars converted into steam engines were parked on sidings off the main track. The atmosphere inside the compound bustled with activity, with soldiers repairing and modifying vehicles, performing calisthenics, or cleaning their weapons.

"Why did you decide to set up camp here?" asked Slava. "Isn't Domodedovo forty kilometers from downtown Moscow?"

"Forty-five, to be exact," answered Melnikov. "When portal opened, this was ideal location. General had decided to use steam engines to get around, so Domodedovo near enough to Moscow we could be there in a few hours, and at time still outside range of demons. After our failed attempt, General decided to hold this compound to launch our next attack once Dr. Frankenstein came up with new plan. He never did."

"Didn't you get swarmed by Demon Spawn?" Jason asked.

"In beginning, yes. When flesh eaters arrived, we stayed quiet and they passed us by. Ravagers were another story. They sensed us in here and attacked on three occasions. We stopped them each time, but with heavy casualties. Last attack happened five months ago. We have not seen any since. They seem afraid to come through portal, as if they're aware of radiation."

"Radiation?" Haneef joined the conversation. "Where did that come from?"

"Every question will be answered in due time." Melnikov pointed outside. "First, I need to introduce you to General Zhirinovsky."

As the other three buses carrying soldiers moved off onto a siding, their bus continued straight along the main track. The driver stopped in front of a warehouse near the wall of the compound. A tall, stout figure stood by the door. He wore the same camouflage uniform as the other Russians, but sported a leather bomber's jacket and a green officer's cap. A large, bushy mustache covered his upper lip. When the door opened, Melnikov stepped out. Upon seeing the captain, Zhirinovsky stepped forward, embraced the junior officer, and slapped him on the back. The two chatted in Russian. As Jason exited,

Melnikov pointed to him. The general walked over and hugged Jason the same way he had Melnikov, then placed his hands on Jason's shoulders.

"Welcome to Moscow," Zhirinovsky said in a heavy accent.

"Thank you for helping us," said Jason.

Melnikov translated Jason's statement and Zhirinovsky's response. "Quarters have been set up for you. If there's anything you need, just ask. Jason, General wants you and me to discuss plans for closing portal this afternoon so I can brief him before dinner. Is that okay?"

"That's fine with me."

"Good." Melnikov passed on Jason's approval. Zhirinovsky headed back to his office. Two young soldiers stepped forward to show the team their quarters.

"Before we discuss plans," Melnikov said to Jason. "Gather your team leaders and meet me back here in thirty minutes. I'll introduce you to Dr. Frankenstein."

CHAPTER TWENTY-SIX

A FTER GETTING SETTLED, Jason met Melnikov in front of Zhirinovsky's building. He asked Haneef and Jeanette to accompany him. Ian begged to come along, saying he wanted to compare notes with the doctor on the Demon Spawn Ian had examined outside of Minsk, so Jason agreed. Father Belsario and Sasha joined them.

Melnikov led the group to the main gate where the buses had entered. Two guards opened it while two more rushed out to open the gate in the chain link fence. Five soldiers armed with AK-47s surrounded the group and escorted them off the compound.

"Where are we going?" Jason asked.

The captain pointed to an isolated building a thousand feet down the rail line. "General wants demons kept separate. We don't know if they can sense each other like animals do. If demons are going to come for their dead, we don't want them trying to break into compound."

"Good idea."

"Plus no one wants to put up with smell."

As the group approached the building, the guards spread out. Four took up position on each corner, and the fifth stood by the entrance. Melnikov paused and removed a jar of Vicks VapoRub from his pocket. He unscrewed the top, scooped up a glob with his index finger, and spread it along his lip under his nose. "Use this. It will help lessen stench."

When everyone else had applied the VapoRub, Melnikov took back the jar and opened the door. Jason had stepped into rooms before that were so hot the air washed over him like a blast furnace. This was the first time he had that sensation with odor. The air reeked of decayed flesh. It generated a burning sensation in his eyes. Jason blinked several times to moisten them. After acclimating for a few seconds, he entered.

Four operating tables were arranged in a square in the middle of the floor. Three held the remains of Demon Spawn—a flesh eater, a soul vampire, and a headless ravager. The remains of a Golem were spread out on the floor against the far wall. Each had their chests carved open from neck to groin. The internal organs and outer skin were coated in a crystalline substance. In the center of the square formed by the operating tables sat a draftsmen desk covered with papers and sketches. A middle-aged man with white hair and a well-trimmed goatee more grey than dark sat on a stool in front of the desk. He wore a stained lab coat over his camouflage uniform. He stared at the sketches, the arm of a pair of eyeglasses clutched between his teeth. He had not noticed them enter.

Melnikov stepped into the room. "Dr. Frank... Dr. Ustagov, our visitors are here."

The doctor raised his head. Upon seeing Jason and the others, he bound off the stool and crossed the floor, folding his eyeglasses and sliding them into the outer pocket of the lab coat. He grabbed Jason's hand and shook vigorously. "You have no idea what a pleasure it is to meet you."

"Thank you," Jason replied hesitantly.

"Is it true you closed the portal in Paris?"

Jason motioned to those around him. "*We* did."

Ustagov clapped his hands together and held them in front of his chest. "I have so many questions. Pardon my manners. Please, come in. I'd offer you a seat but, as you can see, we're not equipped for comfort."

Haneef passed by the corpse of the flesh eater. "How do you preserve them?

"It's all makeshift since we no longer have refrigeration," replied Ustagov, obviously proud of his work. "I embalmed the bodies using a hand pump and covered the exposed areas with salt. It's not perfect, but it gives me enough time to study them."

Ian walked up to the operating table holding the headless ravager and peered inside, not bothered by the odor. "You performed autopsies?"

"I didn't remove all the internal organs. I'm not interested in their physiology as much as figuring out a way to kill them. We tried closing the portal in Red Square and failed. Zhirinovsky won't attempt it again unless we come up with a plan that has a better than even chance of working. The General asked me to find a way to destroy the demons."

"What did you...?" Ian paused and gestured toward Jason. "Sorry, mate. Don't mean to take charge."

"Go ahead," Jason replied. "You know more about this than me."

"What did you find?" Ian asked Ustagov.

"Basically, all dead demons were once human."

"Excuse me," Father Belsario interrupted. "Can you explain that term to us?"

"Dead demons?"

"Yes."

Ustagov paced between the operating tables like a professor lecturing his class. "They are terms I came up with to categorize these things. There are two types of monsters that come through the portal. The first are the living demons. These are living biological units like the giant insects in the subway and the dragons we encountered in Red Square."

"Did you say dragons?" Jeanette asked.

"Yes." Ustagov seemed confused. "Didn't you run into any chemical-breathing dragons when you were in Paris?"

"No," said Jason.

"Allah is full of surprises," added Haneef.

"Interesting." Ustagov became lost in thought for a moment and then got back on track. "As I was saying, the living demons are individual biological units. As far as I can tell, they are indigenous to the other dimension. They make up less than five percent of the demons we've observed. Most of what we've encountered have been the dead demons."

"Why do you call them dead demons?" Father Belsario asked.

"As far as I can tell they're dead. Or more precisely, they are dead humans." Ustagov held up his hands to stop the questions he knew were coming. He stepped over to the flesh eater. "Let me explain. These have the exact same internal organs as humans, only they no longer function. They don't breathe. Blood doesn't flow. The brain doesn't work except for the basest of motor skills. It's true they eat human flesh, but I have no idea why. Whatever they consume remains in the stomach since there is no longer a digestive process. These things are like zombies from your American movies, except that a bite from a flesh eater doesn't make you into one of them." Ustagov walked over and stood by the operating table holding the ravager. "These are the demons that intrigue me most."

"Why's that?" Jason asked.

"Because their internal organs look like those of humans," said Ian.

"Not just look like. They're identical. Although, like the exterior bodies, they have slight mutations, mostly in size, to adapt to the new environment." Ustagov lifted the outer flap of skin, exposing the body cavity. "Because ravagers are violent and powerful, and because their appetite is ravenous, you can see how the heart, lungs, and digestive system have doubled in size to accommodate the physical strain."

"That's what I was trying to tell you earlier," Ian said to Jason.

"You've run into them before?" Ustagov became excited.

"Outside of Minsk," Jason answered. "No matter how much damage we inflicted on them, they healed their wounds in seconds. The only way to stop them was to cut off their heads."

"We had the same problem when we first encountered the ravagers," said Ustagov. He turned his attention back to the body cavity. "I have a theory that these enlarged organs are also why ravagers are able to regenerate. As you can see, all the other organs are unaffected by the transformation. The same holds true for the soul vampire."

"What do you mean by transformation?" Father Belsario asked.

If Ustagov heard him, he ignored the question. The doctor crossed the room and stood by the head of the golem. The team followed. Even dead and decomposing, it presented a frightening sight. It stretched out thirty feet with a massive torso, thick muscular legs, and bulky arms almost as long as the demon's entire body. The bulbous head merged with the shoulders, devoid of all features except a pair of coal black eyes on either side of a ridge that ran down the face and substituted for a nose. Its dark red skin had paled in death, but Jason could still make out that every limb or torso section on the Golem was made of scores of corresponding human limbs stripped of their flesh and molded together, especially the head, which was comprised of a hundred skinless faces.

"Have you dealt with any of these things before?" Ustagov asked.

"Yes." Jason suppressed a shudder when he remembered running into these monstrosities in Paris.

"Good. Then you know the outside of these demons is made up of hundreds of human limbs combined into one massive form. Wait till you see this." Ustagov grabbed a large flap of skin on the Golem's chest and flipped it back as if he were unfolding a blanket, exposing the body cavity. Like the outer features of the Golem, the internal structure comprised scores of organs—hearts, lungs, stomachs, kidneys—joined to form one massive organ. Yards of intestines flowed through its abdomen. Arteries and blood vessels wound throughout the body, packed together and intertwined like the cables on a suspension bridge.

Jeanette retched. Haneef shut his eyes to avoid the sight.

Again, Ustagov seemed unaware of what went on around him. "I counted one hundred and twenty-three identical sets of internal organs."

"That's bloody incredible, mate." Ian crouched down to get a better view.

"What's fascinating, though, is that each of the one hundred and twenty-three sets of organs is separate from the others. They are in tandem with each other but not interconnected. It's the most intricate transformation I've seen yet."

"Excuse me," Father Belsario said, this time more forceful. "You keep on using the word 'transformation'. What do you mean by that?"

"Except for the flesh eaters, all of these demons are deceased humans that have been transformed... changed... altered... whichever word you want to use."

"Altered how?" insisted Belsario.

Ustagov shrugged. "It could have been done surgically or through some occult ritual. I don't know. I know nothing about theology, but my guess is that these things are much more than just demons. They're also tortured souls."

Sasha took Jason's hand. "Maybe that explains why your senses can detect the aura of the dead demons and not the living demons."

"She could be right," said Haneef. "You weren't able to detect the giant wasps in Falaise or the insects in the sewers."

"Wait. Wait. Wait." Ustagov became excited. "You can sense these things when they're around?"

"I can pick up their aura," said Jason. "At least the auras for those demons that were once human."

Ustagov rubbed his chin with his right hand. "Interesting."

"That might also explain why more dead demons pass through the portal than living demons," said Father Belsario. "They see the portals as an opportunity to escape Hell and get back to earth."

"Or they're a vanguard." Ustagov said in a matter of fact tone.

"Vanguard?" Jason asked.

"During World War II, the Red Army used penal battalions of prisoners who had been condemned to death to charge through Nazi minefields and assault fortifications and clear a path so that good Soviet troops wouldn't be killed needlessly. Maybe the living demons are Hell's version of penal battalions."

"Why do you say that?" Haneef asked.

"Let me ask you a question first. How long ago did you close down the portal in Paris?"

"Three months ago," said Jason.

Ustagov thought for a moment. "That sounds about right."

"I'm not following you," said Sasha.

"Let me explain." Ustagov strolled back to the operating tables. "Nine days after the portal opened in Moscow, Zhirinovsky sent a team into Red Square to shut it down. They used small-yield nuclear weapons. The team deployed the device but the effects were disastrous."

"How so?"

Melnikov stepped forward and spoke before Ustagov could respond. "Device failed to close portal."

The doctor ignored him. "In the process, we nuked Red Square. The radiation from the blast contaminated the area. That didn't stop the dead demons from coming through, though. They're already dead and are immune to the fallout. Not so the living demons. After our attack, three more dragons came through to guard the gate. They died within days from radiation poisoning. This happened for a few weeks. After that, the living demons stopped. They knew Red Square was dangerous and avoided it."

"How do you know this?" Father Belsario asked.

"We send recon team in once a week to check on portal," said Melnikov. "General doesn't want to be taken by surprise."

"My point is," continued Ustagov, "it stayed that way until eight weeks ago. Then the recon teams reported that a dragon had ventured through the portal and prowled downtown Moscow. Four weeks ago, they reported seeing two dragons, and last week, four."

"What are the radiation levels like now?" Haneef asked.

"Still high," said Melnikov. "Not enough to kill something immediately, especially something size of a dragon."

Jason shrugged. "Maybe they sensed the area no longer posed a danger and came back."

"Maybe." Melnikov paused. "Or maybe they're trying to protect this portal so you don't shut it down as well."

"By 'they' you mean the living demons?" asked Jeanette.

"Or whoever is controlling them."

It took a few seconds for the implication to sink in. Haneef said, "If the doctor is correct—"

Jeanette finished his sentence. "That means the Demon Spawn are expecting us."

"Shit," mumbled Ian.

"Does this mean you won't be closing portal?" Melnikov asked, a tone of disappointment in his voice.

"On the contrary," Jason asserted. "I want to do this as quickly as possible. Can we go tomorrow?"

"That can be arranged," said Melnikov.

"Good. Is anyone still around who participated in the first raid?"

"Only one person. The rest were either killed in combat or died from radiation poisoning."

"Can I talk to him?" Jason asked.

"That can also be arranged."

CHAPTER TWENTY-SEVEN

A S THE OTHERS headed to their quarters, Melnikov led Jason to the third floor of the headquarters building, which had been converted into a hospital. The captain led him past the nurse's station and down a corridor. A chain stretched across the far end, isolating the last four rooms from the rest of the ward. A metal sign with the words NE DOPUSKAT' and KEEP OUT hung from the center. Unhooking one end of the chain, Melnikov ushered Jason into the restricted area, replaced it, and led him to the last room on the left, stopping outside the door.

"You're about to meet General Budenny. He led attack on portal and received fatal dose of radiation in process. Doctors have no idea how he survived this long. General should be able to answer any questions you have, but you'll have only a few minutes at most before he gets overtired."

"I understand."

Melnikov opened the door and the two stepped inside. Jason paused upon seeing Budenny, taken aback by the man's condition. He sat at an angle in his hospital bed, with an IV inserted in his left arm and a breathing mask over his face. A bladder bag hung on the lower bed frame filled with blood-red urine. He had lost all the hair on his head, even his eyelashes. Red blotches covered his scalp. The general hacked. When he did, he sat upright and the blanket slid off his body. Underneath the hospital gown, scar tissue covered the skin across his chest, neck, and shoulders where second- and third-degree radiation burns had healed. A gold crucifix hung on a chain around the general's neck. On the third cough, Budenny filled his oxygen mask with bloody sputum. Melnikov rushed over to the side of the bed. Removing the mask, he used a nearby towel to wipe out the blood and then cleaned off the general's face. Budenny lifted a shaky hand and clutched the captain.

"Thank you, my son."

"Don't mention it." Melnikov paused. "General, do you think you're well enough to talk? This is Jason McCreary. He'd like to speak with you."

Budenny tried to focus on Jason with tired, blood shot eyes. "Are you the one?"

"Excuse me?"

"Are you the one who closed the Paris portal?"

"Yes, sir. I am."

"Then I have time to talk to you." Budenny took the oxygen mask from Melnikov, held it to his mouth, and inhaled deeply.

"Captain Melnikov told me about the attack on the portal in Red Square. We're going to try again tomorrow. I hoped you could give me some advice."

"Why would you want... my advice? I failed. You're the one... who succeeded."

Budenny had another coughing fit. Melnikov moved to assist him but the general waved him off.

Jason felt guilty for putting the general through this. "I'm sorry to have bothered you. I'll leave now."

"No!" Budenny lifted his left arm as high as possible and weakly waved Jason over. When he spoke, his breathing was labored. "I don't know how... you did it in Paris. I lost several hundred of my men... storming the portal. Those things came after us... like they knew... what we intended. Don't make... the same mistake. Don't charge them. Sneak up on them."

"We intend to, sir," said Melnikov.

"When you closed... the portal in Paris... did you see the other side?"

137

Jason nodded.

"Then you know… what we're dealing with." Budenny motioned for Jason to come nearer. When he did, the general clasped his hand. "I was born and raised… as a Soviet citizen… to not believe… in religion. What I saw… through the portal was… a vision of Hell. There are thousands more demons…. maybe even millions more… on the other side." Budenny lost his breath. He placed the mask over his mouth and inhaled several times.

"We should go now," Melnikov advised.

Budenny clutched Jason's hand and would not release it. After a few more breaths, he removed the mask. "Since looking through the portal… I've embraced religion. Every religion talks about… the end of days. We are seeing that now."

Jason squeezed his hand reassuringly. "It'll be okay. I promise."

"I know it will. Because of you." Budenny took another breath from his mask. "You've been sent… to stop the apocalypse."

Melnikov placed the oxygen mask over Budenny's face. "We need to go now, sir."

"Just one more question, please," Jason pleaded.

"Make it quick."

"When you were at the portal, did you see anyone on the other side trying to get out?"

"You mean anyone human?" Budenny asked through the mask.

"Yes."

The general shook his head and removed the mask. "If there is anyone… on the other side… of the portal… may God have mercy on them."

Melnikov motioned for Jason to leave. As Jason stepped away, the captain said to Budenny, "You rest now. We'll brief you when we get back from tomorrow's raid."

Once out in the corridor, Melnikov asked, "Did you get

everything you needed?"

"I did. Now let's go to your office and plan how we're going to do this."

CHAPTER TWENTY-EIGHT

JASON'S TEAM AND the Purgatoriati sat in the dining hall at separate but adjoining tables. Although the latter did not eat, they sat in silent meditation. Jason's people chatted amongst themselves, keeping the conversation on any topic except tomorrow's mission into Moscow. Only when they were finished did Ian realize someone was missing.

"Where's Jason?" he asked.

"He and Melnikov are finalizing plans and running them by Zhirinovsky," Slava answered.

"Were the Russians able to restock us?" Gaston asked.

"Thankfully, yes." Haneef spooned the last of the beans into his mouth and pushed the plate away. "They had thousands of 7.62mm rounds, more than enough to reload my backpack."

Jeanette wiped her mouth with a cloth napkin. "Will we be taking the horses?"

Slava shook his head. "We'll take the steam buses into the city. Melnikov says it'll be quicker."

"Where are the horses now?"

"They're in a stable on the other end of the compound with the Russians' horses," said Sook-kyoung. "I checked on them this afternoon. The Russians are taking good care of them."

"I'm glad to hear it," said Jeanette. "With luck, tomorrow will be a success."

"Maybe," said Slava.

"You have doubts?" Reinhard finished off the last of his water.

"Not doubts." Slava locked his eyes on the Purgatoriati. He studied them a moment. "Sasha!"

She looked up from the table, the hooded cloak hiding half her features. "Yes?"

"Join us."

Sasha became embarrassed. After a few awkward seconds, she stood up and headed over.

"I mean all of you," said Slava.

Sasha stopped and stared at the Russian, not knowing what to say. She sought guidance from Father Belsario.

"No offense, my son," said the cleric as he kept his gaze fixed on the table. "We prefer to be alone."

"It wasn't a request."

Father Belsario raised his head. His eyes locked on Slava's. They were cold and menacing. "Are you giving us an order?"

Slava refused to back down, although he made his tone less confrontational. "I'm telling you that if you're going to go into combat with us, you need to be part of the group. Every one of us has trained together since this trip began, and most of us have fought together for months. I know these people better than I did my own family. I trust every single one of them to have my back when we go into battle, just as they trust that I'll have theirs. You might think this warrior monk persona and the enhanced physical strength makes you special. That means shit to me. I don't know any of you other than Sasha, and I'm not sure if I trust her anymore. I refuse to go into combat with people I don't know well enough to rely on."

Tense seconds passed. For a moment, no one knew if Slava and Father Belsario would go at each other. Finally, the tallest of the cloaked figures rose. Removing his broadsword from its sheath, he stepped over to the table and stood in front of Slava. The Russian showed no signs of being intimidated. The Purgatoriati placed the broadsword on the table in front of Slava, sat down, and slid the hood off his head. He sported auburn hair and matching beard.

"You have the soul of a warrior," he said. "I can relate. My name is Matthew."

"Is that your real name?" Jeanette asked.

"That's the Biblical name I chose when I joined the Purgatoriati. My real name is not important. I used to be a Knights Templar in the Holy Land at the end of the 13th Century, devoting my life to fulfilling God's will. Only later in life did I realize I had sinned by killing innocents in His name. I left the order and spent what little remained of my life in the Holy Land preaching. I died two years later of typhus. The renunciation of my previous life kept me out of Hell. However, by the time of my death I had not performed enough good deeds to atone for the sins I had committed. That's why I'm here."

Another of the cloaked figures rose, came over to the table, and placed his broadsword in front of Slava. As he sat, he pulled back his hood, revealing a boyish face with a swarthy complexion. "I'm Jonah. I lived in Jerusalem during the Crusades. When the city fell to invaders, I renounced my faith and denounced my god to stay alive. Even though I followed the tenants of my new religion, I was banished to Purgatory because of my disloyalty."

"Which faith were you originally?" Haneef asked.

"Does it matter? Neither Jehovah, God, nor Allah appreciate betrayal."

The last cloaked figure followed the same ritual. Fair in features, with blonde wavy hair and blue eyes, he spoke in a quiet voice. "I'm Luther. My banishment was because I accepted science as my religion. I spent my life in 18th Century Nuremburg discovering the causes for diseases and curing the sick, especially amongst the poor. My good deeds kept me out of Hell while my lack of faith kept me out of Heaven."

All attention focused on Father Belsario. He remained seated, still wearing a stern and angry expression. His countenance softened. Standing up, he removed his broadsword and placed it with the others in front of Slava. "You know my story.

I'm the only person dumb enough to abandon Paradise to come back here and fight Demon Spawn."

Slava rose, removed his hunting knife from its sheath, and laid it on top of the broadswords. "And I'll be happy to have you go into battle with me."

Father Belsario crinkled his lips. "Does that mean you're no longer worried about having us behind you in combat?"

"I still don't want you behind me," said Slava. "I want you beside me where we can cut down Demon Spawn together."

The rest of Jason's team voiced their concurrence. Slava raised his empty hand as if making a toast. "Here's to closing the Moscow portal."

Father Belsario nodded. "And to our new-found friendship."

JASON'S TEAM AND the Purgatoriati had called it a night and left the dining hall for their quarters. Some had gone straight to bed while others milled around and chatted, knowing that sleep would elude them. Sasha did neither. Slipping away from the group, she wandered the compound and stopped to stare at the gates leading outside. When they opened again, she and the others would head into Moscow. The very thought filled her with an apprehension bordering on terror. Not a fear of the Demon Spawn, which she had faced down before, but fear of what the day held in store. The last time Sasha had shut down a portal, it had changed her... her....

Sasha had no idea what to call this new existence. Though resurrected from the dead, she felt no different than before she fell from the bell tower of Notre Dame. Her body functioned normally, only now she never tired and had improved stamina. Father Belsario had warned she would still feel pain as though she were alive, except now her body would be able to withstand thresholds no average mortal ever could. Somehow, she knew those limits would be put to the test in Moscow.

Someone approached from behind. Sasha glanced over her shoulder as Jeanette joined her.

"Hello," Jeanette said.

"Hey." *Please don't talk about Jason,* Sasha thought. *I can still experience emotions.*

"I noticed you were the only member of the Purgatoriati who didn't tell us why you were sent there in the first place."

"That's because I don't know why." Sasha stifled a sigh. "After I died in Paris, I woke up in Purgatory and was eventually drafted into the Purgatoriati."

"You mean recruited?"

Sasha shook her head. "The others volunteered to come back. I had no choice. Father Belsario tracked me down and provided me with two options—come back to Earth to help Jason or spend the rest of eternity in limbo."

"What was the deciding factor?" Jeanette asked, her voice teetering with jealousy. "Spending eternity in limbo or getting another chance to see Jason?"

The question made Sasha painfully aware of the empty void in her heart. "Most people would do anything to get out of Purgatory."

"But getting to see Jason was a perk, right?"

"Do you want to know the truth?" Sasha snapped, allowing her anger to get the better of her. "When Father Belsario gave me the option, for a brief moment I considered taking an eternity in limbo so I wouldn't have to see Jason again."

The statement caught Jeanette off guard. "I thought you liked him?"

"That's the problem. I love Jason." Sasha held up a hand before the latter could say anything. "I'm not here to fight for him, although I'll admit I had hoped he would show a romantic interest when he saw me again. Jason has moved on. He's happy with you, happier than I've ever seen him. Much happier than I ever made him. I won't take that away from him. Trust me, no one knows better than me how much it hurts to lose the one you love. Besides, I had my chance to be with him and blew it, and I'll have to deal with that for eternity. I love him too much to force him to pick between us."

"Thank you."

"A broken heart is the least of my worries," Sasha lied. "Father Belsario has assured me that I'll die several horrible deaths and be resurrected just as many times before this is all over. It doesn't matter. I will do anything to keep Jason alive long enough to complete this quest he has undertaken."

"We both will." Jeanette took Sasha's hands. "He's lucky. It's not everyone who has a real guardian angel fighting by their side."

The comment caught Sasha by surprise. "I hadn't ever thought about it that way before."

Jeanette released her hands. "What'll happen to you when this is all over? Will they let you into Heaven?"

Sasha shrugged. She wanted to avoid this conversation as well. "I don't know. That's a topic Father Belsario refuses to talk about."

CHAPTER TWENTY-NINE

JASON STOOD BESIDE the railroad track and stared at the tunnel entrance located near the southern end of the main runway at Ramenskoye Airport. A slight grade descended between two retaining walls until the tracks ended two hundred feet in front of him against a cement wall with double steel doors blocking the entrance. It reminded him of Nanterre, the city outside of Paris where his team had descended into the subway system. Jason fought back a shiver as the recollection of that underground nightmare flooded his memories. He would be leading his people into battle and needed to present as solid an emotional front as possible.

Behind him, Jason's team, the Purgatoriati, and the thirty-man platoon under Melnikov's command milled around two converted city buses. Neal and Ian each carried an anti-matter device so they would have a backup in case something happened to the primary one. On the opposite side of the tracks, Father Belsario led the Purgatoriati in prayer. Jeanette broke away from the others, with Lucifer and Lilith in tow. She stepped up beside Jason and slid her hand into his.

"Are you okay?" she asked.

"Yeah," he answered with little enthusiasm.

"You're remembering the Metro, aren't you?"

"Who can forget?" Jason had brief images of David, Bill, and Franco, all of whom who were killed by giant insects beneath the streets of Paris. "We lost a lot of good people in that subway."

"You won't lose any here," said a voice from behind them.

Melnikov stepped up to Jason. "We won't be taking subway. It's too dangerous. Giant spiders and centipedes, and swarms of oversized cockroaches that can strip a man clean in minutes. I lost over twenty good men a few months back doing reconnaissance of Moscow subway. I won't make same mistake again."

Jason pointed to the steel doors. "Then what's this?"

"This is emergency exit so government officials can escape Moscow, pick up rescue plane at airport, and fly to safety. This will take us to underground bunker complex Soviet Union built under city so government could survive nuclear war."

"Isn't it also infested?"

"*Nyet.* It's separate system not connected to subways or sewers. Every entrance has steel door creating hundreds of isolated sections. We secure each door as we pass through, so even if Demon Spawn finds way into one compartment, which is unlikely, they can't spread throughout system. We'll have clear path right to Red Square." Melnikov pointed to a young man approaching them who carried a satchel bag draped over one shoulder and a 9mm Tsniitochmash automatic rifle in his right hand. "That is Lieutenant Grachov. He's former FSB, Federal Security Service, our version of your CIA. He knows these bunkers like his own apartment. Grachov will lead us to within few hundred meters of portal so you can deploy device."

"When do we start?"

"Once Grachov opens doors." Melnikov fell in behind the lieutenant. He waved Jason along. "Come on."

The three walked down the slope until they reached the tunnel wall. A handle had been welded onto each steel door. Two separate chains were wound tight around the handles, each secured with a combination lock. Grachov entered the three numbers on each lock and pulled the shackles out of the body. Removing the locks, he slid them into his pocket and unwound the chains. Grachov grabbed the handle of one steel door and pulled it open as Melnikov did the same with the other side. Jason stared into the pitch black.

"It's about forty kilometers to bunkers from here," said Melnikov. He handed Jason a miner's cap with a two-hundred-watt flashlight mounted on the brim. "My men are passing these out to your people. Lights and electric rail circuit were fried during electromagnetic pulse so we will be in dark whole time except for flashlights and these."

"How come these work?"

"Throughout bunker system we have special storage areas built to shield against EMP. We kept these and generators and certain medical equipment in them in case they were needed during emergency."

"Do we have to walk the whole way?"

"Buses will fit. My men will go first. You'll follow five minutes later."

"Why not go together?"

"It gives time for smoke from first engine to dissipate. Besides, even though unlikely, if we run into any demons, you'll have chance to escape and come in another way." Melnikov headed back toward the buses. "Come on."

The others had already boarded. Melnikov climbed into the first bus with his platoon. He said to Jason, "Grachov will go with you and lock doors behind you. If anything goes wrong, listen to him. He will take you back to camp."

"Thanks," said Jason.

The door slid shut and the city bus lurched forward, picking up speed as it descended the slope into the tunnel. Shadows enveloped the vehicle except for embers from the steam engine, and even those were quickly engulfed by the dark. Jason climbed into his own bus and stood by the windshield. Lucifer and Lilith joined him, the latter curling up at his feet, the former tilting his head as he stared into the tunnel. After a few minutes, Grachov barked an order in Russian. The fireman stoked the engine. The bus inched forward, stopping once it entered the tunnel. Grachov jumped off, raced back to the entrance, and closed the twin steel doors. Now the only light came from the lanterns attached to the vehicle's front bumper. After securing the doors with the two chains, which he wound around handles welded onto the inside surfaces, Grachov rejoined the others. The driver released the throttle, and the bus picked up speed, beginning the journey into downtown Moscow.

CHAPTER THIRTY

I T TOOK FORTY-FIVE minutes for their steam-driven bus to reach the end of the line. The driver stopped behind the first vehicle and opened the sliding door. A U-shaped subway platform stretched for two hundred feet down each wall of the tunnel and against the front façade. Grachov led Jason's team and the Purgatoriati to where Melnikov's men had set up a string of flood lights facing a flight of stairs, five steps high and ten feet wide, that ended in front of a pair of six-ton metal doors, each painted battleship gray with a red valve wheel in the center. A chain and combination lock wound between the two wheels. Most of the captain's platoon formed a semi-circle around the doors. Grachov removed the chains.

Slava moved up beside Melnikov. "You know those chains will never keep out Demon Spawn."

"They're not meant to. Electronic locks no longer work, and we can only manually lock from inside. Chains are early warning system. If broken, we know something got inside bunker system."

"What happens then?"

"Then situation become… how you say in English… ah, yes. Situation becomes FUBAR."

The clanking of metal against metal signaled that Grachov had removed the chains. As he spun the valve wheel on the right door and pulled it open, the Russians around him raised their weapons into the high ready position. Jason tensed, expecting a swarm of giant insects to invade the platform. Nothing happened. Grachov waved for the others to join him and headed inside. Jason and Melnikov climbed the stairs and entered an antechamber fifty feet square. The green-painted walls on either side were lined with wooden stools mounted into the cement and, above them, rows of metal cots folded up against the wall. Grachov opened a door like the ones they had passed through, only smaller. Jason maneuvered the flashlight on the miner's cap through the opening. A long red-painted corridor stretched ahead of him until it disappeared in the shadows. Despite a series of metal pipes and bundles of electrical wire running along the right wall, it was wide enough for three people to walk abreast.

Melnikov centered himself in the doorway and faced the others. "Iosif, Pavlov. Secure and lock outer doors and remain here with bus crews. Jason and Haneef will be up front with me. Stay alert and don't bunch up."

"Ready?" Grachov asked.

"When you are," said Melnikov.

The FSB officer led the way. They walked for ten minutes along the foreboding tunnel. It was cold and damp, and the air smelled musty. Jason concentrated on listening for noises on the other sides of the wall, a sign that Demon Spawn might be nearby. Except for the echoing of their footsteps, he heard nothing.

"Are you certain no Demon Spawn can get in here?" he asked Melnikov.

"Every exterior door leading into bunker system made of two feet of steel-reinforced concrete and weighs thirty tons. They are secured on inside by titanium deadbolts ten feet long and eight inches thick. As for bunker itself, entire system is over five hundred feet underground. Walls are twenty feet thick and reinforced with steel bars. If demons exist large enough to get in here, you and I will not live long enough to tell tale."

"Comforting," Slava mumbled from behind them.

The group came to a crossing where their tunnel ended at another that ran north to south. Melnikov pointed to the right.

"A ten-minute walk in that direction would bring us under Dzerzhinsky Square where former KGB headquarters is located. We must go other direction. That will take us to Red Square."

This tunnel was like the others except every few hundred yards it had blast doors built into the walls, all of which were closed and secured. After thirty minutes, the tunnel ended at a slightly larger blast door. Grachov opened it and ushered everyone through. Jason entered a room so large the beams from their flashlights didn't reach the other walls. Dozens of rectangular columns painted light green and arranged in rows supported the roof.

"We are beneath State Palace inside Kremlin. This room is registration area for government officials entering bunker." Melnikov pointed to the wall behind him, hidden in the shadows. "Stairwell over there leads to Kremlin courtyard."

"Let's go," said Father Belsario.

"First we need to survey Red Square and see what situation like. Bunker designers incorporated special access to street level so scouts could go topside without having to open main doors. Jason, you want to see?"

"Of course."

"I'd like to go, too," said Father Belsario.

"Okay, just two of you. I don't want demons spotting us before we're ready. Follow me."

JASON REGRETTED AGREEING to go with Melnikov. The captain had failed to mention that the special access to the street level consisted of a ladder situated inside a vertical shaft not much larger than a manhole cover that ascended over six hundred feet. Fortunately, Melnikov stopped twice to rest, which saved Jason from appearing like a wimp. However, by the time they reached the exit hatch, every muscle in Jason's arms and legs hurt and his lungs felt as if they would explode.

Melnikov raised a finger in front of his lips. "Keep quiet from here on out. We are at ground level. I have no idea how many demons are up here or how near they are."

Melnikov spun the valve wheel, unlocking the hatch. When the captain opened it, Jason felt the aura of thousands of lost souls stimulating his senses. Melnikov stuck his head through the opening, checked the surroundings, and climbed through. He raised his AK-47 into the high ready position and motioned for the others to join him. Jason crawled out and readied his FAMAS. When Father Belsario scurried through, Melnikov lowered the hatch. They were in a small red brick room ten feet square. Melnikov crossed over to a wooden door on the opposite wall, placed his ear against the surface, and listened. When confident nothing lurked on the other side, he swung it open and stepped out. Waving for Jason and Belsario to follow, the captain wound his way up a circular flight of cement stairs. As they approached the top, the glare from the sun forced Jason to squint. When he reached the landing, Melnikov grabbed Jason's shoulder and forced him into a crouch behind a partially destroyed brick wall. It took a moment for Jason's eyes to adjust to the light. When they did, he peered over the top of the wall.

"Oh my God," Jason whispered.

They stood in the ruined Savior Tower near the northern end of the Kremlin's outer wall. Red Square spread out beneath him, or more precisely, its remains. The nuclear explosion had devastated the once iconic landmark. All three towers along the Kremlin's north wall had been ripped apart, and the wall itself had collapsed in several places. Savior Tower, which protected the northeast entrance to the Kremlin, had survived because of its distance from the blast and the massiveness of its foundation; however, the spire and black-faced clock that should have towered above him had been torn away. Off to their left, Lenin's Tomb had survived the explosion despite its proximity, although the top levels that contained the viewing stand had collapsed on itself. Across the square, GUM Department Store lay in shambles. The portion nearest to the blast had been flattened, with the skeletal remains of a dragon lying in front of it. The segment of the façade farthest away had not collapsed, although it was heavily damaged and pocked. At the eastern end of the square, St. Basil's Cathedral seemed relatively unscathed, although all the onion domes had been smashed and the central spire snapped off. The skeleton of a second dragon rested at an awkward angle in front of the structure. Ironically, only the State Historical Museum, which had been directly behind the portal, had come through the incident unscathed because it had absorbed the explosion.

Thousands of flesh eaters wandered through Red Square and around piles of debris, with more stumbling through the portal every minute. The horde spread out and made its way onto the side streets and down to the Moskva River. Two dragons guarded the opening, one on each side. They were curled up asleep, yet Jason knew his team would never reach the portal without disturbing them. A pair of Golem stood several hundred feet away in the other dimension, their attention focused inward.

Several piles of debris stood in eerie mounds across the square, but they did not resemble rubble. Jason tapped Melnikov on the shoulder and pointed toward the one on the opposite side of Lenin's Mausoleum. "What are those?"

"Bones of flesh eaters. After Budenny detonated nuclear device, new dragons pushed them to side with tails so they can travel through square easily. Have you seen enough?"

"Yes."

"Good. Let's go back and get ready. We have tough after-noon ahead of us."

CHAPTER THIRTY-ONE

EVERYONE MINGLED IN two separate groups inside the reception area, checking their weapons one final time. No one spoke. No one had to. Except for a handful of people, every man and woman here had gone into battle against Demon Spawn before. They knew what to expect, and they knew some of them would have only a short time left to live.

Melnikov moved into the center of the two groups. "Grachov, take Jason's team to jump off point and wait. Do not go outside or expose yourself to demons until we are ready."

"Yes, sir."

"Jason." The captain checked his watch. "It's 12:47. At 1:17, we'll commence diversionary fire. Give us few minutes to draw demons away and then storm portal. Don't wait too long, though. Once we make physical contact, we'll have five minutes at best before demons overrun us. Is that clear?"

"Yes."

"Good," said Melnikov. "Let's kick demon ass and make world proud."

Melnikov led his platoon out of the reception hall in the same direction they had entered earlier. Grachov headed for the opposite end of the hall and motioned for the others to follow. The lieutenant opened a blast door in the middle of the wall, revealing a flight of cement stairs that ascended along the outer walls of the well.

Slava shone his flashlight up the center. The beam did not reach the top. "How many flights are there?"

"Twenty-two," Grachov answered.

"Shit," mumbled Haneef, unconsciously hefting the minigun on his shoulders.

"Do you need help with that?" Antoine asked.

"I can handle it."

"No need to worry," said Grachov. "For now, we're climbing only eighteen flights."

"Child's play," Jason joked as he followed the lieutenant. Lucifer and Lilith bounded up the steps beside him, with the others right behind.

When Grachov reached the eighteenth landing he stopped in front of an elevator built into the wall. Removing his bayonet, he wedged the blade between the twin doors and wiggled it until he pried them open several inches. They had not been used in a while and, at first, they would not budge.

"Let me do that." Father Belsario stepped forward. He grabbed the edge of one of the doors and pulled until he had moved it a foot. Sliding into the opening, the cleric placed his back against the door on the right and his hands on the one on the left and pushed. A snap accompanied the grinding of metal against metal, and the doors slid open all the way. The elevator had been built to accommodate patient gurneys, with another set of sliding doors located at the rear of the car. Grachov stepped over and jammed his bayonet between them, and Belsario helped pry them apart. This time they opened with minimal effort.

Grachov led the way down a narrow corridor, four feet wide and seven feet high. Faded white tiles with darkened grout adorned the walls. They walked for several hundred feet. Jason felt claustrophobic in the confined space.

"Where are we?" asked Vicky.

"We're in a secret tunnel that passes beneath Kremlin wall. A handful of government officials know about this. Party built it so we could save the nation's most valued treasure in an emergency." Grachov pointed to the ceiling. "Ground level is one hundred feet above us."

A minute later they came to a metal door with a valve wheel. Grachov spun it, opened the door, and entered the room beyond. It was tiled just like the tunnel but was larger, fifty feet square. A stainless-steel tub sat in the center of the floor, with a hospital gurney on one side and a movable tray of medical instruments on the other. Something sat in the tub. Jason shone his flashlight on it. It was a naked body, the skin yellow and dry, yet not quite mummified. A sewed-up surgical incision ran from its neck to it abdomen where it ended in an opening the size of a baseball. Lucifer jumped up and placed his front paws on the rim of the tub, sniffed the body, and whimpered.

Slava moved up beside Grachov. "Is that who I think it is?"

"That's Vladimir Ilyich Lenin."

"What's he doing here, mate?" Ian asked.

"We are underneath Lenin's Mausoleum. Every year they bring body here for maintenance. You know, to repair any damage and touch up makeup. The curators were in the middle of giving Lenin his annual bath when portal opened." Grachov pointed to a wooden door in the corner. "That's a circular staircase that leads to mausoleum. From this point on there's no talking. Pass it down the line. If demons detect us before Melnikov is in position, we all die in Moscow."

"Gotcha," said Jason.

Grachov opened the door and ascended the stairs.

MELNIKOV'S SQUAD FOLLOWED the underground bunker system to a set of blast doors that exited into the basement of GUM Department Store. The captain grabbed the door's valve wheel and clutched it. The three soldiers standing line abreast in the tunnel raised their weapons into the high ready position and aimed. Melnikov spun the valve wheel until the dead bolts clicked. He hoped that the cave in caused by the nuclear detonation had not affected this portion of the store and that they would not be greeted by a swarm of demons. The captain pulled open the door and stepped through, followed by the three soldiers. The basement remained intact, although chunks of cement had fallen from the ceiling. Even more fortunate, no demons were in sight. He waved on his men. They proceeded south, the last two out of the tunnel securing the blast door behind them. The platoon double timed until they reached a service elevator and accompanying stairwell. Melnikov led the way to the first floor, paused on the landing until his team was prepared, and pushed open the door.

Although this section of GUM had structurally survived the blast, it suffered extensive damage. The glass ceiling had collapsed and most of the store windows were shattered, covering the floor in shards. Melnikov heard a crunching to his right. A flesh eater staggered in front of a Hugo Boss store. Hearing the noise, it spun around and snarled. One of Melnikov's men raced forward, slipped his bayonet from its scabbard, and plunged the blade through its left eye, twisting it at an angle to scramble the brain. A blue eddy of light burst through the top of its skull and the body dropped onto the broken glass with a crunch. When it did, flocks of birds took off from nests along the upper corridor and escaped through the shattered glass ceiling. Nothing else was visible.

Melnikov gestured for his men to shut off their flashlights and then made his way toward the front of GUM. They broke into two columns and followed, checking each store they passed for hidden threats. As they approached the entrance to Red Square, the captain raised his hand, ordering his men to stop, and proceeded ahead alone. He crouched down by the twisted door frames and peered out. They were at the southern-most entrance along the department store's eastern façade. Lenin's Tomb sat across from him and one hundred feet to the right. Thousands of flesh eaters stumbled through the square and the two dragons still rested on either side of the portal. None of them seemed aware of his presence. Melnikov rejoined his team, moving cautiously so as not to make noise.

"We're right where we're supposed to be. Where's Telegrin?"

Senior Sergeant Telegrin stepped forward. He carried an OSV-96 108mm sniper rifle. "I'm here, captain."

"Take a fire team up to third floor and set up position. You know what to do."

Telegrin snapped to attention and saluted. He pointed to the first two soldiers at the head of the team. The three backtracked to the stairwell.

"The rest of you spread out in surrounding stores. Keep within one hundred feet of each other and stay concealed until it's time."

As his team moved into position, Melnikov checked his watch. It read 1:11.

THE STAIRWAY GRACHOV led them up ended inside Lenin's Tomb. The empty sarcophagus sat on a red granite podium in the center of the mausoleum's sunken viewing theater surrounded by a low, red granite wall. A casing of bullet-proof glass rested on top of an intricately carved metal base designed to resemble a funeral bier and tiered with layers of marble. The walls were lined with black labradorite interspersed with red porphyry columns, giving the interior a macabre appearance. Cracks extended across the labradorite, especially on the wall facing ground zero, and several slabs had broken lose to litter the floor of the mausoleum. One of the columns had toppled over onto the sarcophagus, pushing aside the red granite covering and shattering the bullet-proof glass on one side. Grachov led the way up one side of the sarcophagus to the upper lobby maneuvering around the stone slabs. He stopped, pointed to a pair of doors, and whispered to Jason.

"Red Square is right through there. The portal is a few hundred meters away. Are you ready?"

"As ready as I'll ever be."

"Good. Now we wait."

Jason checked his watch. It read 1:15.

MELNIKOV'S WATCH CLICKED over to 1:17. He switched his AK-47 to single shot mode, took aim on the head of the nearest demon, and fired. Its skull exploded. As the corpse collapsed onto the pavement, each soldier along the front façade of GUM opened fire. Another twenty lifeforces were freed from their rotting prison. As the barrage continued, it drew the attention of every demon in Red Square. The horde shifted en masse and shambled toward Melnikov's platoon, clearing a path between Lenin's Tomb and the portal. The commotion also caught the attention of the two dragons. The one nearest GUM scurried toward the sound of gunfire. The second remained in place and scanned the area. Melnikov swore to himself. He had not anticipated this. With the second dragon still guarding the portal the entire plan was now in danger.

Ignoring the approaching behemoth, Melnikov's men concentrated their fire on the demons. The captain watched the dragon, praying it behaved as he expected. It crushed scores of smaller demons as it raced across Red Square. As it neared GUM, it slowed and paced back and forth, studying the situation. The dragon roared defiantly. It lowered the front part of its torso and leaned its head forward. The glowing ridges along its chest and spine shone in intensity.

The fusillade slackened as Melnikov's men focused on the dragon and their impending death.

Come on, Melnikov thought. *What's taking so long?*

FROM HIS ROOFTOP perch on the southeast corner of GUM, Telegrin kept his scope trained on the dragon as it moved across Red Square. Instinct urged him to fire before the creature got too close but his training told him to hold off. He would have one chance to inflict a fatal wound; if he reacted too quickly, he would blow it. Telegrin bided his time. The dragon lowered the front part of its torso and leaned its head forward, pausing for a moment as the ridges along its chest and spine glowed. Telegrin had been waiting for this moment. In the span of two seconds, he lined up the scope on the dragon's right eye, took a deep breath to steady himself, and pulled the trigger.

The 108mm round punched through the eye and into its skull. The monster jerked its head back and howled. It spun around several times, crushing hundreds of demons beneath it, before falling on its side facing away from GUM. It panted as its tail swished in diminishing circles. Telegrin centered his scope on the monster's left eye, taking his time to line up the shot. One squeeze of the trigger and the black orb exploded. The dragon screeched, went rigid, and then fell limp.

The private accompanying him fist pumped the air. "You got him."

"Don't open the victory vodka yet." Telegrin motioned with his head across Red Square.

Upon seeing the death of its mate, the other dragon roared and sprinted from the portal, heading straight for Telegrin's position on top of GUM.

JASON HAD CALLED Neal and Ian to the entrance to the mausoleum, wanting them to be ready to dash for the portal once the area was clear. Grachov stood by the doors, listening to the battle rage outside. When he heard the thunderous stomps of the dragon rushing across the square, the lieutenant ordered, "Let's go."

Grachov unbolted the doors and pulled on the handles. They would not budge. He yanked again. The doors rattled but would not move.

"Shit!" said Grachov.

"Let me help." Reinhard pushed his way to the front and grabbed the handle of the door on the right. Grachov took the one on the left. Both men pulled until the doors gave way. A chunk of red marble from the destroyed reviewing stand that had been leaning against the doors rolled into the entranceway. The German stepped back and waved on the others. "*Schnell!*"

Jason and Grachov emerged onto the black marble foundation. They stopped short upon hearing the blood-curdling death knell of the dragon in front of GUM. As its mate abandoned the portal and rushed across Red Square, it noticed the movement of the two men in its peripheral vision. Whipping to its right, the dragon charged the mausoleum, stopping and crouching when fifty feet distant. The ridges along its chest and spine glowed.

"Back inside!" Grachov shoved Jason through the entranceway. He spun around, slammed shut the door on the right, and tried to do the same with the one on the left. The chunk of marble blocked it. He tried using the door to push the marble, but the stone was too heavy.

The dragon exhaled a cloud of lime green smoke tinted with thousands of crystals.

Reinhard rushed forward and placed his hands on the marble. He made eye contact with Jason. "Don't let this be in vain."

The cloud drifted toward the mausoleum.

Reinhard summoned every ounce of strength and pushed. The chunk of marble moved a few inches, and then some more. Reinhard continued shoving. After a few seconds, it slid across the doorway and out onto the granite base.

The cloud reached the mausoleum.

Reinhard ducked behind the chunk of marble, a futile gesture.

Grachov slammed the door and secured the bolt.

The first crystal touched the remains of the reviewing stand

and burst into a tiny flame, igniting the lime-green gas. A fireball washed over the mausoleum, incinerating Reinhard and leaving behind a charred skeleton and ash.

MELNIKOV WATCHED THE fireball engulf Lenin's Tomb. His heart sank. They had failed again. Their last chance to end this madness had been wasted. He wanted to punch the wall in anger but did not have time. He needed to salvage what remained of his platoon.

The captain slapped the shoulder of the corporal beside him to get his attention. "Spread the word. We fall back on my command. Send someone to get Telegrin."

INSIDE THE MAUSOLEUM'S lobby, everyone instinctively flinched as the fireball washed over the exterior of the structure. It roared like a furnace, only they were on the inside. The temperature spiked, but nothing that would be fatal. After a few seconds, everything settled back to normal.

"Come on," said Grachov as he stepped back to the doors.

Jason shook his head. "That thing will cut us down before we make it fifty feet."

"It takes up to two minutes for a dragon to refill its gas sack." Grachov slid off his tunic and wrapped it around his hand. "We have that much time to get to the portal."

"Then let's do this."

Haneef moved up alongside Jason. "I'll take the rest of the team and distract it. You and the Purgatoriati take care of the portal."

"Thanks."

"May Allah be with you."

Jason patted his friend on the shoulder. "Let's hope he's with all of us."

"Ready?" asked Grachov.

Haneef clasped the minigun in front of his chest. "Yes."

When Grachov opened the door, Haneef raced out and paused twenty feet from the mausoleum. Antoine and Gaston took up positions on either side, providing covering fire. Haneef squeezed the trigger. The minigun whirred to life and spat out a stream of 7.62mm bullets into the dragon's face. The monster arched its head and roared, presenting its back to Haneef and letting the rounds bounce harmlessly off its plated back. The rest of the team took advantage of the distraction. Jeanette led Sook-kyoung and Vicky out of the mausoleum and rushed down Red Square to take up position halfway between Lenin's Tomb and Savior Tower. Slava and Werner followed, and then cut into the square, stopping two hundred feet behind and to the right of the women. When the others were in place, Haneef stopped firing and fell back, running sideways to keep an eye on the dragon.

MELNIKOV SPOTTED JASON'S people rushing out of Lenin's Tomb. He felt a tinge of optimism that they might pull this off, with an emphasis on the word might.

"Captain, are we still going to fall back?" asked a private beside him.

"No. Maintain fire on the demons. We have to keep them from heading back to the portal."

TELEGRIN ATTEMPTED TO line up an eye shot on the dragon, with no success. The creature moved around too much. He had fired two rounds, one which missed and the other which struck the dragon's temple, at this range having as little effect as small arms fire. *Don't get excited,* he admonished himself. *Wait for it. The shot will come.*

WHEN THE BARRAGE of bullets ceased, the dragon spun around. It recognized Haneef as the tiny creature that had caused it so much pain. The behemoth charged, hoping to trample him.

Jeanette's and Slava's squads caught it in a crossfire. The dragon curled into a ball, protecting its head with its tail until the humans emptied their magazines. As they reloaded, it darted toward Jeanette's squad. None of the women noticed it stop twenty feet from them, whirl around, and whip its tail.

"IT'S CLEAR," SAID Grachov as he exited the mausoleum. Jason pushed past him and ran for the portal. Lucifer and Lilith stayed on either flank. Ian, Neal, and Grachov fell in behind. The Purgatoriati brought up the rear.

Several flesh eaters stumbling toward GUM heard the commotion caused by the battle between the last dragon and Jason's people and reversed direction. They numbered a few dozen and were spread thin. Jason wasn't worried about them. His concern focused on the forty or so crossing through the portal. Jason veered to his left toward a ten-foot high mound of skulls. As the others joined him, he took the backpack from Ian, undid the flap, and removed the anti-matter device. Neal did the same with his.

"This is simple," Jason explained to Grachov and the Purgatoriati. "All we have to do is toss one of these into the portal. If anything happens to me or Neal, one of you must finish the job. Got it?"

The others nodded.

Jason rushed the portal. The Purgatoriati and the werehounds formed a circle around him. Ian and Grachov protected Neal. The few flesh eaters in the way were dispatched by the Purgatoriati's broadswords. They covered the distance to the portal in a few seconds.

One of the Golem from the other side emerged through the

shimmering surface. Its right leg came through, planting itself firmly in Red Square, followed by the upper body. Jason broke to the right, gave the demon a wide berth, and stopped. He lifted the device like a football and threw it toward the portal.

The Golem reached out and grabbed the device before it touched the surface.

JEANETTE HEARD THE swish of the dragon's tale as it sliced through the air. She dropped to the pavement and rolled. Vicky reloaded her FAMAS and didn't see the impending threat. Luckily for her, Sook-kyoung did. She dove to the left and knocked Vicky to the ground as the deadly appendage swept by overhead, missing them by inches.

Jeanette came out of the roll into a kneeling position, ready to defend herself against the dragon. It no longer cared about her. It had focused its attention back on Haneef.

THE DRAGON DIDN'T charge Haneef as it had before. This time it approached slowly and cautiously, studying him as a predator would its intended prey. It stopped one hundred feet from the three men. Haneef stood his ground, the minigun aimed and ready to fire.

"What are you waiting for?" Antoine asked.

"Trust me."

The dragon lowered its head. The ridges along its chest and spine glowed.

Antoine aimed his FAMAS at the behemoth. "I hope you know what you're doing."

"So do I."

WHEN THE DRAGON paused, Telegrin centered his scope on its right eye and wrapped his finger around the trigger. He inhaled and held it.

A hand touched his shoulder, spoiling the shot. Telegrin lifted his head and yelled at the private beside him.

"What do you think you're doing?"

"S-sorry, senior sergeant," the soldier stammered through his fear. He pointed toward the portal. "I thought you should see that."

A Golem had stepped through the portal and caught the anti-matter device in mid-throw.

Telegrin swore under his breath. "Private, crouch down and give me your shoulder."

The soldier did as ordered. Telegrin placed the barrel of the OSV-96 on the private's shoulder and centered the scope on the middle of the Golem's face.

SLAVA WATCHED AS the dragon prepared to breathe a cloud of smoke on his friend. He realized what Haneef had planned. Slava dropped prone and yelled for Werner to take cover.

THE DRAGON EXHALED a cloud of lime-green smoke. Haneef waited for it to expand to thirty feet before squeezing the trigger. The weapon whirred to life. The first rounds that struck the cloud ignited the crystals. The cloud erupted into a fireball that flowed back into the dragon's mouth, down its throat, and into the sack where the remainder of the vapor formed. The sack detonated, blowing apart the behemoth's neck and upper abdomen. Chunks of dragon plopped down all around Red Square.

TELEGRIN PULLED THE trigger. Through the scope, he saw the 108mm round strike the skull at the top of the Golem's nose-like ridge.

THE GOLEM WAS pushing its massive hands together, trying to crush the anti-matter device, when the 108mm round struck. The bullet tore through several of its brains, momentarily stunning the demon. Jason turned to Neal. Only then did he realize that a dozen flesh eaters had approached to within ten feet of his squad.

"Quick, give me your device."

"There's no time for that," said Father Belsario. "Jonah, you're with me. The rest of you protect Jason."

Jason unslung his crossbow and fired an arrow between the eyes of the nearest flesh eater; it dropped to the ground with a heavy thud. Beside him, Grachov released a three-round burst into the head of another while Lucifer and Lilith ripped apart two more. Sasha, Luther, and Matthew surrounded Neal, protecting the last device. The latter two lobbed off heads or cleaved away at limbs. Sasha stabbed them in the forehead with her dagger, holding them in place while she used her saber to behead them.

Father Belsario and Jonah charged the Golem, slashing apart any flesh eater that got in their way. The Golem resumed its movement as its other brains compensated for those destroyed by the bullet. Another 108mm round thudded into its head inches from the first entry wound, rupturing another dozen brains and stunning it again. Jonah took advantage of the opportunity. Surging ahead through the path cleared by Father Belsario, he launched himself off the ground, landing on the Golem's chest and driving his broadsword into its hearts. The force of the action knocked both human and demon backward through the portal, each screaming in agony as the shimmering surface ripped apart their internal structure. The last sections of the Golem to fall back through the portal were its hands, which still clutched the device. The outer casing disintegrated on impact, releasing the anti-matter inside.

A blinding flash of light swept across Red Square accompanied by a thunderous roar. Flames engulfed the portal. It burned intensely for a few moments, consuming itself in the conflagration until it collapsed upon itself and exploded. The shock wave from the detonation expanded outward, knocking down everything within a five-hundred-foot radius and blasting away the mound of skulls. Every flesh eater dropped to the pavement, releasing blue eddies of light that swirled into the sky. Ten seconds later, a peaceful calm descended across the square.

Those nearest the blast were either stunned or knocked unconscious. Jason lay on his back, his mind reeling. He became aware of two large tongues lapping at his face. He opened his eyes to see Lucifer and Lilith staring down at him. Reassured that their master was all right, their tails wagged and their licking became more intense. Jason reached up and scratched the werehounds behind their ears and then stood to survey the situation.

The portal had vanished. The only evidence of its existence was the hundreds of demon corpses scattered throughout Red Square and the surrounding side streets, plus the carcasses of the two dragons. He knew that Demon Spawn would litter the area for hundreds of miles. Off to his right, Melnikov and his soldiers stood in front of GUM, hooting and cheering. Around him, the others were getting to their feet and brushing themselves off, all except Father Belsario who crouched on one knee where the portal had once stood, his head bowed in prayer for their fallen comrade.

Sasha came up beside Jason and placed her hand on his shoulder. "Are you okay?"

"I think so. Those things pack quite a punch when they collapse. How are you?"

"I'm immortal, remember?" Sasha chuckled. "I can take a lot more punishment than you."

"Jason!"

Jeanette ran toward him. She dropped her FAMAS and jumped into his arms. Jason hugged her tight. She cupped his face in her hands and kissed him. Neither noticed Sasha walk away or the sadness in her eyes.

Grachov stepped up beside Jason and tapped him on the shoulder. Jason placed Jeanette back on the ground. The lieutenant held out his hand. "Congratulations. You did it."

"No," answered Jason as he shook the hand. "*We* did it. My team never would have gotten this far without you and Melnikov."

"Thank you." Grachov studied Red Square. "We definitely will have something to celebrate tonight."

CHAPTER THIRTY-TWO

G RACHOV HAD NOT been exaggerating about celebrating when they returned to the train yard. Within an hour of their arrival, General Zhirinovsky had organized a party for those who had gone to Moscow in commemoration of their closing the portal. The food was standard fare and far from extraordinary and the atmosphere subdued. Then the general produced three cases of vodka which lightened the mood. Everyone drank except for the Purgatoriati, who attended despite their obvious discomfort. At first, Jason had declined due to his age. Slava, who had been imbibing for nearly an hour, coaxed him into it by showing Jason how a good Cossack drank vodka—place your right hand on the hilt of your sword and your left around the shot glass, and then, after checking on the man to your left to make certain he had not drawn his weapon, down the contents in a single gulp. It took three attempts for Jason to get it right, by which point he was concerned only with having a good time. After what he and his team had gone through the past three months, they deserved it.

Jason studied those members of his team seated around the table. They had made out better this time. Closing the first portal in Paris had cost him thirteen people, including his beloved Sasha. Only two had died in Moscow, losses that were still too high, but he could better deal with that number. Jason realized that they had lucked out in finding Zhirinovsky because the additional firepower provided by the Russians and their knowledge of the terrain had helped achieve victory. Although Jason would not admit it to the others, he knew that one or two more battles like the one they had encountered in Paris would have wiped out his team and prematurely ended their expedition.

Zhirinovsky got up from his chair and tapped his fork against a water glass several times, attracting everyone's attention. Melnikov stood beside him. The general spoke in Russian, pausing to allow Melnikov to translate.

"General wants to congratulate all of you on what you accomplished this afternoon. He calls it historic day, one that will be talked about in Mother Russia for generations. He admits that when he had first heard about what you did in Paris, he was skeptical. After today, he feels ashamed he ever doubted you. Anything you need to complete your mission is at your disposal."

"Thank the general for me," said Jason. "Tell him we're honored to have Russia beside us."

Melnikov relayed the message and waited for the general's response.

"General also reminds us not to forget those who made ultimate sacrifice for mankind today, both among our own people and our new friends."

Zhirinovsky lifted his shot glass. "*Dlya spasiteley Rossii.*"

"To saviors of Russia," Melnikov translated.

Everyone raised their shot glasses.

"*Dlya nashikh pavshikh tovarischey.*"

"To our fallen comrades," Melnikov translated.

Zhirinovsky said in English, "And to closing down the second portal."

CHAPTER THIRTY-THREE

J ASON LOOKED AT the others on his team to see if he had misunderstood Zhirinovsky. The confusion and concern on their faces confirmed he had heard correctly.

"Did I hear the general right? Did he say there's a second portal?"

Zhirinovsky questioned Melnikov. The two men talked for a few seconds. The general pointed toward Jason and sat back down. Melnikov waited for everyone else to take their seat before answering.

"Yes, there is second portal. It's in Siberia, near Lake Baikal."

"You have to be mistaken," said Neal. "When the accident occurred at Protvino and formed an entry portal, it should have created only one exit portal."

"It did. *We* created second portal when we used nuclear device against one in Red Square."

"How?"

Melnikov shrugged. "I don't know science behind it. Ustagov thinks portion of nuclear blast that occurred against surface was channeled through portal and blew out another one in Siberia."

"Are you sure the detonation in Red Square caused it?" Jason asked.

"Yes. We had expedition in Siberia searching for survivors. They were in area when new portal was formed. Expedition noted date and time, and it matched detonation of nuclear device in Red Square."

"Is it an exit or entry portal?"

"It's exit portal. By time our expedition arrived at location, several dead demons had crossed through. Last time we sent recon mission to area they reported most demons were ravagers."

Slava slammed his hand on the table. "Damn it. Why didn't you tell us this earlier?"

Melnikov tried to hide his embarrassment. "As general said few minutes ago, we weren't sure if stories we heard about Paris were true or just rumors. We wanted to wait and see if you really had found way to shut them. Besides, several of us were worried if you found out about second portal you might not be willing to help us."

"That's insane," said Slava.

"When you live so near to portal, sometimes first casualty is rationality."

The dining hall went quiet. All eyes focused on Jason. He remained silent because, if he spoke, he could easily say something he would regret. Jason slowly poured himself a shot of vodka, using the gesture to fill empty space. He was furious at the Russians for not being forthright with him, although given the circumstances he could empathize with their trepidation. Although he understood the Russian's concerns about keeping the second gate secret out of fear his team might not help, it irked him that the Russians had so little trust in them. Of course, he probably would not have put so much faith in his hosts if his team had not been so desperate for support. Jason also chastised himself for allowing himself to believe his mission would be this easy. He wouldn't make that mistake again. Jason swigged the vodka. This time it did not have the same soothing effect as the previous shots.

Zhirinovsky gave Jason time to make his decision. After thirty seconds of silence he asked in heavily accented English, "Will you help us?"

Jason met the general's gaze. "Yes."

"Thank you," replied Zhirinovsky.

"How are we going to pull this off?" Slava asked.

"We have an extra device that Doc created, so we should have enough to complete our mission."

"As long as we don't run into any more surprises." Slava glared disapprovingly at Melnikov.

"And as long as all the devices work properly," Neal added.

"Enough," barked Jason. "I know you're all disappointed to find out that there's another portal to contend with. We all went into this realizing it wouldn't be easy."

Jeanette reached out and clasped his hand. "I'm not complaining, but you do realize it's a long way to Siberia?"

"We're going to have to go through Siberia anyway to get to China and Japan."

"Don't worry about getting to Lake Baikal," said Melnikov. "We have transportation that will get you there in few days. Meet in front of general's office at six tomorrow evening. It'll all be taken care of."

"Damn," said Slava to no one in particular. "Don't tell me we're going to have to spend more time in those shitty buses."

Melnikov chuckled. "Don't worry, comrade. You'll be traveling to Siberia in first class accommodations."

CHAPTER THIRTY-FOUR

THE NEWS ABOUT the existence of a second portal had destroyed the celebratory mood last night. Too bad it didn't have the same impact on hangovers. Thanks to all the shots of vodka, Jason had fallen into a deep sleep ten minutes after climbing into his bunk and did not wake up until well into the afternoon, giving him less than three hours to get ready. At least breakfast would not be a concern. Between the dry, furry sensation in his mouth, the heavy weight in the pit of his stomach, and the pounding headache, Jason did not want a heavy meal. He opted for two scrambled eggs and several strips of bacon, most of which he passed under the table to Lucifer and Lilith. He hoarded the three cups of black coffee for himself. Jason then went back to his quarters to pack and shower. By the time he left, he felt somewhat better.

As Jason approached Zhirinovsky's office, he realized that Melnikov had not been joking about providing first class accommodations to Siberia. A train sat on the siding in front of the main building. Jason counted eleven cars in total. At the front were four sleeper cars and a dining coach. The windows on each were protected by steel bars welded onto the outer surface. Next were two stock cars, also protected by metal plates attached to the roof and outer surface. Russian soldiers were loading the team's horses onto these, with Sook-kyoung overseeing the effort and giving each horse a reassuring pet. Two baggage cars followed, which were being loaded with supplies, as well as a sleeper that Russian troops climbed aboard. The last car in line remained a mystery. Similar in appearance to a caboose, it had reinforced steel plates covering the exterior walls and four makeshift doors built into each flank. A pair of Russian soldiers stood guard outside, each armed with an AK-47.

What attracted Jason's interest were the twin steam engines and coal tenders. They were massive, almost fifty feet in length with a 2-10-2 wheel configuration. The lead engine was black except for the wheels, trimming, cow catcher, and Soviet star mounted on the front, which were all painted red. A metal platform five feet square had been welded onto the top of the cow catcher, extending three feet beyond its tip and reinforced with steel rod supports. The platform served as the base for a triangular cage that ended in a point below the headlight mounted on the boiler. Three thick leather straps were attached to the platform. Behind the front engine sat a second one similar in size and design, only this one was covered in armor. Steel plates protected the crew cab and formed a seven-sided polygon around the boiler while a series of plates shielded the wheels. The engine and tender were both painted in military gray. Jason noticed writing underneath the observation slit in the armor around the cab and stepped over to read it. From top to bottom in black paint were a dark silhouette of a dragon with a single vertical mark to the right, a silhouette of a golem with three vertical marks, and a silhouette of a ravager with seventeen sets of five marks.

Jason's team and the Purgatoriati stood by the engines, some admiring the power and design, others gawking. He walked up to Jeanette and Slava.

"Morning," he said, regretting he spoke so loudly.

Jeanette beamed. "Morning, hon."

Slava stared in awe at the engines. "Aren't they impressive?"

Jeanette leaned over to Jason. "More like ostentatious."

"Different sides of same coin, no?"

Jeanette spun around to see Melnikov standing behind her,

an impish smirk on his face. "I-I'm sorry," she stammered. "I didn't mean to sound... um...."

Melnikov laughed. "Don't worry. You're more on mark than my Russian friend here. Colonel Krayevsky is train commander. Been all over Russia, Belarus, and Ukraine searching for survivors and battling more demons than any of us here have seen. Train functional, but colonel feel if going to go into battle then should be able to do so like... how you Americans say... eh, like a boss."

"How are old these engines?" Slava asked.

"Older than you and me. These are LV class locomotives, made by Soviet Union back in late 1950s. Second engine was being refurbished here when we took over rail yard. Krayevsky had it outfitted with armor plating and took it out on rescue runs. Three months ago, we found first engine in working condition as tourist attraction in Caucasus and commandeered it. We've not had chance to upgrade it yet, but we don't need to for this mission."

"What exactly is our mission?" Haneef asked as he joined the group.

"To close other portal."

"I mean, what are the details of the plan to do that?"

"We have plenty of time on trip to go over and revise them."

"How long will it take to get there?" Jeanette asked.

Melnikov did the calculations in his head. "About two and a half days. We'll arrive around mid-morning."

Slava pointed toward the rear of the train. "What's going on there?"

A pair of Russian soldiers escorted eight men and women toward the last car in line. They wore uniforms stripped of insignia. Each had their hands cuffed together in front of them and their right legs shackled to a long chain. As they ap-proached the end of the car, one of the two soldiers standing guard opened the door and placed a wooden set of stairs in front of it. He helped the men and women enter as the other soldiers kept an eye on them.

"They are prisoners," Melnikov answered.

"What crimes did they commit?" Jeanette asked.

"Serious offenses. Murder, rape, stealing food or supplies."

"What's going to happen to them?" Jeanette asked.

The captain ignored the question. He pointed to the sleeper cars, starting with the last two in line. "They are for Russian units that'll be accompanying us. It'll be same platoon that escorted you into Moscow. This second is reserved for your team. You should be quite comfortable. First sleeper belongs to Colonel Krayevsky. It serves both as personal quarters and command car."

"Will you be going with us?" Jason asked.

"Of course, my friend. I wouldn't miss this for anything. Colonel is in charge of overall mission. I command ground unit." A commotion came from the direction of Zhirinovsky's office. Melnikov pointed in that direction. "Here comes colonel now."

Zhirinovsky exited his quarters talking with a woman whom Jason guessed to be in her early thirties. She was tall, approximately six feet in height. Chest-length silky red hair flowed from under a black fur cap that bore the red star and gold hammer and sickle of the former Soviet Union. She wore the same camouflage uniform of the other Russian soldiers accessorized with black leather boots that came up to her knees and a gray wool overcoat with a black fur collar. A 9mm Makarov pistol hung from a utility belt against her right hip and a saber on her left. Two things struck Jason about this woman. First, her bearing, a blend of confidence and audaciousness tinged with showmanship. Second, her face, for she possessed a natural beauty between her sensuous, pouty lips and soulful blue eyes. The only physical feature that detracted from her attractiveness was the scar that ran from the center of her forehead, across her left eye, and part way down her left cheek. She wore a black eye patch.

Zhirinovsky whispered something to the woman that made her eyes widen. As they approached, the woman stepped over to Jason.

"General Zhirinovsky says you're Jason McCreary and that you're the one who closed the portals in Paris and Moscow. Is that true?"

"My team and I did."

The woman nodded her approval. "I like this one. He's modest and cares about his people. Let me introduce myself. I'm Colonel Svetlana Yakolevna Krayevsky of the Russian Army."

"*You're* Colonel Krayevsky?"

"You were expecting some dowdy old timer or a by-the-book officer?"

"To tell you the truth, yes."

The colonel laughed. "And you're brutally honest. We're going to work well together."

"I hope so, colonel."

"You can call me Svetlana." She winked at him and then caught the captain's attention. "Melnikov, I have to oversee the final preparations before departure. Show Jason's team to their cabins and let them get settled in. We leave in half an hour."

"Yes, ma'am."

Svetlana faced Zhirinovsky and saluted, and then headed toward the lead sleeping car. She addressed Jason while walking backwards. "Someday the world is going to write songs about us. They will either be praising us for saving the world or will be ballads about how we died gloriously fighting for the cause. Let's make sure it's not the latter."

As Svetlana proceeded to the command car, Melnikov stepped toward the three sleepers in front of them. "Let me show you where you'll be bunking down for trip."

Jeanette stepped past Jason and flashed him a disapproving glare. "I can see the next two and a half days are going to be real fun."

JASON SAT ON the bench in his private cabin in the lead sleeper car, with the werehounds curled up at his feet. He had stowed his gear and the four remaining anti-matter devices in the storage compartment above his bunk and settled down to enjoy the ride. The sun rested low on the horizon, casting long shadows across the train yard. Jason considered lighting the candles in the wall-mounted candelabra by the door, but he did not have the energy. Instead, he stared out the window, lost in thought and dozing off. The blare of the engine's steam whistle cut through the silence, jarring him awake. A moment later, the train lurched forward and sluggishly picked up speed. Lucifer and Lilith jumped up and stared out the window, their tails wagging. Never having traveled in this manner before, they were fascinated by the sensation. Jason checked his watch. Seven o'clock on the dot. He didn't know whether to attribute that to traditional military efficiency or Svetlana's flare for the dramatic. A few seconds passed, and the train left the yard and proceeded through the countryside.

Unlike Mont St. Michel, no community of survivors flourished outside the Russian compound. As far as he could determine, only the Russian military that had established itself in Domodedovo lived in the region. Being so near to ground zero, the civilian population could have fled the area for safer ground, been recruited by the military, or been wiped out by Demon Spawn. Weeks after his team returned from Paris, Jacques had started to rebuild society around the island city. Jason wondered how long it would take for the same to happen around Moscow, or if there were enough people left in this region to do so. He wanted to come back once all the portals were closed and see how things had changed here in western Russia.

Assuming he lived that long.

The swaying of the train and the clickity clack of the wheels lulled Jason. He yawned. Lucifer cocked his head in his master's direction. Without even bothering to convert the bench into a bed, Jason spread out along its length. Lucifer walked over and curled up on the floor beside him while Lilith stared out the window, still fascinated even though she could not see anything in the dark. Jason reached down and scratched his pet behind the ears until both fell asleep.

BOOK THREE

CHAPTER THIRTY-FIVE

SOMETHING BRUSHED AGAINST Jason's forehead. At first, he ignored it, hoping it would go away. The brushing continued. Jason assumed either Lucifer or Lilith wanted attention. Without opening his eyes, he swiped his hand across his face to shoo away the offender.

"Go lie down. I'm trying to sleep."

"I'm one of the dogs now?"

Jason opened his eyes. Jeanette sat at on the bench beside him, stroking his forehead with her left hand. She leaned forward and kissed him. "Just so you know, I don't do tricks or play fetch."

"Sorry." Jason sat up and leaned against the wall. Wrapping an arm around Jeanette's waist, he pulled her into him. She sighed with contentment and laid her head against his chest. Lucifer sat on the floor beside him, watching the two humans, his tail wagging. Lilith lay curled up asleep on the other bench.

"I thought you were one of them trying to wake me up. I wanted to sleep in a little before breakfast."

"I got news for you. It's almost noon."

"You're joking."

"Nope."

Jason reached out and petted Lucifer. "These guys must be starving."

"No. I took them to breakfast this morning."

"You were here this morning and I slept through it?"

Jeanette grinned impishly. "You looked so peaceful I didn't

have the heart to wake you."

Jason felt his face flush. Jeanette let him off the hook. "Seriously, you needed to rest."

"I'm not used to drinking vodka."

"It's more than that. You've been on the go ever since we left Mont St. Michel."

"We all have."

"We're not bearing the burden of command. You can't take everything on yourself otherwise you'll burn out. Then where will the rest of us be?"

"I want to make sure as many of us walk away from this as possible."

"I want you to be one of them." When Jason tried to protest, Jeanette placed her fingers against his lips. They were soft and warm. "There is nothing you can do for us for the next two days, so take it easy and recharge. I have a feeling we're all going to have to be at our best once we reach the new portal."

"I will, but I—"

"No buts." Jeanette leaned forward and kissed him, winning the argument. "Now that is settled, are you ready for lunch?"

"Yes."

Before they could leave, a knock sounded on the door. Lilith's head came off the bench, her ears perked and pointed toward the door.

"Come in," said Jason.

A Russian soldier slid it open halfway and leaned inside. "Excuse me for bothering you. Colonel Krayevsky wants to have a strategy session after lunch at 1300 in the command car. She asked that you and your principals attend."

"Tell the colonel we'll be there," responded Jason.

The soldier shut the door behind him.

"Let's grab something to eat while we can." Jason took Jeanette's hand and led her out. As the two stepped into the corridor, Lilith whimpered. The two werehounds stared at him, their eyes pleading. "You're included. Come on."

Lucifer and Lilith rushed forward, pushed past Jason and Jeanette, and raced toward the dining car.

CHAPTER THIRTY-SIX

SASHA STOOD IN the alcove at the end of the first sleeper where it connected with the command car, her gaze centered out the sliding exit door and onto the ground below as it rushed past. She wished the train would go faster so they could get to the portal, do their job, and move on to the next one. Sadly, things would pan out at their own pace and nothing she could say or do would hurry it along. Truth be known, Sasha wished she had not come along in the first place.

"I hope you're not thinking of jumping," said Father Belsario, who had moved behind Sasha without her hearing him.

"I'm not," she lied.

"I'm glad to hear that. If you committed suicide, you wouldn't wake up in Purgatory again."

"I know." Sasha debated whether to ask the next question. "What happens if I get killed by one of the demons?"

"Allowing the demons to kill you is still suicide."

"I'm not referring to that." Sasha faced Father Belsario. "If I die in combat with Demon Spawn, can I opt not to come back to Earth?"

"You can, but the contract will be nullified. You'll be excused from your time in Purgatory once you helped Jason with *all* the portals. If you back out now, you'll be banished to Purgatory until you've served your penance."

Sasha let her gaze fall to the metal floor. "It would be worth it."

"You knew ahead of time you wouldn't be allowed to be with him in a physical way."

"I know that. It's the… isn't there any way you can get rid of the emotional attachment I feel toward him?"

"You know I can't do that. Only those who go to Heaven are spared emotional burdens. It's the rule."

"Can't you bend the rule?"

"It's not my rule."

Sasha sighed and leaned against the door. "I didn't volunteer to come back. You made me do this."

"I understand. There are good reasons why I did."

"You keep saying that but you never tell me what they are."

"You'll find out in due time."

"That sounds like the shit they preached in Catholic School. 'Be a good and pure girl and someday you'll get into Heaven.'" Sasha regretted her sarcasm. "Sorry, Father. I shouldn't get mad at you."

"You're absolved this time," he chuckled. "I understand your frustration. If you trust me…."

"I do."

"Then have faith. You will know all the reasons why you were chosen to come back at the proper time. Sasha." Belsario waited until she made eye contact. "Right now, all you need to know is that Jason has taken on an impossible task to rid the world of evil and he needs all the help he can get."

"He has Jeanette."

"It's not enough. There are three people whom Jason loves and trusts unconditionally. His mother, but the trust was shattered when her calumny opened the portals. Jeanette, but in many ways, she's still a child. And you."

Sasha became excited. "When you say love…."

"He thinks of you as his closest and dearest friend. And yes, at one point he hoped you would be intimate."

The excitement drained away as fast as it had risen. "I blew that opportunity."

Father Belsario placed his hand on Sasha's shoulder. When

he spoke, his voice contained a warmth and understanding she had not heard from him before. "Do you still love him?"

Sasha didn't answer for several seconds. "I love him with my heart and soul."

"Then show Jason how much you love him. If you can't be with him physically, be there spiritually. He has a dozen friends who will support him and fight beside him. What he really needs is someone who will give him alternate advice, who will warn him when he's overextending himself, who will tell him he's letting his emotions dictate his actions. You're the one with the ability to do that and whom he will listen to. That's one of the reasons why I brought you back."

"Who's going to guide me in telling Jason what he should and shouldn't do?"

Father Belsario pointed toward her heart. "You'll find the answers in there."

"You know it pisses me off when you're cryptic like this."

He chuckled again. "Then I won't tell you that the Lord works in mysterious ways."

"Please don't."

"Are you okay?"

"I'm better," Sasha lied.

"Good. Now come with me. Jason has asked us to attend a planning session with Colonel Krayevsky."

CHAPTER THIRTY-SEVEN

WHEN JASON AND Jeanette entered the command car, it reminded him of the movies he had seen as a kid about Russia prior to the revolution when the aristocracy traveled in elegance. The walls were covered in red velour wallpaper. A strip of cherry wood stretched above the windows from one end of the car to the other, with smaller sets of three stained glass windows above each main frame. Ornately carved cherry wood beams were placed along the ceiling at five-foot intervals and, between each beam, dangled a small crystal chandelier, now rendered useless by the lack of electricity. Polished, sand-colored hardwood covered the floors, marred in numerous places where the original furnishings had been ripped up to accommodate the car's current role as a command post. The new furnishings contrasted sharply with the décor. In the corner near the door to Natasha's quarters sat a white metal desk, scuffed and dented, with a worn black leather chair behind it. A rectangular table dominated the center of the car. On it sat several maps stacked on top of each other. The top one showed Siberia, with a red line marking a path from Moscow to Lake Baikal.

Melnikov and Dr. Ustagov were waiting for them in front of the table.

"Afternoon," Jason said as they approached.

"Afternoon," Melnikov said.

Ustagov grunted.

"I'm surprised to see you here," Jason said to the doctor.

"Not half as surprised as I am. Thirty minutes before departure, I was told that I'm part of the expedition. I guess Her Highness felt she needed scientific expertise on this one."

"We've not had a monarchy for over a hundred years," said Svetlana as she exited her quarters and stepped up to the table. "If you're going to talk about me, at least use an insult that's contemporary."

Ustagov's shoulders slumped and he lowered his head. "Forgive me, Colonel. I didn't mean any offense."

"Yes, you did," said Svetlana. "But that's not important. You're here because of your scientific expertise. Is this everyone?"

As if on cue, the door between cars opened and Haneef and Slava entered, followed by Father Belsario and Sasha. Haneef gave a slight bow to Svetlana. "Sorry we're late."

"Is this everyone on your side?"

It is," answered Jason.

"Good." Svetlana paused a moment. "I want to apologize for the rush, but I'm afraid it's necessary. The doctor believes the demons tried to protect the Moscow portal following your success in Paris. If he's correct, then I want to close down the Siberian portal as soon as possible."

"It makes sense," said Jason.

"Why didn't we leave earlier?" Slava asked.

"It's a sixty-five-hour trip to Lake Baikal, if we're lucky. Departing when we did means we will arrive shortly after dawn. You do not want to be near that area after dark." Svetlana took the top map and swung it around so it faced Jason and his team. "We're in luck in two regards. First, there is very little between us and Lake Baikal, so the demons have little interest in this area. They're all concentrated around the lake region."

"How's that lucky?" asked Ustagov.

"It means we don't have to fight our way to the portal like we did in Paris," said Jason.

"Or like we would have had to do in Moscow if Melnikov

hadn't found us," Jeanette added.

Svetlana reached under the first map and pulled out a second one of the southern Lake Baikal region, which she placed on top. "The second piece of good luck is that the portal opened directly on a spur line off the main Tran-Siberian Railway, thirty miles from Irkutsk. That means we don't have to trudge over the tundra to get there. We can drive a train right into it."

"Which explains why you have a second steam engine," said Slava.

"Exactly. I had my men modify the cow catcher of the first engine with a reinforced platform for your anti-matter device. I have a crew up front who is maintaining the engine so it can move on a moment's notice. When we get near Lake Baikal, we'll transfer some of your team to the first engine, mount the device on the platform, and ram it into the portal."

"What about the crew aboard the train?" Sasha asked.

"They can jump off before impact," Jeanette answered.

Haneef scrunched his face as he thought about that. "The train would have to be traveling slowly so that those who jumped didn't get killed or seriously injured."

"But you don't see that as a possibility," said Jason, his gaze locked on Svetlana. "You're assuming there'll be a slugfest to get to the gate. Why else would you modify the cow catcher to clear the tracks of things larger than a cow?"

Svetlana flashed Jason a smile of respect. "Based on previous trips to Lake Baikal and the doctor's observations, I'm expecting a battle royale when we try and get to it. Whoever is on that engine will be on a suicide run. However, isn't the goal to close down the portal at all costs?"

"It is." Jason agreed with Svetlana.

"Why can't we just let the first train run on its own?" asked Haneef.

"There are too many variables," explained Father Belsario. "If we abandon that engine, we lose all control over it. The

Demon Spawn could try to remove the device, derail the train, block its path, or any number of scenarios."

Jason nodded in agreement. "And with no one on that train, we'd be powerless to stop them."

"Just so you know," said Svetlana. "I intend to have two of my crew stay on that engine to provide support in case anything happens, so the sacrifice won't be yours alone."

"Thank you."

"This is insane," Jeanette protested.

"If you have a better idea, please share it." Svetlana said it with no malice or sarcasm.

"There is no better idea," Jason said after a few moments. "What you've come up with is our best option."

"For what it's worth," said Melnikov. "Colonel ran this by me and my staff yesterday morning, and we couldn't think of better scenario."

"We'll stay behind you with the rest of the train to provide cover fire and, hopefully, draw some of the demons off you." Svetlana focused on Jason. "You'll need to decide which of your team members will make the run on the first train."

"That's easy," said Jason. "Slava and I will do it."

"I want to be up there with you," Jeanette responded.

"You should let me do it rather than you," added Haneef.

Jason held up his hands, ending all further conversation. He made eye contact with Haneef. "No offense against you, but I'm in charge and need to be on that train in case things go wrong and snap decisions have to be made. Besides, if something happens to me and Slava, I expect you to take command and complete this mission. Are you okay with that?"

"You're the boss."

Jason turned to Jeanette. "We can't afford to lose too many people out here. There are still three other portals to deal with after this. Understand?"

"Yes," said Jeanette, fighting back tears.

"May I make a suggestion?" Father Belsario asked.

"Go ahead."

"Maybe you should let Sasha and I ride the train into the portal. We can't die. If something happens to us, we'll be back a few days later so you don't lose any of your numbers."

Jason thought about it for a moment. "I still need to be on that train for the reasons I gave Haneef, but I would like you both up there with me and Slava. It might give us a slight advantage."

Jason did not see the disapproving look Jeanette gave him.

"I have a question," said Slava to Svetlana. "You said you're expecting trouble because of your previous trips out here. What have you run into before?"

A little bit of Svetlana's confidence drained away. "Not many types of demons come through the portal. We've seen no dragons or giant insects, only one Golem that guards it and a single swarm of living demons that wandered off into the tundra. What comes through regularly are ravagers, scores of them. The last time we were out there about two weeks ago we counted a pack of about forty."

"Why just them?" Haneef asked.

"We don't know," Ustagov answered. "Maybe they're attracted to the inhospitable terrain."

"Or it could be that ravagers inhabited that particular portion of other dimension where the portal opened," added Father Belsario.

"That's possible."

"We know the ravagers need flesh," said Svetlana. "They set upon the local population, what few there were. There is one small city and dozens of towns around the lake. Most of the people fled once the ravagers appeared. Those that stayed didn't last long. The ravagers haven't traveled far from the lake and, since their food supply has been wiped out, they are hungry and highly aggressive. I lost eleven men last time I was in this area, and almost didn't make it back alive. If the doctor's theory is right, if these things are aware of what we're attempting to do and try to stop us, I'm anticipating we're heading into a full-scale war."

No one responded.

"It's settled then," said Svetlana. "We'll meet again tomorrow afternoon before dinner to go over any final details. By the next morning, we will be approaching Lake Baikal."

CHAPTER THIRTY-EIGHT

JASON AND JEANETTE were the first to leave the command car. Lucifer and Lilith sat waiting for them by the door leading to the sleeper. The werehounds jumped to their feet upon seeing him, their tails wagging. He scratched behind their ears and led them down to his room. Opening the door, the two rushed in, each scurrying to get a seat on the bench.

"Can I come in for a minute?" Jeanette asked.

"Sure." Jason stepped aside. "Good luck finding a place to sit, though."

"I'll sit next to you."

A knock sounded on the door. Jason called out, "Come in."

The door slid open and Ustagov stuck his head in. Upon seeing Jeanette, he became embarrassed. "I'm sorry. I didn't know you had company."

"It's okay. What can I do for you?"

Ustagov stepped in and slid shut the door. "I've been watching you interact with Lucifer and Lilith the past few days. One of your people said they're not real dogs but werehounds that came through one of the portals."

Jason became defensive. "Is that a problem?"

"Not at all. Do you have a minute?"

"Sure." Jason pointed to the end of the bench.

"Thanks," said Ustagov as he sat down. "How did you train them to be so docile?"

"I didn't."

Ustagov was confused. "I don't understand."

"As long as Lucifer and Lilith have been with me, they've

never been wild. I picked them up on a search and destroy mission outside of Calais. They came up to me in this form and seemed friendly enough, and they followed me back to Mont St. Michel. I adopted them. Three weeks later, they morphed into werehounds to defend my team when it was attacked by soul vampires."

"Interesting." Ustagov leaned forward to examine Lucifer. The werehound lifted his head and wagged his tail. "And they don't show aggression toward you or other humans?"

"No."

Ustagov reached his hand toward Lucifer and paused. "May I?" he asked Jason.

"Go ahead."

Ustagov stood and inched his way toward Lucifer, his hand open with the palm down. Lucifer stretched his nose out, sniffed the doctor's hand, and then lowered his head to be petted. Ustagov scratched behind his ears. "These are the first werehounds we've ever encountered. They're also the first living demons we've encountered that haven't tried to kill us."

"It's the same for me."

Ustagov stopped petting Lucifer, much to the latter's disappointment, and sat back down. "Do you sense their aura?"

Jason shook his head.

"Interesting."

"Doc seemed to think...." Jason paused. "Doc was a scientist like you.... Doc seemed to think that the reason I can detect the aura of the dead demons is because they were once human. He reasoned that the link is with their souls."

"That makes sense. Did you have a sixth sense like this before the opening of the portal?"

"No."

Ustagov sat back in the bench and stared at the wall for a moment, lost in thought. "Without studying you more, I can't say anything for certain. However, it sounds to me like the opening of the portals triggered your ability to sense whatever came through."

"How come I don't sense the aura of the living demons?"

"Probably because it's harder to detect them since they're not derived from humans. That doesn't mean with practice you won't be able to."

"How am I going to practice?"

"With them." Ustagov gestured toward Lucifer and Lilith. Jason protested when the doctor held up a hand. "I wouldn't recommend it if I thought it would hurt them. This ability to sense demon aura is a gift that's already saved your life on several occasions. If you can develop it so you can detect every demon out there, you increase your chances of success."

"He's right," said Jeanette. "We'd never be ambushed by Demon Spawn again."

"How should I do it?" Jason asked.

"What do you do now to detect the dead demons?"

"I don't do anything. I automatically sense their aura whenever they get near."

"Interesting." Ustagov pondered for a moment. "Spend time every day and meditate on the werehounds. It may be for nothing. If you're lucky, you might be able to train yourself to sense their aura."

"I will. Thanks."

"Don't mention it." The doctor stood and headed out, pausing for a moment by the door. "Please keep me posted on any progress you make. See you tomorrow."

Lilith lifted her head at the sound of the door sliding shut, and then lowered it back on the bench.

"What do you think?" Jeanette asked. "Are you going to try it?"

"It couldn't hurt."

"Good." Jeanette stood up to leave. "I'll let you get busy."

Jason jumped up to stop her. "You don't have to go."

"I do." Jeanette took Jason's face in her hands, leaned forward, and kissed him. "I'll see you in the morning."

Jason delayed sighing until Jeanette had left. He had promised Jeanette he would wait until she was ready and intended to stand by that pledge. What he had miscalculated was how long that might be. It didn't matter. No one else he knew had found love in the middle of the apocalypse, and he was grateful for what he had. He loved Jeanette with his heart and soul. By the way Jeanette smiled when she looked him in the eyes, or the gentleness with which she touched him, he knew she felt the same. That is what mattered most. He only hoped he and Jeanette would get to spend a night together before the Demon Spawn wound up eating his heart and stealing his soul.

Sitting down on the bench across from the sleeping werehounds, Jason patted his knees and said, "Well guys, it seems we're going to have a long, dull night ahead of us."

CHAPTER THIRTY-NINE

THE NEXT DAY passed without incident. Everyone was bored but on edge because tomorrow the train would arrive at the portal. Most people tried to find something to occupy their time, dealing with the monotony and tension in his or her own way. Everyone cleaned their weapon at least once or, in the case of the Russians, checked their battle stations multiple times. Many of the Russians drank heavily until they passed out in the early afternoon. Others napped. Jason busied himself by inspecting the anti-matter devices, removing each from its case and examining it for defects, which was a useless gesture; if there had been a defect that allowed the anti-matter to interact with the surrounding environment, they would all be dead by now. He then checked on the horses, made certain Haneef's minigun worked, and spent a few hours playing with Lucifer and Lilith until the late-afternoon planning session with Svetlana. Even that did little to fill the time because nothing had changed from the original session the previous evening.

After dinner, Jason asked his team to stick around for a few moments to go over last-minute strategy. Once the Russians had left the dining car, Jason began.

"I want to make certain everyone is clear about what's going to happen tomorrow. According to the engineer's calculations, we've made good time and should reach Lake Baikal ninety minutes after sunrise. Right after breakfast, Slava and I are going to head up to the lead engine and place the device. We're expecting the Demon Spawn to concentrate on taking out the engines, so Sasha and Father Belsario will join us to provide cover. Haneef, Sasha will take the minigun this time."

Haneef attempted to hide his disappointment. Jason tried to comfort his friend. "Again, there's nothing personal about this. If something happens to me, I need you to take over the team."

"I understand," said Haneef.

"Besides," said Father Belsario. "We want to put as few people as possible in harm's way. If Sasha or I get killed, we'll be resurrected and will rejoin the team later. If anything happens to one of you…." The sentence did not need to be completed.

Jason focused on Neal. "You'll be in the command car with Dr. Ustagov, Melnikov, and Lucifer and Lilith. You'll have a second device. If something happens to us, it's your responsibility to deploy it. Lucifer and Lilith will protect you. Melnikov will do what he can to get you close enough."

"I won't let you down." Neal's confidence belied his nervousness. "I do have one question. What if I fail?"

"That'll leave us with only two devices. Whoever is left will grab one and attempt to deploy it."

"If it gets to that point," said Slava, "this whole mission is a failure, so it doesn't matter."

Jason sneered. "That's not very optimistic, but it's accurate. Let's not let it come to that. Understood?"

The two men nodded.

"Luther and Matthew, Father Belsario and I volunteered you for a tough assignment. You will station yourselves on top of the train to clear off any Demon Spawn that board us."

"No problem," said Luther. Matthew agreed.

"Just to be clear," added Father Belsario. "I would join you topside if I wasn't needed on the front engine."

"It's not an issue," said Matthew. "It's our duty to serve any way we can."

Jason motioned to Sook-kyoung, Vicky, and Gaston. "You

three will station yourselves in the stock cars and guard the horses."

"Are you serious?" Sook-kyoung made no attempt to hide her displeasure.

"What's wrong?"

"I'm one of your more experienced fighters and you have me babysitting?"

"Hey?" said Gaston.

Sook-kyoung looked over at Gaston and softened her tone. "I meant the horses."

"You're not babysitting anyone or anything," Jason snapped. "We need the horses alive. If anything happens to them, we walk to China."

"Sorry."

Vicky mumbled something that no one could understand. Jason asked, "What was that?"

"I don't know if I can do this," said Vicky. "I nearly got killed in Red Square because of my own stupidity. Sook-kyoung saved my life. I'm not cut out for this. I'm here for all the wrong reasons. I'm more of a liability than a—"

Sook-kyoung reached over and squeezed Vicky's hand hard enough to stop her in mid-sentence, and then eased up. "You'll be with me. You'll be fine."

"And if I screw up again, or freeze?"

"Then you'll get yourself killed, and probably me along with you." Sook-kyoung rubbed Vicky's hand. "I know you won't let that happen."

Vicky sat up in her chair, seeming more confident.

"As for the rest of you," continued Jason. "You'll join the bulk of the Russian troops in the sleeper and dining cars. You'll be under Melnikov's command, though, so if any of the Russian officers give you orders, obey it like you would an order from me. Understood?"

Everyone responded or gestured in the affirmative.

"Werner and Ian, stick by my people who have been doing

this for a while."

"You don't trust us?" Werner asked.

"It has nothing to do with trust," Jason answered. "You newer members have seen combat three times. Red Square was nothing compared to what we faced in Paris. We're about to experience what could well be the toughest battle yet, and I want to make sure you survive it by pairing you up with my more experienced people."

"When you put it that way...." Werner laughed, using humor to hide his being chastised.

Jason made eye contact, one by one, with each member of his team as he spoke. "The truth is, I have no idea what we're going to face tomorrow. Dr. Ustagov thinks the Demon Spawn realize what we're trying to do and will send as many demons as possible to stop us. If so, then we can expect the fight of our lives. And if we succeed tomorrow, then China, Japan, and the States will be even tougher."

"Way to give pep talk, mate," joked Ian. Nervous laughter accompanied the remark.

Jason chuckled. "Whatever happens, I'm proud of all of you. It's been an honor to lead you, and I hope to see all of you on the other side. Now, everybody get some rest. We're all going to need it."

CHAPTER FORTY

T HE POUNDING STARTLED Jason awake. He bolted upright in his bed, his heart racing and his adrenaline pumping. At first, he thought they might be under attack. Instinctively, he suppressed the fear and let his senses scan for demonic aura. There were none. Then he heard the pounding again. It came from the corridor, this time accompanied by Melnikov's voice.

"Jason. Are you awake?"

"I am now."

"Sorry. It's almost dawn. Colonel wants everyone awake and ready for when we get near portal. Breakfast is in ten minutes."

"No problem. I'll be there."

MELNIKOV'S SOLDIERS HAD eaten before dawn. Jason's team filed in one by one as the sun broke the eastern horizon. Breakfast was filling if somewhat unusual—hard boiled eggs, sliced cucumber, wedges of canned meat, and gallons of strong coffee. Several members of his team were too nervous to keep anything down. However, everyone had at least three cups of coffee. Jason found that amusing because no one would be dozing off today, no matter how little caffeine they had.

Svetlana dined with the second breakfast shift, although she didn't eat. The colonel provided moral support, walking through the dining car and chatting with every member of Jason's team, trying to get their minds off the next few hours.

She adapted her manner to the mood of those with whom she dealt, showing deference when talking with Father Belsario and the Purgatoriati, displaying a cheerful and supportive demeanor with most of Jason's team, and being more flamboyant with Ian. She even petted Lucifer and Lilith and slipped each of them a hard-boiled egg. Jason appreciated the gesture. Unlike the past two days, the mood this morning was somber because everyone knew they would soon arrive at the portal and would engage a horde of Demon Spawn in battle.

When Svetlana reached the opposite end of the dining car, she picked up a glass of water and faced Jason's team, calling for their attention. "I'm not going to make a long speech. We all know how important today is, what success will mean for the world, and the difficulties we're going to face. To those of us who are not around tonight to celebrate our victory, may the sacrifices we make today be talked about for centuries." Svetlana raised her glass. "To the closing of the portal!"

Everyone raised their glasses and repeated the toast.

IN THE PRISON car at the rear of the train, Klimenko sat in the right swivel seat of the extended-vision cupola, scanning the horizon for signs of demons. Barzukov sat across from him, struggling not to doze off. Klimenko leaned over and slapped the back of Barzukov's head.

"Wake up, asshole."

Barzukov massaged his skull. "What was that for?"

"If the major or Melnikov catches you asleep, you'll wind up down there with the prisoners."

Barzukov mumbled something under his breath that Klimenko could not understand and went back to scanning the horizon. Klimenko did the same. He wanted to be especially alert this morning. The train was within forty kilometers of the portal, so at any minute they should—

Movement on the horizon in front of and to the right of the

train caught his attention. Taking the binoculars from their cubby hole, Klimenko raised them to his eyes. A wave of nausea churned up his stomach.

"Dear God."

"What?" Barzukov asked. He grabbed his own binoculars. "You've got to be kidding."

Klimenko snapped out of his initial shock. "Sound the alarm and pass the word. The rest of you, prepare the prisoners."

Barzukov jumped to the floor and rushed forward to where the hand-cranked air raid siren had been set up by the door leading to the rest of the train. He turned the handle. The siren increased in volume until its wavering wail sounded above the clacking of the train. A moment later, a Russian soldier slid open the door to the baggage car. "What's going on?"

"Pass the word down. We have demons at our one o'clock."

Klimenko went back to viewing the approaching horde. He thought to himself, *this must be what the end of the world looks like.*

JASON AND HIS team were finishing up breakfast when they heard the faint wail of an air raid siren from the rear of the train. A minute later, a Russian soldier slid open the rear door of the dining car.

"Lookouts report demons approaching on our one o'clock."

Jumping up from the table, everyone ran to the windows along the right side. A black moving mass emerged along the horizon. Svetlana took a pair of binoculars that hung from a hook and viewed it. Jason noticed that her body tensed and the usual expression of confidence that she wore momentarily cracked. Without saying a word, she passed the binoculars to Jason. When he raised them to his eyes, he understood Svetlana's reaction.

Over twenty ravagers were charging across the tundra heading straight for the train.

CHAPTER FORTY-ONE

JASON HANDED THE binoculars back to Svetlana. "How long before they reach us?"

"Ten minutes, if we're lucky."

"Then we don't have much time." Jason moved away from the window. "Neal, grab two of the devices from my cabin and bring them here. Slava, get the minigun. The rest of you know what to do."

Svetlana made eye contact with Melnikov. "I'm heading up to the armored engine so you're in charge here. Have two of your men join me."

"I will."

She caught the attention of Jason, Sasha, and Father Belsario. "Come with me. I'll show you how to get to the engines."

Sasha shook her head. "I need to wait for the minigun. Slava and I will catch up."

As Jason fell in behind Svetlana, Lucifer and Lilith attempted to follow. He knelt in front of them. "You two stay here until I get back."

Lilith whimpered. Lucifer widened his big brown eyes and tilted his head.

"It won't work this time. You protect Neal." Jason leaned forward and hugged the two werehounds. "I love you guys."

Lilith whimpered again. Lucifer licked Jason's face.

Everyone on the train headed for their combat position.

IN THE ARMORED steam engine, Leonid thought he heard an

unusual noise. Moving to the tender, he crawled up on the coal pile and listened. He picked up the air raid siren above the din of the moving train and the roar of the boilers. Climbing up higher onto the coal, Leonid scanned the horizon. After a few seconds, he spotted the horde of approaching ravagers.

"What are you doing up there?" Mikhail asked.

Leonid pointed to their right. Mikhail stepped over to the engine's window and stared out. Upon seeing the ravagers bearing down on the train, he rushed back to his station and opened the pressure gauges all the way.

BECAUSE OF THE noise, no one in the lead engine detected the air raid siren. Vladimir realized they were isolated, so as a precaution he spent most of his time staring out the cab's windows searching for demons. He spotted the approaching ravagers when they were still nine minutes out. He leaned over and tapped Iosif on the shoulder.

"What?" Iosif brushed his fireman's hand away.

"We have company."

"What are you talking…?" Iosif joined Vladimir and swore under his breath when he spotted the ravagers. He jumped back to his station and throttled the steam engine to full capacity. "Shovel more coal."

JASON'S TEAM GRABBED their weapons and deployed through-out the train. Ian and Werner stayed in the second sleeper car along with the Russian soldiers, each manning the cabins on the right side of the train, while Antoine teamed up with the soldiers in the dining car. Since the windows did not open from the inside, they smashed the glass with the butts of their weapons to allow a field of fire. When Luther and Matthew reached the opposite end of the dining car, they opened the door, exited onto the ladder, and climbed to the roof. Sook-kyoung, Vicky, and Gaston passed through to the stock car. The animals were already agitated, sensing the approaching danger. Haneef continued ahead, making his way to the prison car.

Neal ducked into Jason's cabin, opened the overhead storage compartment above the bunk, and removed two of the anti-matter devices. Slinging one armband over each shoulder, he raced back to the dining car.

Slava ran into the cabin he shared with Haneef and grabbed the minigun. As he tried to exit, Jeanette centered herself in the doorway. "I'll take it to Jason."

"That's foolish," he replied, his irritation obvious. "I'll bring it with me."

"I'm taking your place."

"When did Jason authorize this?"

"He didn't." When Slava argued, Jeanette cut him off. "If I'm going to die, it's going to be beside Jason. There's no time to argue. Give me the minigun."

Slava shrugged and handed it to Jeanette. The woman's body slouched under the weight. "I hope you know what you're doing."

"I do. And thanks."

As Slava ran off to man a position in the third sleeper car, Jeanette lugged the minigun to the command car.

SVETLANA PASSED THROUGH her private quarters to the front end of the command car and exited. Jason shut his eyes and lowered his head as a combination of fifty-mile-an-hour wind and soot slammed into his face. Svetlana seemed not to notice. She stepped to the edge of the platform, reached out to a metal ladder attached to the rear of the tender, and ascended. Jason and Father Belsario followed. Once at the top of the ladder, they climbed over the outer rim into the bin and slid down the pile of coal. Leonid spun around at the noise and aimed an

AK-47 at Svetlana's head. Upon seeing it was the colonel, he lowered the weapon.

"Sorry. I thought you were a ravager."

"You're on your toes," she said. Svetlana motioned for Leonid to step to the rear of the cab, and then led Jason and Father Belsario to the front right corner. She opened a small hatch two feet wide and four feet tall mounted on the front wall that exposed a small dark crawlspace not much bigger. "That's the walkway on the outside of the engine. It's been enclosed in armor. At the far end is another hatch that opens onto the front of this engine. You can access the first engine the same way we did this one."

Jason crawled up and paused as he gazed down the crawlspace. "Are you sure we can fit?"

"It's cramped, but it's doable. Now hurry. We're running out of time."

Jason checked on the ravagers. They were six minutes away.

NEAL ENTERED THE command car with both backpacks. "Where's Jason?"

"He went forward already," Sasha answered.

Neal's eyes widened. "Do I have to bring it to him?"

"Slava will once he gets here."

Ustagov arrived a moment later. Melnikov took one of the backpacks from Neal and handed it to the doctor. "You're responsible for keeping this safe. If others fail, we'll need this to complete mission."

"What will you do?"

Melnikov pointed to Neal. "I'm protecting him."

Two Russian soldiers entered the command car. Melnikov snapped his fingers to get their attention. "Colonel is waiting for you on armored engine."

They raced forward.

Jeanette barged through the door lugging the minigun over one shoulder. She headed for Sasha. "Turn around."

"Where's Slava?" Sasha asked as she presented her back.

"I'm taking his place." Jeanette lifted the 10,000-round ammunition pack onto Sasha's shoulders and helped her strap it on.

"Is Slava okay?"

"He's fine." Jeanette helped Sasha strap in. "I want to be with Jason just in case."

Sasha understood the sentiment. Hefting the minigun in her hands, she asked, "Ready?"

Neal handed Jeanette the backpack containing the anti-matter device. She slid it over her shoulders. "Let's rock."

CRAMPED WAS AN *understatement*, thought Jason. He had to crouch to make it through the crawlspace and kept banging his head and shoulders on the armor plating. The flashlight he held in his left hand barely lit the path ahead. It didn't help that the confined space intensified the sounds of the engine and the drivers racing along the tracks as well as the heat from the boiler. When he opened the hatch at the far end, he felt relieved to be blasted by soot and high wind.

He and Father Belsario exited the crawlspace. They descended the access stairs to the coupling platform, clutching the single guardrail attached to the boiler. Once on the coupling platform, Jason steadied himself. The metal ladder on the rear of the lead tender was four feet away. Beneath him, the tracks raced by at over fifty miles per hour. He inched forward and stretched out his hand, terrified that one bump would knock him off balance and he would fall under the wheels. When his fingers touched the metal rung, he clasped tight and swung his legs over. Jason climbed up and slid down the coal into the cab.

"*Vy zdes' chtoby bombu?*" Iosif asked.

"I don't speak Russian," Jason yelled over the roar of the

steam engine.

"Are you here to plant bomb?"

"Yes."

"Where is it?"

Jason gestured over his shoulder. "Someone is bringing it."

"They better hurry."

Jason stuck his head out the cab window. The ravagers were five minutes away.

HANEEF ENTERED THE prison car and stopped short.

Two swivel mounts had been built into the floor on each side of the car at the center mark. In front of each mount, a slit five feet wide and one foot high had been cut into the armor plating along the wall. A Russian soldier attempted to fasten a two-wheeled M1910 Maxim heavy machine gun onto the mount, having difficulty due to the weapon's size and weight.

What caught Haneef off guard were the two Russians at the rear. They dragged a young female prisoner from her bunk in the middle of the car to an open cylindrical cage the size of a coffin that stood against the starboard wall. Even though her wrists were bound in front by handcuffs, she struggled, kicking with her legs and trying to bite the guards. One Russian placed a hand on her chest and shoved her into the cage with such force that, when she hit the bars, it knocked the wind out of her. The other soldier took advantage and closed one cheek plate of a second pair of handcuffs around the chain of the female prisoner's handcuffs and the other end to the top bars. When he finished, the first guard slammed shut the cage door and secured it with a padlock. Three other prisoners had been locked in similar cages along the starboard wall.

Klimenko, who struggled with the machine gun, noticed Haneef and motioned for him to come forward. "Help me get this damn thing mounted."

"Who are these people?" Haneef pointed to the cages.

"Prisoners."

"What are they doing in cages?"

"They're bait."

"What?"

"To distract the ravagers," Klimenko huffed with growing frustration. "The demons go after the food and leave us alone."

"That's barbaric!"

"Do you want to debate our methods or do you want to live?"

Haneef wanted to respond but could not. As horrific as the practice may be, with a score of ravagers bearing down on them they would need every advantage they could get. He would find a way to atone for this sin later, if he lived that long.

Klimenko waved him over. "Help me get this damn thing mounted."

From the cupola, Barzukov called out. "They're four minutes out."

WHEN JEANETTE, SASHA, and the two Russian soldiers reached the armored engine, they found Svetlana waiting for them. The colonel ushered the women toward the crawlspace between the engine and the plating. "This will take you to the front engine. Now hurry."

"I can't fit through there with this," said Sasha, referring to the minigun. "I'll have to crawl along the top."

"Be careful," said Jeanette.

"I will." Sasha jumped up, grabbed the roof of the cab, and lifted herself topside.

Svetlana pushed Jeanette toward the hatch. "You. Through the crawlspace. Now."

As Jeanette climbed in, Svetlana pointed to one of the soldiers that had accompanied them. "Boris, follow her. Once she and Sasha are on the other engine, decouple us."

ANTOINE STOOD BY the shattered window, shivering as the frigid air rushed through the cabin. He barely noticed the cold, his attention focused on the horde of ravagers stampeding toward the train. Binoculars were no longer needed to see them. Although he could not make out each individual Demon Spawn, a distinct line of rampaging flesh approached.

MANEUVERING THROUGH THE crawlspace was hard enough without having to pull the backpack with the device along behind her. Jeanette breathed a sigh of relief when she reached the other end, until she emerged onto the access stairs. The ground raced by beside her. For a moment, she froze. Something touched her back. Jeanette cried out.

"We must move quickly." Boris pointed to the coupling platform.

Summoning her courage, Jeanette slid the backpack onto her shoulders and made her way down the access ladder. She concentrated on her footing, ignoring the rails racing past beneath her. Once on the platform, she inched forward until she had gone as far as possible. She reached out, grabbing a rung with one hand and then the other. Jeanette stepped out, placing one foot after another on the ladder, and climbed.

Boris knelt, took hold of the cut-lever, and yanked up, lifting the coupler lock. The couplers disconnected and the first engine lurched forward.

When it did, Jeanette lost her footing and slipped off the ladder.

"WE'RE ALL GOING to die," the soldier beside Slava whined, his terrified eyes fixed on the horde.

"What's your name?" he asked.

"Yuri."

"Yuri, if you panic, you'll die. If you don't let fear get the better of you, you have a good a chance of living."

"How do you know that?"

Slava patted Yuri on the shoulder. "Because this is the third time I've done this, and I'm still here."

"HELP ME!" JEANETTE cried as she dangled from the ladder. She frantically kicked to get a foothold, but her feet hung a yard below the lowest rung. Boris reached out to help. By now the first engine had pulled too far away and he could not get to her. Jeanette felt her grip giving way. Any second now she knew she would slip off and fall beneath—

A hand wrapped around her wrist. Sasha leaned over the rim of the tender, her other hand clutching the top rung. She lifted Jeanette so the latter could plant her feet on the bottom rung. Once Jeanette felt secure, she waved to Sasha who released her grip. The two women climbed to the top of the tender and paused.

"Thanks for saving me."

"You'd do the same for me." Sasha pointed to starboard. "Come on. We don't have much time."

The ravagers were less than two minutes away.

THE HORSES BORDERED on panic. Sook-kyoung assumed the ravagers must be near. She wished the stock car had windows.

"Are you two all right?" she asked Vicky and Gaston.

Vicky nodded, but the way her finger kept switching the FAMAS' safety on and off belied that.

"Yeah," said Gaston. "I'm just worried."

"You'll do fine."

"I'm not worried about that." Gaston gestured toward the stalls. "If these horses panic during battle and break free, we'll be trampled to death."

JASON HEARD A commotion behind him as Jeanette and Sasha slid down the coal mound. As the women rushed over to him, his eyes narrowed. "Where's Slava?"

"I switched places with him," said Jeanette.

"Why?"

"Because I love you and want to be with you." Jeanette handed him the backpack and then leaned forward and kissed him. She spun him around and pushed him toward the hatch. "Go."

Jason didn't argue. Opening the hatch, he stepped onto the walkway and headed for the front of the train. Sasha followed, pausing to maneuver the minigun and ammunition pack through the small opening.

"What are you doing?" Jason asked.

"I'm providing you with cover."

"Okay, but stay here. I won't be long."

Jason rushed along the walkway and down the access ladder at the front of the engine. He crouched on the metal platform, steadying himself by leaning against the steel supports of the extended cow catcher. Glancing up, he hoped to see the portal in the distance, but it was still too far away. Jason unzipped the backpack, removed the device, and placed it on the platform. He draped the three straps over it and tightened them.

HANEEF AND KLIMENKO finished securing the M1910 onto the swivel mount. As Haneef loaded the ammunition belt, Klimenko stepped over to the cupola and called up to his friend.

"How long before the ravagers reach us?"

Barzukov replied, "They're already here."

CHAPTER FORTY-TWO

THE RAVAGERS DID not swarm the train in a single line. They approached like a stampeding herd. While they numbered twenty when counted abreast, their ranks were four or five deep stretching to the rear. Although the humans did not realize it yet, they faced over one hundred ravagers.

The first ten to reach the train jumped onto it as it raced past, tearing into the separate cars in a desperate effort to get at the food inside. As the train pulled away, the rest of the horde gave chase.

ONCE HE HAD secured the device, Jason climbed back up the access ladder. He had taken a few steps when an object flashed by in his peripheral vision. A moment later, a ravager landed on the walkway ten feet in front of him, facing Jason. Its cold black eyes bore in on him. With a hiss, the ravager lunged.

HANEEF AIMED THE M1910 at a ravager charging the prison car and fired a two-second burst, targeting its head. Instead, the rounds tore into the demon's chest, blasting off chunks of flesh and shredding internal organs. The ripped-apart carcass collapsed. Haneef knew it would regenerate and return. Three other ravagers trampled its body as they neared the prison car. Haneef swung the heavy machine gun in their direction.

Beside him, the female prisoner chained inside the cage pleaded. "Please don't do this! I'll never steal food again! I prom—"

The guard clasped a lever above his head and pulled down. When he did, the section of wall behind the cage swung to the side and a panel on the floor beneath the cylindrical cage tilted at a forty-five-degree angle, ejecting it out of the prison car. The female prisoner shrieked as it hit the ground, bounced once, and somersaulted end over end. Releasing it had the desired result. The three nearest ravagers veered from the train and chased after the cage.

Haneef swung his gun back toward the flank, scanning for another target.

VICKY CRIED OUT when something heavy landed on the roof of the stock car. Two more thuds followed a moment later. Frightened, the woman pointed her FAMAS toward the roof.

"Calm down," ordered Sook-kyoung.

"Shouldn't we be shooting them?"

"This car is covered in steel plates. It won't do any good. Conserve ammo. Wait until you can see your target."

"By then it'll be too late," quipped Gaston.

Scraping sounded against the roof as the ravagers used their talons to try and break in.

A RAVAGER LEAPT onto the dining car, coming to rest on the window in front of Antoine. It shoved its right arm through the bars and swiped at him. Antoine ducked out of the way. Leaning forward, he placed the barrel of his FAMAS against its skull and fired a three-round burst, blowing its head apart. The ravager fell away.

YURI FIRED RECKLESSLY into the approaching horde. Most of the Demon Spawn were too far away, and his bullets thudded harmlessly into the tundra.

Slava placed his hand on the kid's arm. "Slow down."

"I'm trying to stop them before they get to us."

"It's not going to happen." Slava raised his weapon into the high ready position. "Wait for them to come to us."

IAN STUCK THE barrel of his FAMAS out the broken window and fired at a ravager as it rushed past the first sleeper car. The rounds thudded into its thick flesh, not even slowing its pace. Turning left, the demon headed for him. Ian emptied the remainder of his magazine into it with no affect. It jumped onto the car, landing on the bars covering the window in front of him. Reaching in with its right hand, it slashed at Ian. Ian jumped back out of its reach. Popping out the empty magazine, he reached for a new one, fumbled with it for a second, and dropped it.

Werner stepped up and aimed his FAMAS at the ravager's head. It snarled as he squeezed the trigger. The three-shot burst decapitated the demon. The carcass slumped and slid off the car, its right arm caught between the bars. Werner slammed the stock of his weapon against the hand and wrist until the bones shattered and the ravager fell away.

NEAL JUMPED WHEN he heard the ravager land on the roof of the command car and cringed when its talons scraped across the metal surface. Then silence. He hugged the backpack with the anti-matter device against his chest. To his right, Lucifer and Lilith morphed into their demonic forms. To his left, Melnikov eyed the roof, trying to detect movement.

I MAY BE immortal, thought Luther, *but this in insane*. From atop the dining car, he had a better view of the approaching horde of ravagers, and for the first time realized how many they faced. Movement to his left and right caught Luther's attention. Three ravagers were on top of the stock car, and another had landed on the command car. He stepped over to Matthew and nudged his shoulder.

"You go help Neal and the others. I'll take care of those three."

"GET DOWN!" SASHA yelled.

Jason dropped to the walkway and covered his head as the minigun whirred to life. A two-second burst shredded the ravager's torso, splattering blood and gore across the boiler. The tattered remains dropped with a sickening plop. Jason climbed to his feet. The ravager had already begun to regenerate. Pulverized internal organs reformed and shredded skin healed. Jason reached for his crossbow and paused, going instead for the FAMAS. He unslung the weapon and released a five-round burst into the ravager's head. The lifeless corpse slid off the walkway. Sasha waved him on. Jason clutched the handrail and inched his way through the demonic detritus. Once on the other side, he raced for the cab.

"Thanks," Jason said when he reached Sasha. "That's the second time you saved my life."

"It's more like the fourth or fifth, but who's counting."

Jason crawled through the hatch into the cab and offered Sasha his hand. "I'll help you."

"I'm staying."

"Why?"

"It's too confined in there. I can defend us better from out here."

Jason wanted to argue, yet knew she was right. "Good luck."

"I'll be fine."

Jason kept the hatch open in case he needed to help Sasha.

"What now?" Jeanette asked.

"Now we fight our way to the portal." Jason tapped Iosif's shoulder. "How much longer until we get to the portal?"

"It's about fifteen miles from here, so another twenty or twenty-five minutes."

"Damn," Jason mumbled. He stepped over to the edge of the cabin and studied the horde.

Father Belsario came up beside him. "We're not going to make it, are we?"

Jason shrugged. "I don't know."

SVETLANA LEANED OUT the cab window and gauged the distance between her train and the steam engine up front. She brought her head back inside and ordered Mikhail, "Keep a thousand feet between us and Boris. I want to be close enough to help if anything happens."

"Yes, colonel."

Svetlana leaned out again, this time to check on her train. She noticed the four ravagers on top of the stock and command cars and realized how vulnerable they were. "Boris, Constantin. Climb up on the coal tender and make sure none of the demons get to us."

THE RELEASE OF another cage distracted several ravagers attempting to board the prison car. Those not lured away were brought down by gunfire from the heavy machine gun. Haneef took his time and chose his shots, waiting until a ravager got near before riddling it with bullets. He lined up his sights on a fast one that rushed through the horde and headed for them. When it got to within fifteen feet, Haneef squeezed the trigger. Five rounds spurt from the barrel before a clunk sounded from the weapon.

"Why'd you stop?" demanded Klimenko.

"It's jammed."

"Shit." Klimenko pushed Haneef aside and detached the ammunition slide.

Something heavy struck the side of the prison car. To Haneef's left, three talons slid through the gun slit. He fell to his right, the tips missing his face by inches. Although the ravager could not see inside the prison car, it flung its hand wildly, hoping to wound something. Haneef felt around with his right hand for his FAMAS. His fingers brushed against the stock. He grabbed the weapon and rolled onto his feet.

Before he could fire, the two guards had finished shackling a male prisoner into one of the cages to the left of the M1910. The prisoner screamed obscenities and kicked at them between the bars. One of the guards pulled the lever, opening the section of wall and tilting the floor panel. The cage slid out, bounced once, and toppled down an embankment. When it did, the ravager attached to the outside of the prison car joined five others in chasing the cage. The guard pushed the lever back into the closed position.

A ravager appeared in the opening, positioning itself between the door and jamb, preventing the former from closing all the way. The guard jiggered the lever yet succeeded only in attracting the ravager's attention. It slashed its hand downward, two of the talons slicing deep wounds across his face, opening the skin down to the skull and carving two long gouges in the bone. The third talon sliced across his chest and shoulder, nearly severing the left arm. The guard shrilled once and fell back against the wall, his body convulsing as it slid to the floor. The ravager pushed its way into the prison car.

Haneef stepped forward. It swung its head toward him and snarled. Haneef shoved the barrel into the ravager's mouth and fired two three-round bursts, blowing away the rear of its head. The demon slumped forward, its upper body caught between the door and jamb, its legs dangling over the rails. Haneef rushed over to the controls, leaned over the body of the still convulsing guard, and pulled down on the lever. The door opened, allowing the ravager to slide out. As they closed, Haneef noticed another ravager leaping toward the opening. He braced for death.

A burst of machine gun fire caught the demon in the chest, throwing the carcass into another charging demon.

"It's fixed." Klimenko waved to Haneef. "Take over. I have to help with the rest of the prisoners."

LUTHER DREW HIS broadsword and jumped from the dining to the stock car. The three ravagers were more interested in tearing their way through the steel-plated roof and did not notice him. Raising the weapon above his head, he brought it down across the nearest ravager's back, cleaving a two-inch-deep gash from its right shoulder to its left waist. The blade had fractured its spine but had not severed it. The ravager fell face down onto the roof. It tried to crawl back to its feet yet could only flail its limbs due to the damaged spinal column. As it regenerated, it bellowed in pain, which attracted the attention of the other two.

The ravager at the far end disappeared over the edge, dropping down between the stock and first baggage cars. The one in the center spun around to face Luther. It crouched, twisting its head from side to side as it sized up the threat. Luther raised the broadsword beside his head, waiting for the demon to attack. After a few seconds, it snarled and lunged. Luther slashed down with his weapon, slicing into the demon's right shoulder. It shrieked and jumped back, dislodging the blade and ripping away flesh and muscle. The ravager backed up to the end of the car, crouching again and examining its wound. Luther knew he had seconds before it healed. Lifting the broadsword to chest level and holding it horizontally, he charged.

Three talons scraped against Luther's lower right leg. A

bolt of fear shot through the Purgatoriati as he expected to be mauled. The crippled ravager had not yet fully regenerated and could only tear at his cloak. Still, it presented a threat that needed to be dealt with. Luther repositioned his broadsword so it pointed down and plunged it into the ravager's skull, twisting the tip so that it scrambled the demon's brains. Lifting it out of the shattered skull, Luther swung the blade vertically, using it like an axe to decapitate the ravager.

By now the wounded ravager at the far end of the stock car had regenerated enough to lunge again. Luther didn't have time to raise his weapon, so he dropped and rolled. It tripped and sprawled onto the roof. Both human and demon struggled to their feet. Luther rose first and swung his broadsword in a wide arc toward the ravager's head. The demon raised its left arm to block the blow, only to have the blade slice off its hand below the wrist. It cried out. Enraged, it jumped at the human. Luther swung his broadsword in the opposite direction. The blade connected with the ravager's abdomen, slicing through until it struck the ribcage. The force of the blow knocked it to one side. It toppled off the roof and slammed into the tundra, the body tumbling down the embankment.

Luther steadied his footing, raised the broadsword into the attack position, and scanned around him, searching for the third ravager.

SOOK-KYOUNG HEARD A fourth body land on the roof followed by a scuffle.

"What's going on?" Vicky asked.

"Why don't you go up and find out," Gaston chided.

"No!"

"Both of you, shut up." Sook-kyoung listened as one of the ravagers scrambled over the edge. Her eyes followed the noise, focusing on the door at the far end. A moment later, a pounding came from outside. "Shit."

"What?" Vicky asked.

"I got it," said Gaston as he pushed past the two women and rushed to secure the lock. He got within ten feet when the jamb gave way. The door sailed down the length of the car, slamming into Gaston and knocking him to the floor. The ravager jumped through and landed on the door, pinning Gaston beneath it. It cupped the back of Gaston's neck in its left hand and lifted his head, its fangs inches from his face.

Sook-kyoung switched her FAMAS to single shot mode, aimed, and yelled. When the ravager lifted its head, she fired. The demon shifted to one side so that the round thudded harmlessly into its shoulder. Before Sook-kyoung could shoot again, it lunged. She ran backwards and tripped over a pail of food. As she fell, the ravager plunged on top of her, squatting on her legs and pinning her chest to the floor with its right hand. Raising its left hand, it aimed its talons at her face and thrust. Sook-kyoung raised her FAMAS, deflecting the attack. Its talons dug into the floor beside Sook-kyoung's head.

"I could use some help here!"

Vicky stood at the other end of the car, frozen in fear. A wet patch formed around her crotch.

"Snap out of it!"

By now, all the horses were in a state of panic. The one beside Sook-kyoung kicked at its stall in a desperate attempt to escape. Its hind legs shattered two of the slats, showering the ravager's face with shards of wood. The demon swung its head in that direction. Sook-kyoung yanked her FAMAS from under its hand and slammed the weapon as hard as she could across the side of its head. The blow merely angered it. The ravager knocked the weapon away, pinned both her arms, and leaned into her face. Opening its mouth, the demon roared. Sook-kyoung screamed back, both out of terror and in defiance.

Watching her friend about to die snapped Vicky out of her fear. Firing her FAMAS at this range would catch Sook-kyoung in the crossfire. She looked around for another weapon and found it in a pitchfork stuck in a mound of hay. She grabbed the handle and held it in front of her. "Hey, asshole."

The ravager lifted its head. When it did, Vicky drove the prongs into its eyes. It howled in agony. Vicky lifted the pitchfork, forcing the demon to stand. It flung its head around, trying to break free. Vicky drove the prongs deeper into its head until the tips scraped against the back of its skull. She moved forward, directing the ravager around Gaston and toward the rear of the car. It shuddered and occasionally took a desultory swing at her. When it began to regenerate, Vicky would twist the prongs, reopening the wounds. After several seconds that seemed like an eternity, she reached the opening and shoved the ravager through. It toppled backward, bounced off the baggage car, and fell onto the tracks where the wheels ground up the carcass. Vicky took several steps back until her feet stumbled against the unhinged door. Keeping her eyes on the empty jamb, she knelt and shook Gaston.

"Are you all right?"

"I think so," he replied.

Sook-kyoung joined them and helped Vicky lift the door off Gaston. He stood and moved his arms and legs. "Nothing's broken, but I'm going to be sore in the morning."

Sook-kyoung handed Gaston his FAMAS. "Let's hope we live that long."

LUCIFER AND LILITH circled around Neal and Ustagov, their gaze fixed on the command car roof. Every time the ravager moved, its talons scraping against the metal, the two were-hounds growled. Melnikov stood off to one side, his AK-47 aimed at the ceiling.

"Do you think it's scared of them?" Ustagov asked, motioning to Lucifer and Lilith.

"I hope so," said Neal.

"Don't count on it." Melnikov followed the scraping to the

end of the command car. "If it was scared, it would have run away by now. It's trying to find—"

Talons punctured the roof and ripped along its surface, creating three long gouges. They tore through again, this time perpendicular to the first set, creating a hashtag pattern. A moment later, the ravager crashed through the weakened section. It scanned the car, searching for a target. Ustagov grabbed Neal by the arm and shoved him toward Svetlana's quarters. Melnikov raised his AK-47 as the ravager lunged.

Lucifer dove into the demon. He pushed it against the wall, his horns and the spikes around his shoulders digging into the ravager and holding it in place. Its talons raked against his back but could not penetrate the scales. The ravager grew frantic, bellowing and thrashing to break free. Lilith moved in for the kill. Slinking up on its right, she plunged her scorpion-like tail into its chest, injecting it with paralyzing fluid. At first the fluid had no effect. The ravager screeched and flailed its talons at Lilith's tail. After a few seconds, it grew sluggish, and the shrieking tapered off into a whimper. Its body went limp. Lucifer inched away, prepared to attack again if the ravager reawakened. Lilith removed her stinger. As Melnikov walked up to the ravager, the werehounds moved aside. The captain raised his AK-47 and fired ten rounds into its head, shattering its skull and splattering brains along the wall.

"Do you need help down there?" Matthews knelt by the gouged-out section of roof, peering down into the command car.

Melnikov shook his head. "We're fine. Stay there and let us know if any more ravagers are coming."

FOUR RAVAGERS CLOSED in on the lead engine. Sasha stepped away from the cab to get a better line of sight, shifting her gaze from one to the other. All four lunged at the same time. One aimed for the front of the train and two for the tender, while the fourth headed for her. Sasha would have to time this perfectly. She fired a three-second burst into the nearest one. The hail of bullets shredded the demon, showering her in blood and pieces of body parts. Without wasting time to wipe herself off, Sasha spun to her left as the second ravager landed on the walkway. Rather than charge, it rushed toward the anti-matter device. Sasha fired. A dozen rounds tore into its back, dropping it to the walkway. Despite its wounds, it clawed its way toward the device. Sasha kept up the barrage until the ravager stopped moving and rolled off the train.

Sasha did not notice the ravager on the roof of the cab until it pounced onto her back.

FATHER BELSARIO HAD started to crawl through the hatch to help Sasha when the two ravagers launched themselves at the tender. He jumped back inside as the first landed on the coal and lunged at those in the cab. Jeanette pulled Iosif out of the way. Vladimir attempted to duck as the ravager swiped at him, but the bottom talon sliced through his head above the eyes.

Father Belsario did not have room to use his broadsword, so he bent over and body checked the ravager, pushing it toward the edge of the platform. At the last second, it reached out and dug its talons into the walls of the cab and the accompanying tender. The cleric did not have the strength to dislodge it, and the ravager could not risk releasing its hold to attack the human. Iosif grabbed the shovel from the tender. He drove the blade into the ravager's neck, slicing three inches into its throat. It still could not be pushed out.

"Get out of the way," warned Jeanette as she raised her FAMAS. Belsario and Iosif jumped to the side. Jeanette emptied half a magazine into the ravager's arm, severing it above the elbow. With nothing left to support it, the ravager tumbled out of the cab.

Jason missed all of this. He had been focusing on the second ravager to jump onto the tender, preparing to take it down. Instead, the demon vaulted over the roof of the cab, tackling Sasha from behind and pinning her to the walkway. Because of the ammunition backpack, it could not get to her. Jason hurried through the hatch. Raising his weapon above his head, he charged the ravager and slammed the stock against the base of its skull, hoping to snap its spine. He succeeded only in infuriating it. The ravager spun around and lashed out with its right hand. Jason stumbled back, the talons missing his face by inches. When he fell onto the walkway, the FAMAS dropped over the side. The ravager lifted its left arm to slice open Jason.

Sasha rolled onto her side and raised the minigun in front of its arm so it could not attack Jason. The ravager snarled at her. Jason took advantage of the opportunity. He grabbed the handrail, placed his legs between the steam engine and the ravager, and twisted his lower body to the right, knocking the legs out from under it. The ravager crashed onto the walkway and rolled off, its talons digging into the metal at the last second to prevent it falling. It kicked with its legs, trying to get a foothold. Sasha aimed the minigun at its head and squeezed the trigger. The gun whirred but nothing happened. The ammunition belt had come unfastened during the melee. Sasha kicked at the ravager's claw, catching it with the heel of her boot. It slid back a few inches, enough that its legs became intertwined with the drivers. The drivers ripped the ravager loose and flung it under the massive steel wheels, which ground the demon into pulp.

Jason stood and helped Sasha to her feet. "Are you okay?"

"I'm immortal, remember." She stepped over to him. "The ammunition belt came lose. Help me connect it."

It took Jason a few seconds to reattach the belt. As he finished, Sasha mumbled, "Oh dear God."

Jason followed her gaze back toward the train, not prepared for what he saw.

HANEEF HAD LOST count of how many ravagers he had taken down or how many had abandoned the chase to go after the prisoner cages. He figured another fifty or sixty, probably more, still bore down on the train, as well as the wounded ravagers that would regenerate and rejoin the fray. The number surrounding the prison car increased steadily.

The guards had shoved another prisoner into the last cage on the starboard side, a young man so frightened he offered no resistance. When the guard released the cage, it slammed into a ravager, ricocheted off the train, and then across the tundra where five more ravagers went after it.

"We're done here," said the guard.

"Fill the cages on the other side," Klimenko ordered. "We have to get these things off us."

"How much ammunition do you have?" Haneef asked.

"Not enough. We never expected this many before."

As if on cue, five ravagers bore down on the prison car. Haneef took aim at the nearest. The ravagers diverted away from the prison car and raced forward. After a few moments, Haneef could no longer see them through the firing slit. Neither could Klimenko. The Russian leaned back and yelled up to Barzukov.

"What's going on?"

He got no answer.

Getting to his feet, Klimenko stepped over to the cupola and shook Barzukov by the leg. "Didn't you hear me? What's going on?"

Barzukov sat still, his gaze fixed out the window toward the front of the train. After a few seconds he mumbled, "We're all going to die."

SLAVA AND THE other Russians in the third sleeping car had maintained a steady stream of fire against any ravager that came near. Despite the horde swarming around the train, only a dozen or so had attacked, all of which had been dispatched. Without warning, forty ravagers descended on the sleeping car at once, jumping onto the roof or clamoring onto the starboard side, digging their talons into the walls and clutching the bars over the windows. Throughout the car, gunfire increased in intensity. Slava and Yuri each took down one, only to have others take their place. At least none of them would be able to break through the barred windows.

"What was that?" Yuri asked.

"What are you talking about?"

The sleeping car swayed gently. "That."

What had started as a gentle rocking motion became more intense. The realization struck Slava.

"Clear these things off the sleeper! Now!"

"COLONEL," BORIS CALLED from the top of the tender. "You have to see this."

Svetlana crawled up the coal pile and joined Boris. For the first time in dealing with the demons, she felt true fear.

Most of the surviving horde had attached themselves to the three sleepers, covering the cars like locusts and rocking back and forth. With each sway, the cars tilted more to starboard. Svetlana had underestimated the intelligence of the ravagers. This wasn't a swarm attack. They were trying to derail the train!

"We have to detach the engine."

ANTOINE FELT THE rocking motion. At first, he attributed it to the train's speed until it became more pronounced. Moving over to the window, he watched as the ravagers swarmed the sleeping cars, trying to derail them. Nothing attacked the last five cars of the train. He wouldn't have time to evacuate everyone from the center, but at least he could save a part of the train.

Rushing to the rear door, Antoine pulled it aside, knelt, and lifted the iron plate that covered the gap between the dining and stock cars. The cut-lever sat along the edge of the dining car beneath his feet. He grabbed it and yanked. The coupler lock lifted and the couplers disconnected. A series of pops sounded as the brake lines detached, followed by a ripping noise as the protective covering between the two cars tore apart. Once separated, the last six cars fell behind the rest of the train. Everyone inside those cars would survive the inevitable derailing but would be left vulnerable to the ravagers.

"SOMETHING STRANGE IS going on," Matthew shouted down to the others.

"What?" Melnikov asked.

"The ravagers have swarmed the sleeping cars and are rocking them."

Ustagov raced over to one of the windows and twisted his head to get a better view. "They're trying to tip the train over! We have to uncouple the engine!"

"No," argued Neal. "That'll strand us and leave us at the mercy of those things."

"If they derail the engine, we're all screwed." Ustagov shifted his gaze to the captain. "Do it."

Melnikov rushed to the door leading to the sleeper cars, with Matthew moving along the roof to cover him. Melnikov lifted the iron plate between the two cars and yanked up on the cut-lever, disconnecting the couplers. The command car jerked forward as the steam engine, running at full speed, pulled away from the rolling stock, knocking Melnikov off balance. He grabbed the door railing as the protective covering tore apart around him, exposing him kneeling in the open doorway.

"Watch out!" yelled Matthew.

Melnikov glanced up. A ravager on the edge of the sleeping car had spotted him, shifted its position, and lunged. The captain moved back. The ravager reached out with its right claw and dug its talons into Melnikov's chest, pulling him out of the doorway. The two crashed onto the rails to be crushed beneath the rolling stock.

At that precise moment, all Hell broke loose.

THE SLEEPER AND dining cars tilted farther to starboard with each rock of the ravagers until the port wheels lifted several inches off the tracks. They teetered for several seconds. The weight of the ravagers swarming the starboard walls became too great and the three cars tipped. The lead sleeper toppled first, crushing more than twenty ravagers beneath it and churning up rocks and dirt. The eight Russian soldiers inside were tossed about. Those not killed outright died when the second sleeper clipped its rear end, spinning the first one hundred eighty degrees and snapping it in half. With its structural integrity weakened, the car collapsed, crushing everyone or spewing bodies across the tundra.

As the first car derailed, the ravagers on the remaining two jumped clear to avoid being killed, scattering like cockroaches. In the second sleeper, Werner and Ian felt the car going off the tracks. Werner grabbed onto the framing for one of the bunks. Ian rushed into the corridor and placed his back against an interior wall. When the sleeper fell onto its side, both men were showered in shattered glass. The car shuddered as it collided with the lead sleeper. Werner bounced around, slamming repeatedly into the bed frame. Ian slid across the wall and dropped into the adjoining cabin, grabbing the windowless frame at the last second. In some of the other cabins, Russian soldiers screamed for help. After five seconds of sliding along the ground, the sleeper came to a stop.

Being preoccupied with clearing ravagers off the side of the train, Slava did not realize they were about to derail until the sleeping car he was in toppled over. He reached out to grab hold of anything. Instead, he was thrown against the roof and knocked unconscious.

In the dining car, Antoine had anticipated the derailment. He dove into a pantry on the port side and yelled for the others to hang on. The diner rolled onto the dirt and slid for several seconds before coming to rest at a twenty-degree angle to the tracks. Because of the warning, and being the last car to derail, those inside suffered minor bumps and bruises. For a moment, everything went eerily quiet. Then two sounds penetrated the silence: the moans and cries for help from the wounded and the ravagers swarming in for a second attack.

CHAPTER FORTY-THREE

"**T**HERE IT IS!" Iosif pointed to his left. Jason stepped over to the port side of the cab and leaned over the side. Off in the distance, the portal shimmered above the tracks. At this distance, it appeared no larger than a baseball. He could not tell if any Demon Spawn guarded it.

"How far is it?" he asked.

"About six miles from here," answered Iosif. "Another ten minutes, probably—"

"Jason!" yelled Sasha. "The rest of the train is in trouble."

Jason scrambled up to the top of the coal tender, with Jeanette and Father Belsario behind him. From their vantage point, they watched the four cars derail until clouds of dirt obscured the crash scene. Only the armored train remained visible a thousand feet behind them.

"We have to go back and help," said Jeanette.

"No." Jason slid down the coal pile.

"They'll die if we don't."

"They'll die even if we go back," snapped Jason. He softened his tone. "Our best chance of helping them is to close the portal and kill the ravagers."

When Jeanette protested, Father Belsario placed a hand on her shoulder. "As heartless as it sounds, he's right. Closing the portal is the most important thing."

"You're right." Jeanette's gaze fixed on Jason, her eyes pleading for forgiveness. "Sorry."

Sasha leaned into the cab again. "Save the group grope for later. We have company at two o'clock."

Jason moved over to the starboard side of the cab. Ten ravagers charged them from a thousand feet out.

"WHY ARE WE slowing down?" Vicky asked. "And what was that noise?"

Sook-kyoung ignored the questions. Instead, she made her way through the stock car. When she opened the forward door, she gasped. The derailed rolling stock spread out for several hundred feet in front of them. Cries of help came from inside the wrecked cars. Despite the cloud of dust hovering over the site, she detected movement in the dining car.

Something dropped onto the platform at the other end of the stock car. Sook-kyoung, Vicky, and Gaston spun around and raised their weapons. Instead of a ravager, Luther stood in the center of the opening. "Shut that door and come here."

"Why?"

Luther walked to the center and spun around to face the other door, his broadsword drawn and ready to attack. "We have a dozen ravagers bearing down on us."

BARZUKOV HAD BEEN providing his comrades with a blow-by-blow description of what he witnessed from the cupola, including the derailment of the four forward cars.

"Did anyone survive the crash?" Klimenko asked.

"I can't tell. There's too much dust." Barzukov leaned from one side to the other, trying to get a better view. "Shit!"

"What?"

"The ravagers are swarming the derailed cars. If anyone survived, they won't last long."

"How many are coming toward us?"

"None," said Barzukov.

"We have to help them," said Haneef.

"Are you nuts? If we let those things know we're here,

they'll come after us next."

"Don't be an asshole," barked Klimenko. "Once they kill off the others, they'll come after us anyway."

Haneef knelt by the heavy machine gun and unfastened the weapon from its mounts. Klimenko walked past and tapped him on the shoulder. "Don't waste your time with that. We'd have to set it up outside where we'd be exposed."

"What will we fight them with?"

"This." Klimenko opened a locker and revealed a pair of flamethrowers. He offered one to Haneef. "Have you ever used one of these before?"

"Never."

"Then today's your lucky day."

Klimenko helped Haneef strap on his flamethrower before donning his own. The two men made their way to the rear of the car and exited onto the platform. Haneef used the access ladder to crawl to the roof. Klimenko leaned back inside.

"Barzukov, stay here and keep an eye on the prisoners."

IAN DANGLED FROM the windowless frame of the cabin he had nearly fallen in to, his hands bleeding and throbbing from being sliced open by shattered glass. Something moved up behind him. Ian braced himself for death. Instead, a Russian lieutenant with blood streaming down his face from a gash across his forehead grabbed Ian under his arm and lifted him up to the interior wall.

"Thanks, mate" said Ian.

"You okay?"

Ian nodded. "How many others survived?"

The lieutenant yelled something in Russian and received three responses. He excused himself and made his way forward, careful not to fall into the empty cabins.

From two cabins down Werner called out. "Ian, is that you?"

"It's me."

"I could use some help here."

Ian crawled toward the cabin. He found Werner dangling from the bed frame. Lying prone, Ian wrapped one arm around the shattered window frame and reached down with the other. "Come on, mate."

Werner took Ian's hand in his left and pulled himself up enough to clasp the door jamb with his right. Once he had the leverage, Werner climbed up onto the interior wall. He tried to catch his breath.

"Are you hurt?"

Werner shook his head. "I'm banged up and bruised, but nothing's broken."

The lieutenant came back with two other soldiers. "I have one man up front with two broken legs. We'll have to come back for him. Right now, we have to get out of here."

"What about the ravagers?" Ian asked.

"Let me check." The lieutenant stood and stuck his head through one of the shattered window frames along the port wall where the bars had been torn off. A blood-curdling screech emanated from outside. The lieutenant's body stiffened. A second later, his head fell through the window, bounced off the interior wall, and rolled into one of the cabins. The body dropped beside Ian and draped over a section of interior wall. A ravager stuck its head through the frame where the lieutenant had stood a moment ago. Five more dropped through a gash in the port wall at the front end. Three of them slunk into the cabin that held the soldier with the broken legs; his screams echoed through the sleeper. The other two spread out, eyeing the remaining humans.

Upon seeing Ian, the ravager that had butchered the lieutenant curled its lips back and exposed its fangs. Ian shoved the barrel of his FAMAS into its mouth and fired off seven rounds, vaporizing its head and propelling the carcass backwards off the train. Before the body hit the rails, Ian yelled, "Let's go!"

A ravager pounced on one of the soldiers, driving the talons of its right hand through his shoulders and pinning him to the interior wall. The demon used its other set of talons to slice open the Russian's left side, spilling his intestines across the interior wall. The second soldier removed his Makarov from its holster and fired three rounds into the ravager's chest. It collapsed onto the eviscerated soldier, its talons still imbedded in his back. Shifting his aim, the Russian emptied the rest of his magazine into the face of the approaching ravager. The demon mewled once and went limp across a door frame, the weight of its upper body dragging the carcass into the cabin. Still clutching the Makarov, the soldier lay prone across the door jambs and crawled as fast as possible toward the end of the car.

Werner also headed for the rear exit, slowing at every jamb to navigate the opening so he didn't fall into a cabin. Ian moved up to the roof of the sleeping car where the interior wall ran above the doors, allowing him to scurry toward the rear exit with ease. When he reached the end, he crouched on the interior wall, aimed his FAMAS at the door, and grabbed the handle with his left hand. As he opened it, he half expected a ravager to lunge. The last sleeper sat thirty feet away, and there was nothing between the two cars. Ian swung himself outside. Planting his feet on the door railing for support, he leaned back inside and held out his hand to Werner.

"Come on, mate!"

Werner quickened his pace, pulling himself along the interior wall. He was crossing over the last door jamb when a ravager plunged through the window above him. The two fell into the cabin. Ian winced when he heard Werner's body thud against the shattered glass and metal of the cabin wall and puked when he heard the ravager sink its teeth into his friend's body. He backed out of the car. Before Ian could slide the door shut, the sole surviving Russian called out.

"Don't lock me in here."

The soldier was twenty feet from the exit. Ian waved him

on. Behind him, the three ravagers emerged from the first cabin, their faces and claws covered in blood. The one that had been shot in the chest had regenerated and fixed its gaze on the Russian. All four raced toward him.

"Move your ass!" Ian aimed his FAMAS and fired a three-round burst into the face of the nearest ravager. It flipped onto its side, the body slamming into the one behind it, slowing it down. The soldier crawled faster. Ian shifted his aim onto the third ravager, which raced up the uninterrupted stretch of interior wall, and fired. Anticipating the attack, it jumped to one side and moved in on the soldier. Ian switched aimed and emptied the remainder of his magazine into the demon. It cried out and collapsed.

As the soldier neared the exit, Ian reached in and yanked him to safety. Behind the Russian, the fourth ravager closed in for the kill. It lunged toward the open door.

SLAVA VAGUELY HEARD the screaming and gunfire around him. His senses spiked, however, when something grabbed his shoulders. His hand felt around for his FAMAS as his eyes popped open. Instead of staring into the face of a ravager, Yuri stared back at him with a sense of relief.

"You've been out a full minute," said Yuri. "I thought you were dead."

"I feel like it." When Slava moved, every muscle in his body ached. As Slava struggled to his feet, he realized he had been lying in a pool of blood, demon body parts, shattered glass, and twisted metal. A section of the cabin roof had broken away, exposing a three-foot wide hole partially buried by dirt. The only thing that had saved him from being torn apart like the rest of the cabin was the mattress that had landed beneath him when they derailed. Rolling onto his hands and knees, Slava attempted to stand. His left leg throbbed, causing him to cry out.

"Is it broken?" Yuri asked.

"No. It hurts, though." Slava put pressure on the leg and winced. "It's sprained, that's all."

Above them, yelling and gunfire mixed as a group of ravagers ripped their way through the sleeper and attacked the Russian soldiers in other cabins.

"We have to get out of here," said Slava.

"What about the others?"

A terrified scream came from the adjacent cabin. "It's too late for them."

Slava bent down and used his hands to shovel dirt out of the hole in the roof until he cleared away enough to fit through. Slava rolled onto his back and stuck out his head. Ravagers swarmed the four derailed cars. He didn't see any on the ground. It was a long shot, yet they had no other choice.

Slava pushed back inside the cabin. "Where's my weapon?"

"It fell out while the car slid along the ground."

"Shit." Slava thought for a moment. "Follow me."

"Where are we going?" A burst of automatic weapons fire tore through the bulkhead above Yuri's head, forcing him to duck.

"Any place but here."

Slava crawled out and stood with his back against the roof of the sleeper. A three-foot-long section of metal pipe sat in the debris field ten feet from the wreck. Slava rushed out, picked it up, and dashed back against the sleeper, praying none of the ravagers spotted him. They had not.

Yuri emerged through the hole and climbed to his feet. "Where to now?"

"Which car has the most armor plating?"

"The prison car at the end of the train."

"Then that's where we're heading. Stay low and move fast."

ANTOINE OPENED THE door to the pantry and crawled out. Blood, shattered glass, and debris covered the starboard wall of the dining car. Several tables had broken loose from their floor mounts and sat at awkward angles. In the middle of the carnage, a ravager with no right arm or leg twitched uncontrollably, its regeneration taking longer than usual due to the extent of its injuries. Throughout the car, the Russians stood up and rummaged through the debris for their weapons.

"Is everyone alive?" Antoine asked.

"Yes, but some of us are hurt badly. We're well enough to fight, though."

"We'll be doing a lot of that soon." Antoine examined the windows above him. All the bars appeared to still be in place over the panes.

"What are we going to do?"

"Hang on a minute." Antoine went over to the rear door. He knew the derailed portion of the train presented a sitting duck for ravagers. If the rest of the rolling stock had not derailed, maybe they could fight their way to them and make a last stand from there. Grabbing the handle, Antoine slid it open and exhaled audibly. The last six cars had not derailed and sat less than two hundred feet away. If they could make it there before the ravagers got them, they might—

A ravager centered itself in the doorway and snarled. Antoine raised his FAMAS and fired several rounds point blank into its face and chest, ripping the demon apart and flinging its body onto the tracks. No sooner had he shot the first ravager when three more pushed their way through the opening and into the dining car.

THE HORSES WENT wild as ravagers landed on the sides and roof of the stock car. Sook-kyoung and Luther had taken up position near the rear door, with Vicky and Gaston in the middle as back up. Sook-kyoung knew that at any moment ravagers would swarm through the opening. Their chances of surviving were small. One made its way along the roof and dropped onto the platform outside. On spotting the humans, it snarled. Luther drove the tip of his broadsword into its face, pushing the blade until it smashed through the back of its head. Luther placed his right foot on the demon's abdomen and shoved. The ravager slid off the blade and fell onto the tracks. Alerted by the first ravager, the others swarmed along the stock car toward the door.

Sook-kyoung took down the next ravager that landed on the platform with two three-round burst that flung it against the baggage car. Five rounds had punctured its chest and the sixth struck it in the forehead above and to the right of its eye, blowing out a portion of its skull. It lay against the wall, mewling and twitching as its head wound healed.

Two more entered one after the other. They came in over the upper lip of the door and crawled along the ceiling like spiders. Before Sook-kyoung or Luther could stop them, the ravagers split up and descended into the first two stalls on either side, tearing into the horses. The cries from the slaughtered animals were chilling, causing the remaining horses to panic. Vicky ran up to the first stall on the left and emptied her FAMAS, killing the ravager as well as putting the terrified animal out of its misery. Gaston did the same on the right, using three three-round bursts.

A fifth and sixth ravager attempted to push through the open door, one dropping to the platform and rushing in, the other spider walking along the ceiling. Luther disposed of the latter, slashing the broadsword from left to right and cleaving off its head. Sook-kyoung fired on the ravager on the platform, emptying the remainder of her FAMAS into its face. The headless carcass slumped across the floor. "I need to reload," she said. "Someone spot me."

"I've got it." Gaston moved up on Sook-kyoung's right. He raised his weapon into the high ready position and gently applied pressure on the trigger, waiting for the next ravager to attack.

Sook-kyoung heard six more scurrying around the roof.

AS HANEEF REACHED the second baggage car, he spotted the six ravagers hovering around the edge of the stock car, searching for a way to break inside. He stopped in the middle of the roof and motioned to the prison guard accompanying him.

"Fire a burst into those things."

The guard stepped in front of Haneef and released ten rounds into the pack of ravagers. The bullets thudded into them, succeeding in attracting their attention. Upon seeing the new prey, all six broke into a run, charging across the top of the baggage cars. The guard fell back behind Haneef, taking up a position ten feet to his rear. Haneef raised the barrel of the flamethrower and waited. When they were halfway across the second baggage car, he squeezed the trigger.

The first three ravagers caught the full force of the attack. The flames washed over them, incinerating them. The lead one collapsed onto the roof of the baggage car, thrashing around for several moments before the flames cooked its muscles and melted its brain. The other two fell over the side and rolled in the dirt. A stream of fire caught the fourth ravager in its face; it jumped off the baggage car and rushed into the tundra, screeching at the top of its lungs. Untouched by the flames but frightened, the last two dove off the train and scurried toward the shelter of the derailed cars.

Haneef ran up to the edge of the first baggage car. The guard stayed with him, his eyes scanning the area in case the ravagers doubled back. Haneef dropped to one knee and leaned over.

"Are you all right?"

"Yes," answered Sook-kyoung. "Do you need help?"

"No. Stay where you are and protect the horses. We've got things up here." Haneef said to Klimenko, who had just joined him, "You stay here and keep those things from getting into the stock car. We'll check on the others."

"LET US OUT," pleaded one of the remaining prisoners.

"Shut up," snapped Barzukov.

"We're no good to you now that the train has stopped. We can help you fight these things."

"I said shut up!" Barzukov stared through the front window of his cupola, watching as Haneef set fire to the ravagers around the baggage car. He had already taken down four of them in under a minute. Maybe their crazy scheme would work aft—

One of the female prisoners screamed. Barzukov glanced down. She stood in her cage, terror etched across her face. He followed her gaze out the rear door and down the tracks, and immediately understood her reaction.

Barzukov had forgotten about the ravagers that had given up chasing the train to go after the caged prisoners they had dropped along the way. With that food supply now gone, those ravagers, eighteen in total, as well as another half dozen wounded ones that had fallen in battle and regenerated, had given chase and were closing in on the immobile prison car.

JASON STUDIED THE pack of ravagers closing in on the engine. They were less than five hundred feet away. Sasha and Father Belsario took up position on the starboard walkway, ready to defend the train. Jeanette stood behind him watching their rear. Yet something bothered Jason. This attack seemed different. Ravagers usually swarmed their target en masse. This time, while half the demons descended on them, the rest veered right and rushed to a location in front of the train.

"What's ahead of us?" Jason asked Iosif.

"You mean Lake Baikal?"

"No." Jason pointed to the ravagers moving away from the engine. "Where are they going?"

Iosif leaned out the window and swore. "Shit. They're heading for the junction box."

"What's that?"

"It's where the main rail line branches off onto the spur that leads to the portal. Last time we were here, the colonel set the junction to put a train onto the spur. If those things change it, we'll have to stop to reset it."

"Which will make us sitting ducks."

"Exactly."

Jason climbed out onto the walkway, maneuvered past Father Belsario, and made his way to Sasha.

"Get back inside," she warned him. "We're about to be attacked."

"Never mind about them." He pointed in front of the train. "Concentrate on taking out the ones ahead of us. They're going to switch the junction box and send us away from the portal."

Sasha rushed down to the front of the walkway. Jason stayed near to provide cover. The engine barreled toward the junction yet had not lessened the distance enough for her to get an accurate shot. Sasha waited until the first ravager approached to within a hundred feet of the junction box and fired a two-second burst. At this distance half the rounds missed, although enough struck that the ravager ran away to avoid the pain. She fired at the next two. These did not break and run. They raced ahead until they reached the junction box. Sasha fired a five-second burst that took them both down.

Jason missed this, concentrating instead on the six ravagers about to swarm the engine. One launched itself at Sasha. Jason opened fire with his FAMAS, catching it with a burst to the chest that tossed it back onto the tundra.

Two ravagers landed on either side of Father Belsario. The one on the left spun around to lunge at Jason. Belsario stepped to his left and swung his broadsword in a wide arc at waist level. The blade sliced half-way through the demon's abdomen and lodged in its internal organs. From behind him, the second ravager attacked. Belsario flattened himself against the boiler, allowing the second ravager to land on the first. Father Belsario grabbed the railing with his left hand and the hilt of his sword with the right and kicked the wounded ravager Spawn off the train. It hit the ground and somersaulted, spilling its guts and intestines in the process. The second ravager also slid off, but at the last moment managed to grip the edge of the walkway and pull itself up. Father Belsario repositioned the broadsword and sliced off its head. The ravager spasmed once before its lifeless body slid off the train.

The last three attacked the cab. Two landed on the tender and rushed Jeanette and Iosif. Jeanette sprayed her FAMAS back and forth between the two ravagers. One collapsed onto the coal, kicking and screeching from a wound that tore open its abdomen. The other leapt over the tender and attached itself to the rear wall, out of Jeanette's line of sight. She switched her aim back to the wounded ravager, emptied her magazine into its head, and reloaded. The third ravager mounted the cab roof and paused, waiting for Jeanette to be distracted so it could attack, its back to Father Belsario. He held the broadsword in his hand like a spear and chucked it. The blade sliced into the ravager's back, severing its spinal column. It went limp, collapsed to the roof, and rolled off, taking Belsario's broadsword with it.

By now, three more ravagers reached the junction box. One grabbed the mechanism to shift the tracks. Sasha blasted it apart with a five-second burst of gunfire from her minigun. The other two attempted to take its place and met a similar fate. Having doubled back, the first ravager raced for the switch. The engine reached the junction first and veered left onto the spur leading to the portal, tilting precariously for several seconds due to its high speed. Jason and Sasha clutched the railing and braced themselves. Father Belsario had not seen the curve approaching and would have been thrown off if he had not grabbed the rim of the open hatch at the last second. As the engine cleared the junction, the ravager reached the switch and swung the mechanism, shifting the tracks back to the main line.

Jason placed a hand on Sasha's shoulder. "We made it. It's clear sailing to the portal."

"I hate to disappoint you." Sasha's eyes were tired and desperate. "But it's not."

SVETLANA GRINNED AS Jason's engine made the turn and proceeded toward the portal. In less than five minutes they would deploy the anti-matter device. With luck, they might just–

The major had not noticed the ravager as it manipulated the junction switch, so she was shocked when her engine continued straight along the main rail. Nor did she see the ravager give chase to the train as it rushed past. Svetlana stepped over to the driver's controls and applied the brakes. The drivers locked and the engine lurched at the sudden decrease in speed. Metal squealed against metal and sparks flew from the tracks as more than one hundred tons of steel skidded along the rails. The driver and fireman were thrown against the boiler's bulkhead. Svetlana slammed into the controls. On top of the tender, the two soldiers standing guard fell forward, toppling down the coal until they hit the interior wall of the bin. Because of this, neither of them noticed the ravager jump onto the roof of the command car and scurry toward the hole ripped into the roof.

Inside the command car, the sudden drop in speed tossed everyone and everything around. Lucifer and Lilith slid forward, banging into furniture along the way. Knocked off balance, Neal dropped the backpack containing the anti-matter device and staggered against the port wall. Matthew, who had been staring out the back window keeping watch, grabbed hold of the door handle. Ustagov, who stood beside him, stumbled backward and tripped over the backpack. As his shoulders hit the floor, the ravager dropped through the gash in the roof and landed on his chest. It raised a claw above the Russian's head, pointing the talons at his face.

"No!" Neal pushed himself off the wall and charged the ravager, hoping to shove it off Ustagov. It spun around at the sound of his voice and swung its hand, slicing three deep gashes across Neal's chest. He stopped, his body going into shock. His eyes fell onto the wounds. Blood trickled from the gashes, which soon began hemorrhaging. The wounds opened, spilling his internal organs and intestines. Neal dropped to his knees, landing in his own gore, before collapsing. The ravager jumped to its feet to feed off Neal's viscera. It did not notice Matthew come up behind it, his broadsword drawn. With one swing, Matthew decapitated the demon.

Ustagov crawled over to check on Neal, his knees smearing blood across the floor. Although his eyes were open, Neal stared into space. His breathing grew labored. Ustagov patted him on the cheek. "Kid, are you still with us?"

Neal's lifeless eyes stared up at the ceiling. "Doc?"

"It's me."

"Are you okay?"

"Yes. You saved my life."

"Good." Neal tried to lift his hand but did not have the energy. "Do me a favor."

"Anything, kid."

"The devices. Help Jason with them. Please."

"Of course, I will."

"Thank—" Neal's head slumped forward.

ANTOINE FELL BACK, spraying the three ravagers with gunfire as they swarmed through the open door until his FAMAS ran out of ammunition. Two of the Russian soldiers joined him. The demons were gunned down before they made it to the humans but would recover quickly. Attracted by the noise, five more rushed inside. Two tackled the soldiers on either side of Antoine, knocking them down and ripping into their flesh. The other three charged the Moroccan.

With no time to reload, Antoine dropped his weapon and grabbed the central base of one of the dining tables that had been dislodged. He swung it back and forth, knocking the three ravagers aside. Antoine retreated halfway down the dining car, past where the two soldiers were being slaughtered, and brandished the table in front of him like a sword. As each ravager attacked, he slammed the top into its face. It kept them away for several seconds, but Antonine knew sooner or later they would overwhelm him.

BARZUKOV SAT FROZEN in terror as the pack of ravagers rushed through the open rear door and tore into the last four prisoners. He wanted to cover his ears so he didn't hear the screams of those being devoured alive and the maddening slurping of the ravagers as they fed yet knew, if he moved, he would give away his presence. He shut his eyes and tried to drown out the hellish sounds. The tortured screeching soon died out, leaving only the sounds of the rending and chewing of flesh. Despite his fear, Barzukov slowly opened his eyes. Down below, one of the ravagers stared up at him, its head cocked to one side. Barzukov yelled. When he did, the ravager sprang into the cupola, ripping apart Barzukov with its talons and splattering blood across the windows.

A burst of gunfire from the forward part of the train attracted the ravagers' attention. As a pack, they raced out and swarmed toward the derailed cars.

IAN PULLED THE Russian soldier through the exit and slid the door shut a moment before the ravager reached it. The demon slammed into the metal, the force of the blow knocking Ian backwards onto the ground. The Russian soldier he had saved lifted him up.

"Thanks, mate" said Ian, brushing off the dirt.

"I should be thanking you."

From inside the car, the ravager howled and scratched at the door.

"We need to get out of here," said Ian.

"But where?"

Ian stepped away from the car to check out the situation. The armored engine raced down the tracks a few miles ahead of them, much too far for them to make it. Behind them, the rest of the train sat two hundred feet from the derailment. Reaching it would be a long shot, but it was better than the alternative. Ian pointed toward the rolling stock that still stood on the tracks and pushed the soldier in that direction.

"Let's go!"

"SCREW THIS." SOOK-KYOUNG made her way along the stock car to the open door. "I'm going topside."

"I'm with you." Luther fell in behind her.

"Haneef told us to stay here and protect the horses," Vicky protested.

"Those things are not coming after the horses with us top-side. Haneef needs us. Are you coming?"

Vicky hesitated but eventually nodded.

Sook-kyoung fixed her gaze on Gaston. "What about you?"

"I'm in."

Leading the way, Sook-kyoung led her squad outside and onto the roof.

SLAVA AND YURI reached the end of the crash site and leaned against the roof of the dining car, ignoring the melee going on inside. Slava peered around the corner. Haneef stood on top of the stock car. The Russian scanned the surrounding area to make certain no ravagers were nearby and stepped away from the dining car, waving his arms to catch Haneef's attention. His friend spotted the gesture and motioned for him to join them. Slava and Yuri dashed across the two hundred feet between the derailed cars and the stock car.

JUST AS SLAVA and Yuri broke into their run, more than a dozen ravagers emerged from the three sleeping cars after having fed off the soldiers inside. They sniffed the sky and, upon detecting fresh meat, scurried across the derailed cars, converging on the stock car.

"We've got company," said Haneef.

"I have this." Klimenko used the end ladder and climbed down, followed by one of the Russian soldiers. Once on the ground, he moved to a spot between the two sets of rolling stock and fifty feet from the tracks to catch the oncoming ravagers in a crossfire.

JASON FOLLOWED SASHA'S gaze to the portal, now less than two miles away. A pair of Golem had passed through and took up position on either side of the rails as a third emerged from the shimmering surface and stood on the tracks. The three leaned forward onto their knuckles, locked their elbows, and leaned into each other, presenting a massive wall of flesh to stop the approaching engine.

"How are we going to break through that?" Jason asked.

Sasha lifted her minigun. "With this."

Jason shook his head. "There has to be another way. That's suicide."

"Jason, I'm immortal. I can't die again."

"No!"

Sasha cupped his cheek in her left hand. "It's the only way. We both know it."

As much as Jason hated to admit it, Sasha was right. That did not negate the fact that he would lose his best friend for the second time. Knowing she would come back eased the pain, but he still felt that soul-sucking void in his chest. Taking Sasha's hand from his cheek, he kissed the palm and hugged her. "Make it count."

"I will." Sasha hugged back. "Now get back with the others. We only have a few minutes left."

Jason raced along the walkway back toward the cab. He paused for a moment for a final glimpse of Sasha. She crawled down the access ladder at the front of the train and braced herself beside the platform carrying the anti-matter device. Jason continued to the cab. When he passed through the hatch, Jeanette and Father Belsario stood in the coal bin of the tender, and Iosif knelt by the coupling. Iosif waved anxiously.

"Hurry up. I need to get us uncoupled from the engine while we still have time."

As Jason stepped forward, the ravager that had been hiding along the rear wall of the tender raced around the side and jumped into the cab.

THE BATTLE AROUND the crash site entered its final stage.

Slava and Yuri were halfway across the gap when three ravagers jumped from the derailed cars and rushed them. Sook-kyoung and Vicky crouched down on either side of Haneef and fired into the ravagers, slowing them enough for Slava and Yuri to reach the relative safety of the stock car. Once they were out of the line of fire, Haneef let loose with a jet of flame, washing it over the ravagers. They threw themselves onto the ground and flayed about for several seconds before being consumed. Upon seeing what had happened, the rest of the swarm split into two, each flowing off the derailed cars and closing in on the humans from the flanks. Haneef kept his eyes on the pack moving in on the left.

Klimenko and the Russian soldier with him took aim on the ravagers charging from the right. Neither man noticed the pack from the prison car rushing up behind them. One jumped on the soldier's back and sliced his throat open with a single swipe of its talon, killing him instantly. He was the lucky one. Four others swarmed Klimenko. One landed on the Russian, shoving him forward into the dirt. It slashed at him, gouging the fuel canister. Compressed fuel burst through the rupture and ignited. The flames flowed back into the canister, turning the stored fuel into a fireball. The explosion shredded Klimenko and the ravager on his back. The other three were incinerated.

Ian and his Russian companion reached the end of the dining car as the ravagers raced past. One noticed the two men crouched in the shadows and veered off to attack them. Ian grabbed the only weapon he could find, a broken section of wooded paneling five feet long, and raised it in front of him like a spear. The ravager impaled itself, the jagged end plunging through its chest and bursting out below the left shoulder blade. Instead of killing the ravager, the wound infuriated it, It lashed out at Ian with its talons.

Inside the dining car, Antoine's arms were growing weak from using the table as a combination shield and battering ram. The Russian soldiers moved up beside him and took down four of the ravagers. The fifth lunged, slamming into the top of the table and pushing Antoine backward. As it swept past the four soldiers, it lashed out, first with its right hand and then left. One of the soldiers went down with a severed arm. The other three dived away to avoid the talons. With nothing left to stop it, the ravager shoved Antoine against the wall, knocking the wind out of him and causing him to release his grip on the table. It slapped the table aside, stepped up to Antoine, and raised its claw above his head to finish the kill.

Seven of the ravagers from the prison car veered left and charged at the humans on top of the stock car. With the addition of the two packs from the derailed cars, nineteen ravagers were closing in on the survivors. Haneef switched from one side to the other, releasing a burst of flame at the nearest demon before doing the same on the other side. Those that avoided the fire launched onto the car and climbed the walls, only to be blasted off by automatic weapons. Some died instantly while others, only wounded, retreated and approached again from a different angle. The two that made it to the roof were sliced down by Luther's broadsword. However, the survivors knew the tide of battle was about to go against them. There were too many ravagers to keep away and their ammunition would soon run out.

JASON TRIED TO raise his weapon to fire on the ravager, but events happened much too fast. It landed on Iosif as he proceeded to unlock the coupling device. Being off balance, Iosif tumbled forward. Both he and the demon dropped between the engine and tender onto the tracks beneath.

Jason rushed forward and finished the uncoupling process. When the two separated, he didn't expect the train to pull so far ahead so quickly and tumbled toward the edge of the cab.

"Jason!" Jeanette rushed forward to help him, but Father Belsario held her back.

"I'm all right." Jason caught himself at the last moment. By now, a six-foot gap had widened between the two vehicles. He had seconds to get to safety. Jumping to his feet, Jason backed up against the controls and ran across the cab. When he reached the edge, he kicked off and hurtled the gap. He had misjudged the speed of the tender, so he landed much harder than expected into the pile of coal. His body slumped down and came to rest on the floor of the bin. Jeanette knelt beside him, running her hand across his face and forehead.

Father Belsario threw himself on top of them, shielding them with his body.

SASHA WAITED UNTIL the engine had approached to within a thousand feet of the portal before squeezing the trigger. The minigun whirred to life and spit out rounds at the rate of three thousand per minute. The shells ripped into the three Golem, tearing away chunks of flesh and punching their way through internal organs. Each behemoth bellowed in pain and defiance but held its ground. Yet even the most resilient Demon Spawn could not withstand the assault from the minigun. The barrage severed limbs and ravaged their bodies. In the few seconds it took the engine to close the gap to the portal, the minigun had churned the Golem into a mound of shredded tissue and flesh. When the engine struck the demonic barricade, the cow catcher plowed through the detritus as if it was a mound of freshly-fallen snow.

A second later, the train collided with the portal. Sasha experienced an excruciating pain as her body vaporized in the interdimensional rift. The agony lasted a few milliseconds. Her physical anguish in this realm was replaced by an inner peace as she drifted toward a bright light emanating from a black void.

When the platform carrying the device connected with the portal's surface, its outer casing disintegrated, releasing the enclosed anti-matter. A blinding flash of light and a thunderous explosion emanated from the point of impact. Flames engulfed the portal, burning intensely as the conflagration consumed it. After a few seconds, the portal collapsed on itself, sending out a shock wave that radiated across the tundra.

FOR THOSE BATTLING the ravagers around the derailed rolling stock, and who were about to be overwhelmed, the explosion signifying the closing of the portal came as a Godsend. The ravagers went lifeless and dropped where they stood. An eerie silence descended over the tundra.

Gaston spoke first. "What just happened? Why are they dead?"

"Jason closed the portal." Haneef slid one strap of the flamethrower off his shoulder.

"Are you nuts?" Gaston asked. "There could be more of those things out there."

Haneef shook his head. "Their existence is linked to the portal. Once it collapses, everything that came through it dies. We're safe now."

Haneef climbed down from the stock car, followed by the others. The rest of his people and the one surviving Russian soldier gathered around. He took a quick survey of the situation. "I'm going to find Jason and the others. Luther and Slava are with me. The rest of you, comb the area for survivors."

THE JOLT WHEN the tender rolled into the back of the stopped engine jarred Jason awake. As he lifted his head, Jeanette wrapped her arms around him and hugged him tight.

"I'm so glad you're all right," she gushed. "I was worried about you."

"I'm fine," he answered groggily. "I assume we were successful?"

"We were," said Jeanette.

Jason attempted to stand. His head spun. Jeanette and Father Belsario each took an arm and lifted him to his feet. He wobbled and reached out to support himself on the rim of the coal bin. The dizziness passed after a few seconds. Jason crossed over into the engine cab, crawled down the ladder, and headed for the front of the train.

"Where are you going?" Jeanette asked.

"I want to see for myself." Jason proceeded forward, steadying himself on the drivers. Jeanette and Father Belsario followed.

No evidence remained that the portal ever existed except for the break in the tracks and the damage done to the steam engine. Everything from the cylinders and smokestack forward had been vaporized by contact with the portal. Water from the boilers flowed out the front of the engine and poured onto the tracks, sizzling and generating clouds of steam. Jason did not see any signs of Sasha, although he did not expect to. At least in Paris there was a body that he could have grieved over if he had possessed the courage to view her remains. Now nothing existed to mark her second final resting place. Jason shut his eyes and silently wished Sasha well on her journey back to Purgatory.

Jeanette slid up beside him, wrapped her left arm around his waist, and pulled him into her.

Father Belsario placed his hand on Jason's shoulder. "We shut down another portal."

"At what price?" asked Jeanette.

"This is the way it's going to be until we close all of the gates," Jason answered.

Jason faced the devastation behind him. Off in the distance, he saw the derailed cars and the surviving rolling stock stopped behind the pile up, as well as the armored engine backing toward the accident scene.

"I hope it was worth it," said Jason.

"It was," answered Father Belsario. "That's not for me to decide, though. Only God can do that."

Jason wondered if God knew or cared about what happened down here on Earth. He took Jeanette's hand. "Let's join the others."

Jason never looked back at the train.

CHAPTER FORTY-FOUR

IT TOOK MUCH longer to reorganize after the battle than anyone had anticipated.

Lucifer and Lilith warmly greeted Jason after he and the others hiked back to the crash site, jumping on him and licking his face. For his part, Jason was surprised to discover that the losses to his own team were limited to Werner and Neal, although the latter hit him hard. That piece of good news was tempered by the fact that Svetlana had lost twenty-four people in battle, including Melnikov.

Thankfully, the derailment had not caused any damage to the tracks, and none of the overturned cars blocked the rails, so Mikhail backed up the train and coupled the last six pieces of rolling stock. While half of Jason's team sorted through the wreckage for anything salvageable, the other half worked with the Russians to scavenge material from the derailed cars to patch the hole gouged out of the command car's roof and construct a makeshift cover over the rear door of the stock car. Both parties undertook the unenviable task of clearing the blood and bodies out of the surviving cars and of burying the dead. The prison car was too gore-laden to be salvageable so, with the help of the Purgatoriati, the Russians toppled it off the track and out of the way of rail traffic. Because all the sleeping cars had been destroyed, everyone would have to camp out as best they could in the surviving rolling stock, the Russians taking the troop car at the end of the train and Jason's people sharing the command car with Svetlana. As two work crews readied the train for the completion of their journey, a third dug graves for those lost in battle, twenty-four for the Russians and one each for Neal, Werner, and Sasha. Jason noticed that the two slaughtered horses and the corpses of the four dead prisoners all shared one large, unmarked grave.

Since the preparations for departure took until after midnight, Svetlana decided to wait until morning before continuing. Everyone rose at dawn. After a quiet, uncomfortable breakfast of canned food heated over an open fire, the survivors gathered by the grave markers to remember their fallen comrades. Following a moment of silence, Svetlana stepped forward and faced the others.

"I'm not going to belabor this. We all knew what we were getting into by coming here. Most of us thought our chances of success were zero but that we had to at least try for the sake of humanity. We *were* successful, and that's something every one of you… every one of us, should be proud of."

"Was it worth it?" Ustagov asked, gesturing toward the grave markers. "Was closing the damn portal worth all this?"

"Yes." Svetlana spoke the words without anger or recrimination. "I've buried hundreds of men and women, and dozens of friends, trying to shut down the portals. For the first time, those deaths are not in vain. It may be difficult for us who are going through it now, but someday mankind will remember what we did here, and what Jason's team is doing around the world."

Jason nodded in agreement. The Russians had given him something much greater than their support in ridding the motherland of the portals. They had given him hope for the future. When his team had left Mont St. Michel, Jason had feared that those he encountered along the way would be like Jacques and Bishop Fiorello, narcissistic and petty men who would take advantage of the situation to enhance their own selfish desires. Running across people like Zhirinovsky, Melnikov, and Svetlana, who willingly made sacrifices for the common good, encouraged Jason that there certainly were others out there like the Russians whom he could rely on and whom, with their help, would take back their world from the Demon Spawn. For the first time since departing on this quest, Jason felt they had a better than even chance of succeeding.

Svetlana stepped away and headed toward the train. "Pay your last respects. We move out in twenty minutes."

The Russians spent a few moments saying goodbye to their friends and rushed off to prepare the train, all except Ustagov who stayed with Jason's team.

"What happens now?" Haneef asked.

Jason glanced around the survivors, making eye contact with each of them as he spoke. "Svetlana has agreed to take us to China and get us as close to the next gate as possible. Once she does that, she'll head back to Moscow."

"And then we'll be on our own again?" Antoine asked.

"Yes."

Jeanette tried to brighten the mood. "Hopefully Uncle Reno has been able to contact groups in China who are willing to help us out like the Russians did."

"We have to be realistic about this," said Jason. "Even if Reno did reach them, these groups have no idea where Svetlana will drop us off and when. If we meet up with anyone, it's not going to be until we near the portal."

"What about the Purgatoriati?" Vicky asked.

Jason winced at the thought and hoped Jeanette had not seen him.

"Gabriel, Jonah, and Sasha will meet up with us somewhere during the journey," said Father Belsario.

"Are you sure they'll want to come back to this?" Gaston joked.

"We have no choice," Luther answered. "Part of our penance is to stay with you until all the portals are eliminated, no matter how many times we die and resurrect."

Sook-kyoung whistled in disbelief. "That sucks."

"Tell us about it," said Matthew.

Ustagov stepped up to Jason. "If you don't mind, I want to join your team."

Ian laughed.

"What's so funny?" Ustagov snapped.

"You are, mate. You've been pissing and moaning about being forced on this trip ever since we left Moscow. Now you want to join us?"

Ustagov let the anger slip away. "Neal died saving me from a ravager. He asked that I take his place in helping you complete your mission."

Ian grew somber. "I didn't know. I'm sorry."

Ustagov patted Ian on the shoulder, letting him know they were cool. "So, am I in?"

"Of course, you are." Jason offered his hand. "Glad to have you."

The train whistle blew for three seconds.

"We need to get going," said Jason. He lingered behind as the others paid their final respects and made their way to the command car. Lucifer and Lilith remained by his side.

Jeanette also stayed back, waiting until the others were out of earshot. She reached out and took his hand. "What's wrong?"

"Nothing," Jason lied.

"It's Sasha, isn't it?"

"It's Sasha. It's Neal. It's Werner. It's everyone who died out here." Jason stepped away from the grave markers. His voice grew quiet and depressed. "And it's everyone who is going to die before we're through."

Jeanette faced Jason, taking both of his hands. The eyes that locked on him were filled with love and compassion. "Like you said earlier, what we did here was the right thing to do."

The train whistle blew again, this time three long blasts. Jason and Jeanette headed back to the train, with Lucifer and Lilith rushing ahead of them. Svetlana stood in the cabin of the armored engine. She waved to the couple as they climbed on board.

As they entered the command car, Jeanette asked, "Do you want company?"

"If you don't mind, I'd rather be alone for a while."

"I understand." Jeanette clapped her hands to get Lucifer's and Lilith's attention. "Come with me."

The three made their way to the front of the command car where the others had gathered.

A minute later, the train lurched forward. The engine slowly gained speed. As it passed the junction, Jason lifted the binoculars to his eyes and studied the wreckage of the first engine for the final time. If Jason succeeded in what he set out to do, then maybe someday this location, like the ruins of Notre Dame and Red Square, would become a memorial to those who sacrificed their lives to close the portals and rid the world of the Demon Spawn. Deep down he knew that would not happen. Future generations would repair their cities without giving a second thought to the portals or the Purgatoriati and would go about their lives without showing any concern for what might have been. At some point in time, the spur line would be cleared so rail traffic could travel to Irkutsk. Maybe the engine would be placed on the side of the tracks to commemorate what had happened or be erected as a monument in a nearby city. In truth, he knew it would most likely be sold as scrap metal. Everything the Demon Hunters and the Purgatoriati did here, and all the sacrifices made, would one day be forgotten by all but a select few.

Jason placed the binoculars back on their hook and joined the others.

The train headed south along the main line of the Tran-Siberian Railroad. The next stop would be China.

CHINA

CHAPTER ONE

A small village twenty-five miles north of Changchun, Jilin Province, China
The day after the closure of the portal in Siberia

LITTLE AH REMEMBERED the times before the end of humanity. Being only five years old she did not recall much, only the important things like watching television, playing with her toys, meeting her friends in pre-school, sleeping in a warm bed, and always having enough to eat. It had been over a year since the electricity went out and ten months since her parents had abandoned their apartment in Changchun and headed into the country in search of food. By now, Ah had grown accustomed to sleeping on the ground under a worn and dirty blanket, living inside of a tent that only partially kept out the rain and the cold, and eating whatever scraps the villagers could scrounge up that day. She did not enjoy her new life; she had only become used to it. She missed her favorite cartoons, her soft mattress, and hot meals at the table with her family. Most of all, she missed those times when her parents were happy. Although Ah's mother remained cheerful during the day, she cried at night when she thought her daughter had fallen asleep. Her father was the same way, always smiling and rubbing her hair, telling her things might be bad now but

265

would soon improve. Ah grinned and nodded to make her father feel good but deep down she knew things would not get better. She could see the fear and worry in his eyes and decided to make the best of the situation and not upset her parents. Her old life was gone and would never return.

Ah pulled the smelly blanket under her chin and rested her head on the backpack she used as a pillow. She had kept only one connection to those happier, earlier times—Ling Ling, a stuffed panda, the only possession her parents allowed her to bring when they left home. Ling Ling had seen better days. One of her eyes had fallen out and the white fur had become so dirty it blended with the black. For Ah, the stuffed panda was priceless because it comforted her through the uncertainty. She confided in it when she did not want to bother her mother or father. She cried on it when she was sad, or clutched it tight when afraid, both of which happened much more frequently than she cared to admit. Ah kissed the top of Ling Ling's head before going to sleep. She would rather die than leave her panda behind.

A loud commotion outside the tent woke her up. She sat upright, clutching the stuffed animal to her chest. Yelling came from around the camp site and people raced back and forth. In the distance, she heard galloping horses, the noise becoming more intense with each passing second. Someone barked an order about defending the perimeter. Gun fire erupted. It lasted for several minutes and mixed with screams. Then, as suddenly as the uproar began, everything went quiet except for the sound of running footsteps approaching the tent. Ah tried to remain brave, but her body shivered from fear.

The flap flew aside as Ah's mother raced in and rushed over to her daughter. "We have to get going."

"Where?"

"Don't ask questions." Her mother's voice wavered. She grabbed Ah by her left wrist and yanked her toward the exit. Ah dropped Ling Ling. Breaking free from her mother, the child ran back and picked up the stuffed panda.

"Hurry up," her mother snapped.

Ah hugged Ling Ling and joined her mother. Before they could exit, a man carrying a large gun used the barrel to push aside the flap and enter. He wore a uniform that Ah recognized as belonging to the People's Liberation Army, or PLA. Her mother gasped and stepped backward, dragging Ah with her. She wrapped her arms around her daughter and cried. "Please don't hurt us."

The soldier stared at them, his face expressionless. Turning his head, he waved for someone to join them. Ah's mother gripped her tightly and sobbed.

A young woman entered the tent. She wore civilian clothes—leather pants, a white shirt, and a tan leather jacket, none of which were soiled or tattered. Her raven black hair hung past her shoulders, clean and well groomed. She stood five and a half feet in height and, although by no means overweight, she did not have that emaciated appearance the others in camp did. Her deep brown eyes switched between Ah and her mother. After a few seconds, the woman smiled. "My name is Mei. Please, don't be afraid. We're here to help you."

"You shot at us," growled Ah's mother.

"Your people shot first." Mei's pleasant demeanor did not falter. "We only defended ourselves. Now please, gather your belongings and follow me."

"Suppose we want to stay here?"

"I'm sorry. We can't allow anyone to stay behind."

When Ah's mother refused to budge, Mei moved across the tent and squatted in front of the child. "What's your name?"

"Ah." She hugged the stuffed panda.

"That's a beautiful name." Mei reached toward Ah. Her mother held her close but Mei showed no interest in the child. She petted the panda's head. "What's her name?"

"Ling Ling."

"Do you trust me, Ah? Do you think I intend to hurt you or

your mother?"

For some reason, Ah did not feel threatened by this woman. Maybe it was Mei's joyful expression, or maybe the glint in her eyes that promised her intentions were in everyone's best interest. Ah swallowed hard. "I trust you."

"Good." Mei grinned. "Do you and Ling Ling want to come with me?"

Ah glanced up at her mother. "Can we go with her?"

Her mother trembled and, for a moment, Ah thought she might cry. Finally, she gave in to the inevitable. "Promise me you won't harm Ah."

"I promise," Mei said with sincerity.

Taking Ah by the right hand, her mother headed for the exit. Mei and the PLA soldier moved aside, each holding up one end of the flap. Once outside, they followed Mei to a clearing on the western perimeter. Most of the people from the camp were present, while a group of people she did not know, each carrying a gun, stood behind and on either side of them. Ah searched for her father but could not find him. She wondered if he was one of the bodies lying scattered around the field. Before she could ask her mother, something in front of them caught her attention.

Three horses approached camp, one in front and two slightly behind and on either side. The figures riding the rearmost horses wore black cowls that covered their hands and extended below the stirrups. They bowed forward in their saddles so that the hoods draped over their faces and hands. The rider of the lead horse wore a similar cowl, only blood red. Thirty feet from the group, the last two horses stopped. The animals shook their heads and stamped their hooves; the drivers remained motionless, as if there they were not alive. The first horse continued ahead and stopped directly in front of Ah. As the rider dismounted and approached, Ah tried to get a look under the cowl but the features remained hidden in the shadows. Mei spoke loud enough for everyone to hear.

"Ladies and gentlemen, this is Bai, the head of our group. She will lead you to the Promised Land. All you have to do is trust her, like we do."

A flurry of questions followed Mei's statement as those in the group asked at once where they were going, how long it would take, and what they could expect when they arrived. Mei calmed them down when Ah asked, "Are you going to hurt us?"

"We're going to save you."

"Save us from what?" asked Ah's mother.

"From all of this." Mei gestured toward the camp site. "We're going to save you from discomfort and starvation, and from the *Xionghu*. The world as you once knew it has come to an end. Things will never return to what they used to be. We're creating a new way of life and are giving you the opportunity to join us and make this world a better place. You can stay here if you want, cuddling in fear and living like vermin. Or you can come with us and have a purpose."

Ah stepped forward. "Is Ling Ling invited to join?"

Mei began to speak but Bai raised her right hand, cutting her off. Ah caught a glimpse of Bai's fingers and shuddered. She wanted to run away. Then Bai spoke, her voice soft and reassuring, mesmerizing yet unsettling at the same time. "Who is Ling Ling, my child?"

Ah held up he stuffed panda.

Bai reached out and rubbed her forefinger along Ah's cheek. This time the child did not flinch. "Everyone is welcome into this new realm."

Ah grinned and hugged her panda.

Bai remounted her horse, turned it around, and headed back the way she had come. As she passed, the other two horses fell in line behind her. Mei motioned for the others to follow. Ah surged forward, dragging along her mother. One by one, the others followed until the entire camp was on the march toward their new destiny.

A Thank You to My Readers

This is a tradition I began with *Shattered World I: Paris* and liked it enough to continue with it in the sequel. It's unusual for writers to thank their fans for reading their book but this is a heartfelt appreciation. The publishing industry has changed dramatically over the past ten years, and there are now thousands of young adult post-apocalypse novels on the market for readers to choose. I appreciate the fact that you took a chance on *Shattered World II: Russia*. I hope you enjoyed reading it as much as I did writing it.

If you liked *Shattered World II: Russia*, please tell your friends about the book and review it on Amazon. The review does not have to be long—just a rating and a sentence or two about why you enjoyed it. The more reviews *Shattered World II: Russia* receives, the more opportunity other readers have of discovering the book. If you haven't read yet *Shattered World I: Paris*, the first book in the series, it's still available on Amazon, Kindle, and Kindle Unlimited.

The *Shattered World* saga will continue. Future books will take the Demon Hunters to Asia, the United States, and eventually Hell itself. The locations they will visit will be more exotic. The people they encounter will be more colorful and, in some cases, will pose as much of a threat as the Demon Spawn. And of course, the demons they face will be more terrifying. I can't promise that your favorite characters will survive but I can promise action, thrills, and surprises.

Acknowledgments

Writing is very solitary and lonely. Getting a book published, on the other hand, is a complicated process involving many people, all of whom deserve to be recognized.

I want to express my deepest gratitude to Michele Thompson for her excellent editorial skills and for catching those things I missed in the original draft. Her efforts helped make *Shattered World I: Paris* a success and she has done an equally fantastic job on the sequel. Uwe Jarling and Julie Nicholls created the cover art and, as with the first book, their work is phenomenal. Uwe takes my visions of the characters and demons and brings them to life. Many thanks also to Petar Dekic for providing the maps so my readers can follow the adventures of the Demon Hunters.

Finally, a major debt of thanks goes to my family, human and furry. Here in New England my study is in the basement. I have to keep the pets separated because Bella does not get along with my cats, and as such I end up with my Boxers standing at the top of the stairs whimpering for me to come up and spend time with them while my cats stay with me in the study and spend more time walking across my keyboard than I do typing on it. Sometimes it's hard to maintain my writing discipline. However, my family gives me the time I need to write and never holds my self-imposed isolation against me. I couldn't do this without their love and support.

Author's Bio

Scott M. Baker was born and raised in Everett, Massachusetts and spent twenty-three years in northern Virginia working for the Central Intelligence Agency. Scott is now retired and lives just outside of Concord, New Hampshire with his wife and fellow writer Alison Beightol, stepdaughter, two rambunctious boxers, and two cats who treat him as their human servant. He has written *The Vampire Hunters* trilogy, about humans fighting the undead in Washington D.C.; *Rotter World, Rotter Nation,* and *Rotter Apocalypse,* his post-apocalyptic zombie saga; *Yeitso,* his homage to the giant monster movies of the 1950s that he loved watching as a kid; as well as several zombie-themed novellas and anthologies. He is currently working on a new zombie survival series focusing on a young woman learning how to stay alive in a world overrun by the living dead

Please check out Scott's social media accounts for the latest information on future books, upcoming events, and other fun stuff.

Blog: scottmbakerauthor.blogspot.com
Facebook: facebook.com/groups/397749347486177
Twitter: @vampire_hunters
Instagram: scottmbakerwriter

www.ingramcontent.com/pod-product-compliance
Lightning Source LLC
Chambersburg PA
CBHW060859250626
47159CB00008B/2803